MISSING IN ACTION

KATE CANTERBARY

VESPER PRESS

This is a work of fiction. Names, characters, places, and incidents are the product of the author's imagination or are used fictitiously, and any resemblance to actual persons, living or dead, business establishments, events, or locales is entirely coincidental.

Trademarked names appear throughout this book. Rather than use a trademark symbol with every occurrence of a trademarked name, names are used in an editorial fashion, with no intention of infringement of the respective owner's trademark(s).

Editing provided by Julia Ganis of JuliaEdits.

Proofreading by Jen Graybeal of Jen Graybeal Editing Services.

Cover design by Sarah Hansen of Okay Designs.

Created with Vellum

ABOUT MISSING IN ACTION

Former Navy SEAL turned covert agent Wes Halsted spent his days—and weeks and months—being someone else. But with his cover blown and his injuries requiring months of recuperation, he must learn how to be himself again.

Only…he'd rather save his issues for another day and get to know a stressed-out, suited-up businessman instead.

Tom Esbeck has everything under control. Meal plans, workout plans, project plans, five-year plans. A plan for everything and everything according to plan.

Except there's no plan for a surprise—and shirtless—encounter with the built-for-sin spy he'd crushed on years ago.

But crushes—and spies—burn out fast.

BEFORE YOU DIVE IN...

If you need some tunes to set the vibe, check out the Missing In Action playlist.

Join Kate Canterbary's Office Memos mailing list for occasional news and updates, as well as new release alerts, exclusive extended epilogues and bonus scenes, and cake. There's always cake.

If newsletters aren't your jam, follow Kate on BookBub for preorder and new release alerts.

PROLOGUE

WES

Christmas Eve

IT WASN'T the worst of times but this sure as shit wasn't the best of times.

In the best column, I was listing the nun's habit I nicked out of a countryside convent last night. No one fucked with nuns. Most people avoided eye contact with them altogether. Bad memories of wooden rulers and forced recitation of multiplication tables. This vestment was keeping me off the radar and doing a sensational job of concealing both my beard and my injuries.

The convent also yielded a pair of granny glasses, tattered scarves, and a small purse loaded with supplies to treat my injuries. Gauze, alcohol swabs, antibacterial ointment, an old bottle of penicillin, a sewing kit, and a pair of needle-nose pliers.

That was where the best column ended.

As far as the worst of times went, getting shot was at the top of the list. There was a bullet lodged in my flank and I'd been bleeding, slow and steady, for hours. A cold sweat covered my body, my heart was wobbling in my chest, and I could only see straight if I squinted. That was fucking unpleasant but my only objective was getting to the port.

I'd spent the night on the run, zigzagging and back-tracking to shake the secret police from my tail, and didn't have the time to dig that son of a bitch out of my soft tissue. There was also the matter of my broken arm and the electrical current burns on my legs but I could manage those. The gunshot wound though, that thing was going to turn septic in a hot minute.

If those issues weren't enough to earn the distinction of Really Fucking Bad, I had a few more lined up. My CIA handlers had no idea where I was. I hadn't seen my partner Veronica in two weeks, and I suspected she was dead or close to it. My local liaisons were dead, both executed in front of me.

A hostile foreign government had discovered that I'd been spying on them for a wee bit of time. The same hostile foreign government was pissed that I didn't fold under their charming interrogation techniques. I could only imagine they regarded my exit from their off-book detention facility—and all the guards I took out in the process—as an unwanted aggravation.

Based on the activity I'd observed as I made my way

north toward the Barents Sea, that government had dispatched entire armies to root me out. They intended to find me and make an international example. Regardless of whether they succeeded at nailing my nuts to the wall, they would also plan some prime-time retaliation.

I went on squinting at the road ahead, breathing slowly and worrying the rosary beads between my fingers to displace some of the pain streaking through my body. If I could get to the port, I could get home.

I walked with purpose, careful to keep my eyes down and my steps confident. I was playing the part of a local, one who wouldn't normally draw the attention of the heavily armed law enforcement agents on every corner.

It wasn't supposed to go down this way. I figured that was how all agents prefaced their debriefs of operations gone bad. I wouldn't know. My operations never went bad.

Until now.

I'd been working this assignment for almost two years. Two years of cohabitation and marital bliss with a *woman*. Even if that woman was also a highly skilled operative, it was one hell of a long-running hetero con. Two years of chipping away at Moscow's society circles, playing the part of the eccentric antiquities dealer who also trafficked in weapons of war. Two years of planting seeds and watching them germinate.

There was no reason for this operation to fall apart weeks before we were due to get out of town. Our work was airtight and the information we'd gathered was solid gold. There were bumps in the road, for sure, but that was the way with every hop. This hop had been one of the good ones. Difficult, exhausting, grueling—but one of the good ones, until I woke up in a dirt-floored dungeon with my hands and feet shackled to an ancient stone wall.

I stifled a laugh at that. My father liked to say that if you thought an operation was going well, you weren't paying attention.

I had paid attention. I knew this operation, every corner and seam of it.

If I made it home, I was certain he'd tell me I hadn't.

For the first time in my fucking life, I wanted to hear my father tell me I was wrong. I wanted to make it back to the States and I wanted him to take apart this mission and point out my flaws.

A large family came around the corner, and I spared them a warm glance. "God be with you," I said in Russian, affecting my most provincial accent. Nuns didn't rock the upper-crust city accent I'd employed during my time here.

They nodded, mumbling the blessing back to me. I hunched into my habit, hoping to obscure some of my height. Nuns weren't six three.

My thumb and forefinger rolled to another bead as the bone-on-bone pain radiated up my arm and into my shoulder. I was furious about that. The motherfucker who broke it didn't know what the hell he was doing. He just wailed on me with a lead pipe as if that was going to yield any actionable information. Talk about amateur hour. I needed the use of both arms right now, and I didn't have it because some foot soldier with anger issues didn't like it when I told him his mother was bad in bed.

I pressed the pad of my thumb into a rosary bead as a gust of nausea threatened to knock me over. I continued walking, my gaze trained on the stories-high cargo ships and cranes looming tall over Kola Bay. I was almost there, and breathed a small sigh of relief.

A liquefied natural gas tanker was leaving from Murmansk this morning, one with a crew that knew how to look the other way for the right price. The tanker was set to sail around Scandinavia to the Atlantic, and make several stops along the east coast of North America. If I could get on that tanker, I could send word to my handlers. They needed to pull their operatives out of the country and turn down the volume on current assignments, and prepare for the disproportionate response headed their way.

I picked up my pace as I marched through the rows and lanes of shipping containers. Unsurprisingly, I was the only nun in sight, a spectacle in a sea of metal and machinery. The roughnecks and longshoremen eyed me as I passed, and I offered the sign of the cross in response. Something about that gesture, coupled with my rosary beads and exaggerated hunch, earned tolerant nods from the men.

When I reached the far edge of the port, I lifted my arm in greeting to the quartermaster. He eyed me with an appropriate amount of suspicion as I moved toward him. From the habit's deep pockets, I retrieved a small coin purse. It was lined with enough cash to ensure passage to North America, and a little more to keep the questions at a minimum.

No, I hadn't robbed the convent. Even spies had standards. Most of the cash was courtesy of the secret police I took down on my way out of their black site last night. At the off chance the bills were tagged and traceable, I turned them over in small towns throughout the region. Now, all the money was clean and I was a matter of steps away from surviving the worst of this ordeal.

"A beautiful day the Lord has granted us," I said to him, that provincial accent heavier than ever. I worried my beads, forcing his attention there rather than my face. "Do you have room for one more?"

He regarded me for a long minute in which I debated whether I could strangle him without arousing the notice of the other dockworkers and then stow away aboard the tanker. The short answer was yes, I *could* do that, but no, it wasn't a wise move. And I needed to conserve energy like a motherfucker.

"Room," he repeated, pulling the beanie from his head and wiping his hands on the wool. "Headed for America, you know. I have space for one more on deck five, but only deck five. Nothing less."

In other words, he wanted at least five thousand American dollars.

I held out the coin purse. "You're a true servant of our heavenly Father, my child." If I hadn't been holding back a roar of pain, I would've laughed at myself. I figured I'd laugh later, when a steady stream of morphine was coursing through my veins and my humerus bone wasn't trying to tear through my skin. I'd laugh about this whole fucking thing.

Thankfully, the quartermaster wasn't listening to a word I said. He was concerned only with thumbing through the money. He mouthed the numbers as he counted, his head bobbing as he neared five thousand. His eyes lit up when he hit six, and then popped right out of his greedy skull when he closed in on seven.

Every payoff was associated with a moment, a beat where the deal could progress as planned or everything could go pear-shaped. This was that moment. The quartermaster was gripping the cash and sizing me up, debating whether he could shake me down or hold me hostage for more. If I knew his type, I knew he was also thinking about dragging a blade across my throat and throwing me overboard once we left port.

And there was nothing I could do about it. Couldn't reason my way around it. Couldn't walk away. I had to wait it out.

He gestured to the medallions hanging from the rosary beads. "Saint Nicholas," he said, pinching one of the charms between his grubby fingers. "Watches over the seafarers, yeah?"

"The seafarers, yes, of course," I replied. I shook the beads at him. "I've been calling upon Saint Nicholas for safe passage."

He unzipped his coat and peeled back several layers of thermal shirts to reveal his bare chest. He pointed to an old tattoo. "Saint Nicholas." He tipped his head to the gangplank. "Be well, Sister."

I offered him a grateful smile and started up the ramp.

Now I only needed to survive the rest of this journey. I was one step closer but still an ocean away from the other side of this mission. If I made it home, I was taking a long-ass vacation. I was due for some sun, sand, and a sexy man by my side.

"If," I murmured to myself, laughing as much as my broken body would allow. "I'm getting home if I have to steer this motherfucker myself."

1

WES

A WEEK LATER…MAYBE?

I WAS HAVING the weirdest fucking dreams. Nightmares? I wasn't sure.

I'd never given much thought to Peter Pan but my head was filled with nighttime flight and "second star to the right and straight on till morning."

The others were stress dreams. Live action to-do lists screaming at me to get shit done. Time sliding away from me, fast-forwarding as I watched everything go to hell. Bursts of light and whole-body jolts like the bottom was falling out.

And then there were the shadows. The whispers around every corner. Goddamn, I couldn't get away from those shadows. They were worse than the stress dreams. Worse by a lot. They reminded me I'd missed something. I'd missed something and people were dead because of it.

There was flying and stress and shadows but there was quiet too. An uncomfortable quiet, like the silence before a detonation. That quiet made me wonder whether I was dead too. Or close to it.

I was a spy and I'd long accepted the fact I could—and likely would—die on the job. My work necessitated a life lived as if I had nothing to lose. I wasn't afraid but I wasn't ready either. I didn't want this to be the end, not here in a dark, wet corner of a gas tanker somewhere between home and away. Not before—before everything else I needed to do.

"Not here," I mumbled to myself. My mouth was sandpaper. "Not dying here."

I summoned the strength to reach for the wound on my side. I had it packed with a length of fabric from my vestment, the best I could do to slow the bleeding. I yanked the layers away from my skin, hoping to find the dressing dry. Bleeding to death was not the way to go. Too slow, too painful. Give me fast and quick—and blissfully unaware.

But a pair of warm hands stopped me, saying, "Whoa there. Easy, easy." Then, louder, "He's waking up. Seems agitated. Can you give him something to calm him down? The last thing we need is torn sutures or an open incision."

"Not fucking agitated," I muttered, forcing my eyes open. "Goddamn, how fucking bright is it in here?"

I squinted at the woman holding my hand against my chest. Her dark braid snaked over her shoulder and brushed my arm. She wore a slim black t-shirt, long-sleeved and unadorned. There was nothing remarkable about her but I *knew* her. I was certain of it. But I didn't know how or from where.

Then the realization hit me. I wasn't dead and I wasn't on that tanker anymore. I glanced down at the crisp hospital gown covering my chest, the tubes taped to my hand, the blanket covering my legs. The whiteboard on the wall ahead of me announced the names of my care providers. The date too. December thirtieth.

"Where—" I tried turning my head to the side but *fuuu-uuck* that hurt.

"Halifax," she replied. "Nova Scotia."

I blinked up at her. "Why the fuck am I in Canada?" I rasped. "Why stop a hundred miles from the US border? I could've jogged there!"

She squeezed my wrist, offered me a grim smile. "You didn't have another hundred miles. You barely made it here. You lost half your blood volume. Your heart stopped twice. Trust me, this is as far as you could go."

"Me?" I barked. "Please. I had another—" I glanced at my arm, the one on the receiving end of the lead pipe treatment, and found a long, ugly scar from my elbow to wrist. "*Fuuuuuck*."

Now I was really pissed about that lead pipe.

"Like I said," she continued, "you didn't have another hundred miles." She released my hand, stepped back. "There were diplomatic reasons as well."

"Say again, Tomb Raider?" I asked, an eyebrow arching up as I peered at her. Who the fuck was this chick?

The door opened and in limped Jordan Kaisall. "You're awake. Good. We gotta move."

Once again—*fuuuuuck.*

If Kaisall was standing in my hospital room—in Nova Scotia of all the damned places—a couple of bad dreams were the least of my worries. Kaisall was a black ops contractor. He took on jobs too risky, too dark, too plausibly deniable for anyone else. His teams went in after the SEALs, the Green Berets, the Rangers, the CIA operatives. Got them—us—out when shit turned sour.

And he was my brother's business partner.

If Kaisall was here, Will knew everything. Perhaps not everything but he knew my mission was fucked and he knew more about the past couple of days than I did. And if Will knew, my father did too. Not only that, but the CIA hadn't come for me. Either they wouldn't or couldn't.

One more time—*fuuuuuck.*

He dropped his hand on the woman's shoulder, a touch too familiar to be collegial, and she smiled. *Yes.* Then it clicked. Yeah, I knew her. "Mossad," I whispered. Israeli intelligence. "You're Mossad. I saw you a few years ago in—hmm. In Tangier. Right?"

She gave me a quick shake of the head, a fleeting smile. "I'm sure you're mistaken," she replied. "I'm just a cake decorator."

"And I'm just a cultural anthropologist," I drawled.

She shrugged. "I'm told Morocco is lovely in October."

"Especially when taking down terrorist cells." I bobbed my head when she didn't respond. "And Budapest in May? How do you like it there?"

"It's hard to say. I haven't been in ages." She sounded a bit wistful, as if her memories were of the variety kept in scrapbooks and Instagram photos. But they weren't. Nothing we'd seen existed in the light of day. Hell, *we* didn't exist. That singular truth made our work possible.

It also meant my brother's business partner had to fetch me from the North Atlantic because no one else dared come for me.

"Yeah and I hear Russia's delightful in December but thank fuck none of us are there right now," Kaisall added. He beckoned toward me. "I hope you weren't especially fond of your spleen."

I forced a shoulder up in spite of the pain twisting through my body. "No more than any other vital organ."

"Good answer. Couldn't be saved." He tapped his fingers on the footboard. "Do you think you can walk? I've got a jet waiting at a small airstrip outside the city and we'd attract a lot less interest if you could board on your own."

My tank was half full of borrowed blood and I wasn't sure I could feel my feet but I said, "Of fucking course I can walk on my own."

I hadn't survived SEAL training and one deployment after another and *then* CIA training *and* years-long missions *and also* escaping Russia with a bullet in my side and a janky broken arm to give up now. No, son. No. I was walking out of here if it cost me everything. I'd get the fuck through it.

That was how I lived—getting the fuck through it.

"All right," Kaisall replied, skepticism heavy in those two words. "Wheels up in two hours." He wrapped his arm around the woman's waist, kissed her temple. "That's just enough time to get you a clean passport."

I snickered. "How is Nova Scotia's black market? I've always wondered."

Ignoring me, Kaisall said to the cake-decorating killer, "Anything you need before we go, April?"

April. Yeah, that hadn't been her name in Tangier. Or Budapest.

"It's only a quick hop to Hanscom," she said. "I'm good."

I almost whimpered. Hanscom Field was west of Boston and half an hour to my brother's house. There was only one reason we'd fly there. Only one reason to head for the sleepy seaside town Will and his wife called home.

I blew out a breath but I paid for it with a sharp surge of pain from my side. Goddamn fucking gunshot wound. Almost as annoying as the fucked-up arm. "Why Hanscom?"

"Because you need to lie low, Wes," Kaisall replied. "CIA hasn't figured out how to clean this one up yet but they need you to stay the fuck away from anything with facial recognition."

"And my cover?" A wry laugh passed my lips as I thought better of the question. I knew the answer. We wouldn't be hiding out in Canada and sneaking into the States if my cover was intact.

Kaisall and April exchanged a sharp glance. He shook his head. "CIA isn't taking responsibility. They're sticking with your original story—Navy veteran turned cultural attaché buying up antiquities—but the FSB has you on video taking out one of their operatives. It's not good video but it's video and they're not afraid to air it."

Once more for the cheap seats—*fuuuuuck.*

KAISALL TWISTED open a bottle of water and pressed it into my good hand. "Another hour and we'll be on the ground," he said.

It was his best attempt at lightening my mood but it wasn't working. Everything hurt like fire and I was cold sweating straight through the clothes April had snatched for me. The nurses had loaded me up on painkillers after applying fresh dressings to my wounds but it didn't make a dent. If I had to be thankful for something, it was the posh comfort afforded by this private jet. I could dig deep but I didn't think I had it in me to endure two hours in the belly of a C-130 transport plane right now.

"Since we have some time together, why don't you explain how you came to be involved in this situation," I said, offering a jerky nod at April and Kaisall.

Kaisall scowled at his phone before setting it facedown on the glossy table between us. "We picked up an increase in chatter earlier in the month."

"By 'we,' you mean Shaw," April added.

Kaisall tipped his head toward her. "Yeah, Jeremy Shaw. Tracking and deciphering chatter is his ball game. He's our intel guy." He lifted his brows, silently asking her approval. She nodded in response. "Kept listening. Noticed some movement on the chessboard. Kept watching. Then we—Shaw—heard through some friends that your local contacts were missing. Then you and Veronica dropped off the radar."

I stared at him, allowed a stiff smile. "Is there anything you're not watching? Anywhere you're not listening?"

He shrugged a shoulder. "Eyes and ears are the name of the game."

"You're not wrong about that," I muttered. "How'd you find me?"

"Shaw," April said. "He was on the desk when it all went down."

"I gotta meet this Shaw kid," I said. "Buy him a beer or two."

"If you can get him out of the office, you're welcome to it." Kaisall barked out a laugh. "We opened some back doors and grabbed some traffic camera footage near the port cities. We figured you'd head west, head toward the water. The holiday meant fewer ships leaving port so the options were narrow. From there, we ran down manifests and hacked into comm systems to take a listen. It was a process of elimination and chances were good we'd chosen incorrectly but..." His voice trailed off as he reached for his phone.

"But Will sent you in," I supplied.

"Hell no." April shook her head. "We didn't tell him until we'd been there and back again."

"Oh. Oh, okay," I murmured. My brother was a saver. He saved people. He did it as a SEAL and now as the commander of a private military force. I couldn't say for sure but I imagined he did a fair amount of it as a husband and father too. I didn't harbor any illusions about my importance in the world but I knew he'd show up if I needed him. He'd save me too. He couldn't *not* do it.

"How'd you manage that if he knew about the chatter, the movement?"

"He's been out of pocket. He went dark around the same time you did," Kaisall said. "Shannon had the baby a few days ago. You're an uncle. Again."

I closed my eyes. One new development at a time. "I tried to get to the bridge," I said. "I figured I could fire off a message to Langley. Maybe hook onto an NSA channel. But I never got a clean opening. Hell, any opening. Armored guards kept a twenty-four-hour watch and I had to choose between taking them out and not bleeding to death."

April leaned back, crossed her legs as she studied me. "How'd you get that bullet out? The flight surgeon couldn't find it but said it wasn't through-and-through."

"Pliers," I replied. Remembering the pain of fishing the bullet out of my flank was only slightly better than incurring the injury itself. "Wasn't pretty but had to be done. Sepsis is the least interesting way to go."

She pivoted to face Kaisall with a smirk. "Told you."

He rolled his eyes. "Say thank you to April for saving your life. She HALO jumped onto that tanker in less than favorable conditions and I'm still unhappy about it."

"Thank you, April," I said. "If that's your real name."

"It is," she replied. "As far as you need to know."

"Thank her like you mean it," he snapped.

"I fuckin' mean it," I replied, offering a weak gesture at her. I did, I meant it. I was appreciative of the effort and extreme risk that went into a high altitude, low opening jump in the middle of the ocean and everything that went into finding me and dragging me to the safe harbor afforded by North America. "Thank you."

She shifted, recrossed her legs. "No problem."

"It *is* a problem," Kaisall argued. "We were on vacation. In Jamaica. This guy has to go get himself shot and interrupt our damn holiday. I had plans for that time and they didn't involve scrambling a transport plane, tapping a team of medics, and sending my—my April into a no-win situation where she had to small-boat your ass to a fucking fjord. All because you got shot on the job."

"To be fair, the gunshot wound wasn't my biggest issue," I replied, pointing at my busted arm. "This situation was more troublesome but I had it covered."

Another eyeroll from Kaisall. "Okay, sure."

"Hell, I'm happy I didn't have to steer that tanker myself. I thought about it a few times. Take out the crew, head to Greenland, get a little time in the hot springs. That's as close as I'm getting to an island vacation, right?"

"Please don't remind me that I left *my* island vacation to orchestrate your exfil strategy," he said.

"*We* left, Jordan," April said. "*We* left our island vacation."

"To that end," I started, attempting a nod at both of them, "why don't we return to that island vacation? The last thing my brother needs under his roof is an injured spy with no cover." I lifted the water to my lips, gulped down a sip. "Just take me back to Jamaica with you."

"You need ongoing medical attention," April replied.

I gestured to my side. "Come on, Tomb Raider. You've pulled out a bullet or two and kept on going. I'm sure of it."

She spread her hands out in front of her. "Not a one."

"Bulllllllshit," I hissed.

"It's true. Believe me, I've looked," Kaisall replied. "But watch yourself if she gets her hands on a knife."

"The only reason we got off that tanker was my knife skills," she argued.

"Ohhh, that's interesting," I cooed. "Someday I want to hear how you managed that bit." I tried tipping my chin in her direction but it only sent pain screaming through my torso. "But not today. I want you to take me to Jamaica today. All I need to recover is my toes in the warm sand and a dick in my hand."

Kaisall stifled a laugh, saying, "I'm on orders to deliver you to Halsted's house."

"Don't listen to my brother—"

"Not your brother," Kaisall interrupted. "This order came from the Commodore."

My father. Of course my father, the one who loved the Navy and everything about it so damn much he only answered to "the Commodore," was calling me home. It was a matter of days ago that I'd wanted nothing more than my father and his endless critique but now, without death crawling up my spine, I wanted nothing more than an island, a beach, some anonymity.

That was the best and worst part of my life—the anonymity. The ability to exist without anyone noticing, anyone caring. I wasn't sure when I chose a life made remarkable by being forgettable. I didn't think I'd started out with this goal. If anything, I'd joined the Navy, the

SEALs, and then the CIA with the goal of being remembered. Revered, even.

I'd intended to be legendary.

But that wasn't the way of it for spies and SEALs. I'd learned to accept that, and most of the time I loved it. I could be anyone, go anywhere. I could live hundreds of lives and make myself at home in just as many cities and want for nothing. Nothing at all.

"We go to Will's house. Swing by, say hello," I conceded, "then Jamaica."

April and Kaisall shared a knowing glance, one that said, *Unlikely.*

"We'll stop there, prove to my parents that I'm alive and mostly intact, and then head for the islands," I continued.

Another dubious glance.

"If there's video, the Agency won't want anything to do with me until they can bury the shit out of it and hang something more incriminating on the Russians' heads," I continued.

"They're already giving it the fake news treatment," Kaisall replied.

"Good, good," I murmured. "So, we agree. Ten minutes at Will's place and then straight ahead to Jamaica."

Kaisall shook his head. "While I usually advocate for post-mission downtime, that's not how this one is shaking out."

When he didn't go on, I swung my gaze between them. "You've gotta be kidding me. No. There is no way in Satan's rose garden that I'm staying at my brother's house indefinitely. No fucking way."

My brother was one of my best friends. The guy was awesome. But he didn't let anyone off the hook. He didn't let anyone sneak off with their shit and fix it up on their own, without him. That wasn't how fixers rolled. They fixed and they didn't let you out of their sight until they were satisfied the fix was going to stick.

And his wife, god help me. Anything my brother didn't handle, she would. She'd kick my ass and then hug the shit out of me and make me promise to be careful with my remaining organs.

Family was weird.

"Come on, man. You'll love it." Kaisall shared another glance with April before looking back to me with a barely restrained smile. "It's not Jamaica but a house filled with screaming babies is pretty good too."

"Just send me back to Russia," I grumbled.

2

WES

"WHAT'S YOUR PAIN LEVEL?"

I blinked at the doctor as he studied the wound on my flank. If this guy thought I was copping to anything more than mild discomfort while my brother leaned against the wall with his arms crossed over his chest, he was out of his damn mind. It didn't matter that the wallpaper was alive and my arms didn't seem connected to my body and I felt like I'd been fired out of an active volcano.

"Not bad," I said as breezily as I could manage.

"Save the bullshit, Wes," Will ordered.

I didn't know when that motherfucker learned how to read minds but I flipped him off nonetheless. Rather, I flipped him off as best I could with my disconnected limb. Which was not at all, if I had to guess. "Yeah? When was the last time you were shot?"

He shrugged. "Three, maybe four years ago."

"Oh, fuck off," I grumbled.

"This is productive," the doctor murmured, glancing over his shoulder at my brother. "Would you excuse us? I'd like to have a conversation with my patient."

"Bro, I'm not your patient," I said, swatting his hand away from my side. "I just need to get to the islands. Nothing the sun and sand can't cure. Salt water is the best medicine."

"I'm all for natural solutions but the sun and sand are not addressing the infection you've developed from the gunshot wound," he replied. "There's also the issue of the burns on your legs and several bruised bones."

"Fuck that," I roared. "Pour some gin on it. I'll be fine." I pointed at the wall behind my brother. "Would you turn the wallpaper off? It's making me dizzy."

"Can you sedate him, Nick? Just knock him out for a few days?" Will asked. "My parents are going to be here any minute and they're not prepared to see this. I cannot look after this fucking guy, my parents, *and* my wife and babies right now."

"Don't forget about the dogs," I quipped. "There are dogs, right? Don't tell me I hallucinated all that barking. I don't know. Maybe Kaisall was the one barking. He's a fuckin' bloodhound."

"Honestly, Will, I want to help you but this is not my area of expertise. I'm better qualified to assess your kids' neurological development than handle major trauma injuries. Let me call Stremmel and—"

"No way in hell, Acevedo," my brother yelled. "I've seen enough of that guy for a year. Maybe two. You can handle one mouthy SEAL. This should be easy. You worked in a refugee camp in Africa, for fuck's sake."

"I did," the doctor agreed. "But I specialize in kids and their brains." He pointed at me. "This is neither a kid nor a brain."

"Thanks for calling in the B-squad for me. Thanks," I said to my brother. Goddamn him for looking so smug and...upright. He made it seem like standing was easy and I hated him for that. "Seriously. Why would anyone choose that wallpaper?"

Will shot a glimpse to his side and then back at me. "Wes. Buddy. There's nothing on the wall. It's light gray. Shannon said the color is called moondust or some shit like that."

I stared at the flowers and fairies and mushrooms dancing behind his back. That wall was not gray. It wasn't. And all I needed was some penicillin and the sea. "I don't wanna see them," I said, my words fragmented and whiny. "I don't wanna see Mom and Dad right now. Tell them I went to the Caribbean to be a pirate."

"You're welcome to do that," Will replied. "Truly. Go on with your swashbuckling self, Wes. Just drag your ass out of my guest room and pull on a puffy shirt, and I'll buy you a fucking ship."

"You're supposed to steal the ship," I argued. "I'd expect you to know that." I blinked up at the doctor. He was pretty but there was no missing the wedding band on his left hand. "Have we met? I've heard your accent before."

"Yes, at your sister's wedding. You also know my wife. Erin."

"Oh, yeah. The redhead chick the Italian mafia put under their protection. Because that's totally normal." I tried to get a better look at him but his head wouldn't stay still. Or stop multiplying. "When did you guys get married? I wasn't invited. I don't think."

A slight smile lifted his lips as he stabbed a syringe into a vial, slowly filling the barrel. "The night before your sister's wedding."

"She doesn't make house calls with you?" I asked.

"No, not when she's in the Philippines."

"Damn," I murmured. "I like her. You, I'm not too sure about."

"I like her too. This might burn a bit," he said as he tapped the syringe. "But it will hit you before you can count to ten."

"Imma make it to thirty," I replied, winking up at the doctor while he rubbed an alcohol swab on my bicep. "Just watch."

He grinned as the syringe pierced my skin. "Only if you count fast."

I heard the numbers rolling off my tongue—one, two, three, *cuatro, fünf, kuusi, siedem*—but it was the warm sound of my brother's laughter, and "He's some kind of pain in the ass, isn't he?" I remembered as the edges softened and the room went dark.

THE SHADOWS WERE BACK. The voices too.

They swirled and hovered around me, coming in bursts and fading away before I could grab hold of them. And I wanted to hold on. I wanted to come back and I wanted to be here—be anywhere. I didn't know how long it took me to fight my way through. It could've been hours, it could've been weeks. But when I blinked my eyes open and found gray walls, plain and stationary in their moondust glory, I managed a dry laugh. It cracked through me with a bolt of pain that pinged every raw nerve and strained muscle in my body. I felt it in my torso, skull, knees. If it was possible, the beard that'd grown bushy and thick since leaving Russia hurt too.

"You've always snored like a locomotive when you're sick."

I shifted just enough to catch sight of my mother seated in the corner, some variety of sewing in her hands. She didn't look up from her handicrafts.

"What?" I croaked. Goddamn, my mouth was filled with sand. "What did you say?"

"I said you snore like a locomotive when you're sick," she repeated. "It's a quick way of knowing you're still alive but you're going to wake the dead, Wesley." She stabbed her needle through the fabric and dropped it to her lap. Then she leveled her gaze on me. "You've been asleep for almost twenty hours. We need to get you up. After everything you've put me through, you're not throwing a pulmonary embolism on top of it all. And god help me, if you want to be an asshole and do it just to spite me, I will crack your chest open and fish out that embolism myself."

"What?" I blinked at her as her words came to me through a long tunnel. "What?" I asked again.

She stood, paced toward the bed and peeled back the blankets without ceremony. When it came to mothers who'd also served as combat nurses, privacy was an illusion. "You've been in this bed for twenty hours," she said as she inspected the wound on my flank. "Your blood needs to move. If it doesn't, it thickens and gets stuck in places like your lungs."

She poked at a tender spot on my arm and those gray walls turned bright red. "Jesus Christ, Judy," I cried. "Trying to break the bones one more time?"

"It's looking better," she said, ignoring me. "It's going to be sore for a long while."

"Perhaps you could go easy on me," I said, nearly nauseous with pain. "I don't know, maybe don't stab me with your bony little fingers?"

My mother snapped the blankets back up, fisted her hands on her hips. "Wesley," she hissed. "Do you have any idea what you've put us through? You were tortured and shot and your arm—my god, your arm might not heal properly. You lost your *spleen* to this mission and your—"

"And my cover," I whispered. "I lost my cover, I'm probably being charged with war crimes as we speak, and I'll never work in covert operations again, Mom. You don't need to remind me."

She was silent then because she knew. She knew this was worse than any broken bone, any semi-essential organs. My father had served as a Navy SEAL before moving up the chain of command and running SEAL school down on Coronado Island. Will had served before an injury and burnout got the better of him. My mother knew more about the covert life than anyone and she knew I was well and truly fucked.

She brushed her fingers over my forehead, finally giving me the dose of momming I'd needed. "You'll be fine. You'll land on your feet, Wesley. You always do."

I wanted to believe that. I wanted to see a path forward that didn't involve me and my fruit salad of injuries parked behind a desk in CIA purgatory. Or worse—whatever that was.

"Just because you don't see it now doesn't mean you won't see it," she continued. "Your only concern right now is getting healthy." She glanced over her shoulder, frowning. "And that means getting up. Let me grab your father or Will to help you. You've been too big for me since you were five, you little behemoth."

I curled my fingers around her wrist, tugged her close before she could dart away. "Mom, wait."

A flood of memories from my escape washed over me. Determination to get home, to survive. Fear that I wouldn't and then the cold, prickling acknowledgement that my odds weren't good. I hadn't accepted death on that tanker but I'd twirled toward it. I remembered that twirl as if it'd happened five minutes ago.

I'd wanted my mother, as most sailors and soldiers did when they were broken and bleeding and sinking into the darkness as it surrounded them. I'd wanted my family. My brother, my sister, even my father. I'd wanted one more day to tell them I loved them and appreciated them. And I'd wanted to tell them who I was because I wasn't taking all of my secrets to the grave. They couldn't remember a fraction of me, the piece I'd spit-shined since always.

My mother combed her fingers through my hair. "What is it, sweetheart?"

I took the deepest breath my wounds would allow and said, "I need to tell you—"

The door banged open and my father stepped inside, a crisp Navy ball cap perched on his head and an equally crisp plaid button-down tucked into ironed jeans. Fuck it all, it was good to see him. It was damn good to see him but that flashbang burst of military discipline stole my honesty.

"There he is," my father boomed. "I knew you'd come around soon enough. I told your mother she had nothing to worry about. You always come out on top, Wesley."

A laugh that sounded more like a cough rattled through my chest. This was the wrong moment to inform my father, the one with his retirement rank embroidered on the side of his cap, that I was on top only about half the time.

"Quiet, Bill," she said over her shoulder. Then, turning back to me, "What were you saying, Wesley?"

"I, uh," I started, gazing at my father, "I need to pee."

She clapped her hands and pointed at my father. "It's a good thing you're here, Bill. Wesley never liked it when I helped him in the bathroom as a child. I can only imagine he'd put up the same fit if I tried now."

I held back a snort because I was certain it would hurt like hell. But more than that, I was lucky. Lucky to be alive, lucky to have people who gave a shit about me, lucky to have a mother who would yell about getting my ass up so I didn't give myself an embolism. I was lucky, even if I was thirty-six years old, missing a spleen, and still in the closet.

"Thanks, Judy," I murmured. "Thank you."

I was lucky.

3

WES

"CAN I take a look at the burns on your legs?"

I blinked up at the doctor. "What's your name again?"

He plucked a penlight from his pocket and clicked it on before flashing it between my eyes. "Are you having trouble recalling other names? Events? Places?"

I clutched the blanket to my neck as I scowled at him. "No, man, I just don't think we've been properly introduced."

He clicked the light off. "I've seen you four times since you arrived here," he said. "Nick Acevedo. I've mentioned that. Each time."

I blinked at him again. My arm hurt so much I wanted to tear it off. "I wasn't listening. You're married to the redhead who knows everything about volcanoes. See? I remember the important shit and I just wanted to get on a first-name basis before you got in my bikini area again."

"What day is it?"

"Fuck if I know," I replied. I hated the world right now.

Hated the fucking world. It hurt to breathe, stand, think. My partner Veronica was dead and my security clearance had been revoked. My job was sure to follow. "January something. If I had to guess, I'd say the twelfth. Maybe the thirteenth. That's all I've got."

"Where are we?"

"My brother's big-ass house in Massachusetts, where it's really fucking cold and my balls go into hiding every time I look at the ocean. Since you mention this frozen corner of hell, I'll give you twenty grand to put me on a flight to the Bahamas this afternoon."

"Save your money," he said, still frowning at my eyes. "The names of Will and Shannon's kids?"

"Abby and Annabelle. The dogs are Taos and Del, not that you asked."

"You need to tell me if you experience any neurological issues," he said.

If I could've managed a shoulder jerk or a nod without pain ricocheting through my body, I would've done it. Instead, I said, "Sure thing, boss."

"I'm astonished that first infection cleared up so nicely," Nick said. "I expected a secondary infection of some kind. Cellulitis, MRSA, something. There's no reasonable explanation for how well this gunshot wound is healing."

If this was A-plus healing, I didn't want to imagine the average. I required assistance to sit up. The act of speaking zapped my energy. I coughed last night and seriously believed my internal organs were going to burst out of me. I sat down to shower. "Strong immune system."

"That only gets you so far," he murmured as he prodded the wound on my flank.

"Mom's home cooking," I offered.

His brows pitched up. "Chicken soup has never once prevented streptococcal infections following gunshot wounds."

"Then it must be all the thoughts and prayers. They have to be good for something," I said.

He glanced at me with an unimpressed glare. "Hardly. Listen, I'm not ready to sign off on this wound. It looks good but it's not uncommon for infections to crop up late in the game with gunshots. When a bullet passes through human tissue, it creates a passageway but also a vacuum. It sucks in everything it can, filling that passage with foreign matter. Clothing fibers, dust, debris, bacteria, germs on the bullet itself. All of those things are drawn into the affected tissue. That passage will collapse as the force of the bullet moves through the body. That's what we're looking out for right now."

"You're waiting for secret prison dirt to flare up into a killer infection?" I waved at my bruised, broken body. "This isn't enough shit to deal with, might as well throw in some international germs?"

He shrugged. "They take time showing up, especially considering you survived on pure adrenaline for several days."

"What I'm hearing you say is I should eat more chicken soup."

He didn't acknowledge that comment, instead shifting

his attention to the incision on my arm. "This needs another week of immobilization. Probably longer."

"That's really going to get in the way of my combat exercises."

"You're not cleared to hold a pencil, Halsted. Combat is gonna wait." He stretched my arm out and back down to my side. "You'll need extensive physical therapy before you can do anything resembling combat."

"You're killing my sex life, doc."

"You're not cleared for sex either," he said, a laugh heavy in his words. "No lifting, no stairs, no bending or twisting, and no sex."

"I don't know how you get your dick sucked but I can do it without lifting, bending, or twisting, and there have only been a few instances involving stairs, so—"

"If those incisions open, you'll need four to six weeks of intensive wound care," Nick replied. "No sex."

"But a lot more chicken soup?"

He studied me for a moment, my arm still held in his hands. "You're not going back to work for five to six months, Wes. If not longer. We won't know the full extent of the damage until the swelling goes down and the bone starts healing. You have a long recovery ahead of you. If you're anything like Will—"

"I'm not," I snapped.

I loved the guy. He was one of the best. All of that was true but it didn't make us the same person and it didn't mean we handled our shit the same ways. Recovering in his house, surrounded by his children and his wife and his dogs and all the things he kept under his immaculate control, reminded me of that fact. And it reminded me *I'd* fucked up and *I'd* lost control, and now my partner was dead and my cover was irreversibly blown and my career was most likely over.

"If you are," he started, his words soft, "that's not something you want to hear. You're human and you have to put up with all the fragility that comes along with it, even if you have a history of defying that truth."

I wasn't prepared to revisit the topic of my mortality today. I'd spent enough time flirting with it on that tanker.

Thinking about that awareness chilled me to the core and reminded me how I'd longed to get it right if I made it through. How I'd made promises to myself.

But...was I still betraying myself if I broke a promise I never imagined I'd live to carry out?

4

WES

THE HOUSE WAS QUIET. It was strange. In my six weeks of residency at my brother's house, I'd come to learn it was nothing if not routinely loud. This place was filled with dogs, babies, people, my cadre of physical therapists, and old, creaky floors. This newfound calm was unsettling. It set me on edge, sent every worst-case scenario swirling through my mind.

Was it quiet because we were under attack? Had intruders locked everyone in the basement at gunpoint?

Was it quiet because terrorists shot nerve gas into the house? Had I survived because I'd isolated myself in the garage apartment as soon as I could manage the stairs on my own, which had only taken seven mortifyingly long days after my father had shouldered my sorry ass to the bathroom and stayed in there with me to make sure I didn't fall over and die?

Was it quiet because everyone was gone? Kidnapped, maybe killed?

I padded into the kitchen, careful to keep my steps silent. With my functional hand, I pulled a cleaver from the knife block. If my other hand was worth shit, I would've grabbed an apple from the fruit bowl. It wasn't much but my knuckleball was enough to disorient the most skilled attackers. Combat wasn't about advanced weapons. It was about inflicting quick, devastating damage with anything you could find.

That was when I noticed him.

He was walking slowly, his gaze and his thumbs glued to his mobile phone. Medium height, golden skin, dark hair, lean shoulders. *Young*. Too young for me. Retro horn-rimmed glasses, a three-piece gray suit that made me thirsty as fuck with the way it nipped in at his trim waist, and an expensive leather messenger bag. He didn't look like any assassin I'd ever met. Mostly because he wasn't paying attention to a damn thing.

Maybe he wasn't an assassin at all.

"Who the fuck are you?" I barked.

His head snapped up as he sucked in a breath and flattened his phone to the vee of his vest. "Tom Esbeck," he replied, blinking fast. Blinking at the cleaver I pointed in his direction. Blinking back at me. He had gorgeous eyes, a deep, moody brown that reminded me of the first cup of hot coffee after a long, wild night. "Uh, okay. This is interesting. Yeah, I'm Tom and we've met. At Matt and Lauren's wedding. We met there. I told you where to find the good gay bars in Provincetown. Remember?"

I didn't, and I didn't lower the cleaver. "Aren't they all?"

"Gay?" he asked. "Or good?"

I jerked a shoulder up. The only shoulder I could jerk. The cadre of physical therapists hadn't cracked this nut yet. "Both."

He shook his head. "No, not nearly. Not anymore," he replied. "Listen, I'm not sure what this is about but I'm just leaving a few things for Shannon to sign when she gets back. Could we play cops and robbers later? I'm due on the other side of the city in an hour and traffic is such a bitch."

"Where is she?" I hated asking the question. I hated not knowing. But I'd also locked myself away above the garage back in January, ignoring most attempts at interacting with anyone while I watched the month and my life as I knew it slide away. I'd chosen that and I'd chosen this set of consequences too, even if I found them inconvenient now.

He glanced at his watch. One of the new ones that tracked steps and sleep and literally everything about your existence. "Doctor appointments. Her and then the new baby." He nodded toward the cleaver with an eyeroll. "Praise the puppies. It's always something at the Halsted house."

I peered at him as he shifted toward the door, tilting my head a bit to drink him up. He was trim and fit as fuck and...and beautiful. *Beautiful.* His complexion was gorgeous. That vest wanted to be ripped off. Just fucking ripped off. Fabric tearing, buttons flying everywhere, off. I'd destroy that fancy dress shirt too. Leave it in a shredded pile on the floor.

If I'd met him before, I would've remembered. Yeah, I

would've remembered him. I wanted to remember him. "Wait. You're not leaving yet," I called to his back. "Who are you again?"

5

TOM

G.I. JOE WAS BAREFOOT and shirtless.

And wagging a knife at me.

And didn't remember meeting me before this charmed encounter.

When the reasonable part of me thought about it, I could forgive him. It had been a wedding with free-flowing liquor, and it had been more than five freaking years ago.

But when the vain part of me thought about it, I wasn't as forgiving. The vain part of me was my entirety and I wanted to be memorable. I didn't care if that made me petty and self-centered, and I wasn't sticking around to hoard scraps of his bare-chested attention. I shifted toward the front foyer, giving him a tidy view of my ass in this flawless suit and one more chance to dust off his memory.

And my ass *was* juicy in these trousers. Ripe-peach juicy.

I was unconcerned with the knife in his hand and the

fact he continued wagging it in my direction. He wasn't going to hack me to death or throw it at me, or whatever it was these military types did. But the scar running down his flank and the brace on his arm, those were certainly consequential. I'd heard from Shannon that her brother-in-law was staying with her and Will while he recovered from an assortment of injuries incurred while overseas. I'd heard specifics on neither his wounds nor his previous location.

Wes stared in my direction—specifically, his gaze shifted to my very juicy ass—for another moment before dropping the knife to the marble countertop beside him. The clang of steel on stone vibrated between us.

"Wait. You're not leaving yet." He sounded irritable, as if him forgetting me was my problem. "Who are you again?"

I shifted back to face him but couldn't tear my gaze from his body. He was amazing. A real, live G.I. Joe with scars and fresh wounds and unbuttoned jeans and…no shirt hiding that glorious tuft of blond chest hair.

No shirt.

No! Shirt!

Dammit, I was trying to be aloof. He didn't remember a damn thing about me yet I was salivating over his abs and dreaming about pulling on that chest hair while I sat on his face. Why did I do this to myself? Really, why did I turn into a heart-eyed puddle every time a brawny beefcake blew me off? Because that was the situation now…and always. I got nothing and kept getting in line for more of it.

"Like I said," I started, busying myself with the files in my bag to keep from drooling, "I'm Tom. We've met before.

I work for Shannon and I'm dropping off some documents for her." I slapped a purple file folder on the counter. "No need to brandish any weapons on my account, sweet pea."

"Then it's a good thing I don't have any others," he replied, tipping his chin toward the arm encased in a brace. "I should probably start hiding some in here."

In spite of myself, I barked out a laugh. "What is it with you Halsteds and arming yourselves to the teeth? Last I heard, your brother was working on a trebuchet."

"It's the in-depth knowledge of the evil lurking beyond the peace and quiet of this happy suburban town."

His words were easy, almost matter-of-fact, but there was nothing easy about the hard glint in his eyes. And those eyes, they shone like an endless night. Deep enough that I almost fell in and drowned as we stared at each other.

I blinked away, cleared my throat. "Right, well, I need to be in Marshfield before two and—"

"Will you come back?" he asked.

"What?" I laughed to cover my surprise.

"What?" he repeated, his brows quirking. He looked sad. Oh my god, if he didn't knock that off immediately, I was going to papa bear all over his ass. "I just meant, I don't know, I thought you might be coming back and—"

"I mean, maybe? I don't really—"

"No, yeah. It's fine. No worries," he said, shaking his head as we talked over each other. "I just thought you'd—you know, maybe—you'd come back. Here. Again. For Shannon…or something else."

"I can," I said before my attention-starved mouth could consult my no-nonsense brain. "I can come back. Later? Tonight?"

What the hell was wrong with me? What the actual hell was wrong with me?

"Yeah?" A grin pulled at his lips and my belly flipped all the way over. That hadn't happened since I'd tried intermittent fasting last summer. Horrible experience. Then he had the audacity to continue speaking after flooring me with that smile. "Would I be pushing my luck if I asked you to bring some sushi with you?"

"Yes," I replied flatly. "It's broccolini and salmon for me tonight."

Wes cocked his head to the side and rubbed his hand down his abs. Down the thick trail of blond hair and under his waistband. It took real strength to keep from reaching out and petting him. I knew if I did, I'd call him a good boy while I did it and we could not have that. Not at all. And it was bad manners to pet men without their permission.

"You're sure about that?" He tucked his thumb behind his waistband, tugging his jeans down just enough to expose paler skin and muscled grooves and dusky hair that made me stupid. Just fucking stupid.

With a sigh, I asked, "What do you want?"

"I'm sure I'll be happy with anything you give me," he drawled.

"Oh my god, stop it," I snapped, holding up my palm at him.

"Stop what?" he asked, all sweet and innocent.

"You know," I warned, jabbing a finger in his direction. "You know what you're doing."

Those jeans slipped down another quarter of an inch. "Is it working?"

More than it should. "No. Now, either give me your sushi order or you're getting a plateful of California rolls with fake crab."

He dragged his gaze over me, my suit, my wingtips. Then back up. "Let's get a few things straight, honey. First, you don't eat anywhere that serves imitation crab. Just not happening. Second, I would be happy with anything you bring me and that's no exaggeration. In case you haven't noticed, I'm fucking helpless right now. I can't go anywhere or do anything. I haven't been out of this house since I was dropped at the curb last month and I haven't been with family in much longer. *Years* longer. I don't care what you're feeding me. I'll take it."

He wasn't referring to *family* family. He was surrounded by that. It was a different form of family he needed now. That knowledge, more than anything—chest hair and stupid muscles included—softened me for this man. I knew isolation. I knew loneliness. I didn't wish that on him.

"Fine but get a shirt," I replied. "It's too damn cold to be walking around like that."

"This is mild compared to where I've been." Wes rasped out a laugh, one that started in his belly and moved all the way up to his full lips. I knew this because I watched his muscles bunch and jostle as he did it. And I damn near swooned. Wrist to the forehead, breathy sigh, buckling knees swoon. I crossed my arms over my chest, a feeble attempt at keeping myself upright.

"Get a shirt," I repeated.

"I'll try." He ran his hand over his fuzzy chest, a smile warming his eyes. "Can't make you any promises."

Yeah. I needed a fainting couch real quick.

6

WES

"WHERE DID EVERYONE GO THIS MORNING?" I asked, parked in the middle of the kitchen while my family bustled around me.

I'd spent the past two hours torn between the lingering effervescence of flirtation and the itch of my earlier panic over the quiet. Now that my brother's home had returned to its regularly scheduled chaos, I was ready to scratch that itch.

Will stood with his back to me as he poured Cheerios into a plastic cup. He handed it to his daughter Abby, who promptly upended the contents onto the floor. "Call the dogs in, Wes," my brother said, ignoring my question. He crouched down to meet Abby at eye level. "Was that necessary?"

"Apes!" she cried.

"You asked for Cheerios," he replied evenly. "If you'd asked for grapes, I would've given you grapes."

"Apes!" she repeated.

"Are you going to throw them if I give them to you?" Will tucked her hair over her ears. "Because dogs cannot eat grapes and then your mother will decide the floor needs to be washed in the middle of the night, and we can't have either of those situations, Abby. How about blueberries?"

My mother breezed past me with little more than a pat to my shoulder, asking, "Where's the blanket Annabelle spit up on earlier? I want to toss that in with the load of baby clothes I'm washing."

"I don't know, Judy," Will replied, pushing to his feet. "Check the baby bag."

Abby toddled over to me and fastened her body around my leg. "Hello," I said to her.

My father marched through the kitchen carrying three paper grocery bags in each arm. Naturally. Why take an extra trip to the car when you could be a hero instead? "Give me a hand with this, Wesley," he said as he removed items from the bags.

"He's supposed to be calling the dogs in," Will said.

I glanced down at the child hugging my leg. She smiled up at me with a drooly grin and proceeded to gnaw at my jeans as if that was standard operating procedure. "Yeah, just a second with that. I asked where everyone went this morning. The place was a ghost town and no one mentioned a damn thing to me."

"Wesley, please. The babies are listening," my mother chided.

The gremlin on my leg was too busy chewing denim to hear anything but that wasn't my problem right now. "Cool.

Whatever. Where was everyone and why was it a huge secret?"

"Is there something you're trying to say?" Will called over his shoulder.

"Yeah, I'm saying everyone left and no one told me about it," I replied. "What's the story with that?"

My father folded two empty grocery bags into precise halves, smoothing the paper along the crisp edges. "No secrets, Wesley. Your mother and I took Abby to her yoga class and food shopping while Will and Shannon had appointments."

I looked down at Abby. "You have *yoga* classes? And *my father* took you there?"

"Sure did," he called, smiling at the little girl. "We have a lot of fun with our tree poses, don't we?"

The man known to many as the Commodore because he loved military life *that much* set bags of avocados and purple carrots down to extend his arms over his head and flatten the sole of his shoe to his opposite leg. Abby slapped her hand to my shin, shouting, "Shree! Shree!"

"Sorry, kiddo. I can't do that one," I said. "Still kind of amazed your grandfather does."

An overflowing laundry basket tucked to her hip, my mother said, "We love the tiny tot yoga. We do all the poses together and practice deep breathing."

"Forgive me if it takes a minute to wrap my mind around that," I said.

Shaking her head, my mother said, "Take all the time you need. I'll be in the laundry room."

"Have fun with that," I called after her. "Maybe now I

could get some explanation as to why no one told me about this. I thought—I don't know. All I'm saying is, it's weird for this place to empty out. I thought something was wrong."

My father dropped his hands from over his head and studied me for a moment. It was uncomfortable, his scrutiny. "Are you sleeping well?" he asked.

Not at all. "Yeah, I'm fine."

He continued staring. "Do you find yourself worrying often?"

Only about everything. "No, hardly at all."

"Since no one is going to get the dogs, I'll do it," Will announced, disappearing out the back door.

I reached down, ran my fingers through Abby's halo of white-blonde curls. "Don't chew off my leg, okay? I need both of them."

"'Kay, 'kay, 'kay," she answered.

"There's no shame in talking to someone, in getting help," the Commodore announced.

He said this as if it was a simple truth, something he knew and I should know too. But it wasn't simple and we both knew that. It wasn't a matter of bravado. The aftertaste of black ops work wasn't meant to be examined in talk therapy, and only those who could manage the silence were sent down range. We had the psych profiles to prove it. Sitting my ass in front of a shrink would accomplish one thing: prove I'd lost a lot more than my cover in Russia.

"Coming home can be difficult under the best circumstances. You've been through the worst circumstances," he continued.

You don't know the half of it. "I'm doing great. No issues aside from my arm."

He shot a tight-lipped grimace at the brace on my arm, nodding. "No doubt about that. None whatsoever." He flattened his hands on the countertop. "And there's no doubt losing a team member is devastating, especially since you worked so closely with Veronica for such an extended period of time. It might help to talk it out instead of letting her death occupy space inside you."

Thanks for reminding me about my fake wife, the one killed execution-style and discarded on the steps of the American embassy. "Did you learn that at tiny tot yoga?"

"I'll have you know we talked about breathing in good vibes and blowing out the bad ones last week," he replied with a laugh. "I hope you know you can always talk to me, Wesley. Me, your mother, Will. All of us. You can talk to us about anything, good vibes and bad vibes. You know that, don't you?"

There's an entire lifetime I can't share with you and not just the one classified above top secret. "Of course."

He stared at me, unblinking, as if he intended to continue. As if he wanted to have a conversation about all the things we didn't discuss, which was everything. Even if I was at liberty to share, I wouldn't know where to start explaining to him the toll of extended espionage, of faking a hetero relationship, of living to tell about shoddy attempts at torture-based interrogation, of feeling trapped in America after years abroad, of speaking a foreign language for so long my brain required extra processing time to comprehend English.

Of being someone else for so long I doubted whether I knew anything about myself. Except I knew I was living a marginal, fractional life. I was covering up and sweeping away and smoothing off the edges.

He knew I couldn't tell him anything. That was why he returned to stocking the refrigerator and let the moment pass.

"I don't need therapy," I added.

"Didn't say you did," he replied.

"I'd just like some notice if everyone is going to be out of the house."

He closed the refrigerator. "Will do."

"It was weird. That's all. And someone from Shannon's office dropped by. It was surprising. That's all this is about. I didn't expect these things. You don't have to worry about me picking up some PTSD on my last outing."

Shannon stepped into the kitchen from the back staircase, saying, "Why are there Cheerios on the floor? Never mind, I don't need the story. I'll wash it later." She stopped at my side and held my younger niece out to me. "I overheard what you said on my way down. I forgot I'd asked Tom to bring me a few things today. I should've given you a heads-up. Sorry about that. I can't keep track of the days. Would you hold Annabelle for a minute? I need to grab some snacks before feeding her again."

I gestured to my injured arm, the one I couldn't lift beyond shoulder level. "I probably shouldn't."

"It's just for a minute." Shannon settled the baby into the crook of my good arm and tucked the lame one beneath it. "See? Perfect."

Wide eyed, I glanced between the tiny bundle in my arms and the little koala on my leg. "I don't need a detailed schedule," I said. "Just let me know when the place is emptying out."

"I'll see to it," my father said. "We shouldn't have left you without appropriate intel. Won't happen again."

I had no reason to continue harping on this but I couldn't let it go. I couldn't stop scratching the itch. "Out of curiosity, why did it happen this time?"

"I'm sorry about that," Shannon said as she scooped peanut M&Ms into a cup. "We should've—"

"Shannon, sweetheart, you have enough on your hands." My father leveled the stern gaze of a commanding officer on me. It was good to know my issues ranked below forcing an apology from my sister-in-law. "You've made it clear you don't want to be disturbed. We didn't disturb you. If you're looking for someone to blame for this morning's events, blame me." He sliced his hand through the air to punctuate his point. "There's no shame in talking to someone about"—he glanced around with a slight shake of his head—"about anything. Anything you're dealing with from this mission or...anything else in your life. Anything at all, Wesley. It might do you good as you make sense of your next moves."

Thank you again. I really needed a reminder about the fucked-up state of my life and body. "Sir, yes, sir."

Shannon eyed us as she collected Annabelle from me. "Do you think you could help me upstairs with these two?" My father rushed over to assist but she held him off. "No, we're fine, Bill. I wouldn't want to pry Abby away from

Uncle Wes until she's decided she's ready." When I didn't respond, she waved me toward the back stairs. "Come on. We're going to have some quiet time. All of us. You too, Wes."

Since extending this discussion of my mental health wasn't a good choice for anyone, I gathered Abby up with one arm and settled her on my hip. Without another word to my father, I followed Shannon upstairs and toward the master bedroom.

"This one needs to eat," Shannon announced, tipping her head toward the newborn in her arms. "That one"—she glanced at the girl-shaped koala on my hip—"needs to settle down for a quick nap. And you"—she grinned at me as if she saw something I couldn't—"need some baby snuggles."

I gestured to my niece. "This? No, she needed a chew toy. If I hadn't been there, I'm sure she would've found a chair leg or some running shoes to stick in her mouth. I'm not one for dispensing snuggles. I'll just leave her with you."

She set her M&Ms on the table and climbed atop the massive bed with its luxurious navy velvet quilt layered over a thick down duvet and patted the space beside her. "Sit with me, Wes."

It was an invitation but it was also an order.

I didn't know much about my brother's wife. I'd met her the same time he did—our sister Lauren's wedding—but I'd paid little attention to the redheaded steamroller that weekend. As the story went, Will paid a lot of attention to her that weekend. It was her sister, the geologist expat whose need for space and independence from her family was rivaled only by mine, that I'd noticed. Our journeys abroad hadn't overlapped many times since that weekend but whenever they did, I was left with the sense Shannon wasn't the kind of woman you crossed and lived to talk about it.

From this angle, I could see it.

I set Abby on the bed and settled beside her but she immediately crawled into my lap, resting her head on my chest. "Oh. All right," I said, giving her back a tentative pat. She brought her thumb to her mouth. "This is...fine."

"I'm going to offer you some unsolicited advice," Shannon said, propping her elbow on a pillow.

I glanced away as she edged up her shirt. "I'm all stocked up on PTSD diagnoses, thanks."

"Yeah, I caught most of that," she replied, popping a candy in her mouth. "But here's the thing, Wes. He wasn't talking about PTSD back there. That was the gateway he used to start the conversation, to signal that he supports you."

Abby grabbed a handful of my shirt in her fist, dragging a corner of the fabric into her mouth. Her eyes were glazed and lids drooping. The only things she wanted in the world were something to chew on and somewhere warm to rest her head. If only my life could be that simple. "It's pretty great how he requires the shield of psychological trauma to start a conversation."

"Are there better ways to do it? Sure. Is it major progress for a guy who will admit that, until very recently, he didn't appreciate the importance of mental health access for service members? Yes. I maintain that he was trying to open the door for you."

I glanced at Abby, her eyes closed and her thumb still on her lower lip. I guided her hand to my chest to prevent her from startling herself awake. Her curls were insane. Messy corkscrews of the palest blonde, a shade barely above translucence. Fine wisps of the same platinum covered Annabelle's head too. "I would've bet money on these two having your hair."

She shrugged. "What can I say? We make blonde babies."

I watched Abby sleep for several minutes. I couldn't spend any time considering whether my father's insistence I talk to someone was a poorly veiled attempt at discussing —what, exactly? Did Shannon believe he was trying to have a good-natured chat about my sexual preference?

My parents were good, decent people but when my father was a commanding officer in the United States Navy, he'd carried out Don't Ask, Don't Tell. He'd booted sailors from SEAL school for being openly gay and he hadn't seemed terribly remorseful about it. I remembered him talking about it at the dinner table when I was a kid. If anything, he thought it was a good, sensible solution to the "problem."

Even if he wanted to be supportive now, how the fuck was I expected to forget how he institutionalized homophobia? And even if he'd grown and learned and knew better, why did I have to bother with that conversation when there was no earthly need to discuss sexual preference with anyone other than my sexual partners? Will and Lauren hadn't sat our parents down for a chat about preferring the opposite sexes. Why was I obligated to do it based on the simple fact I preferred men? And why did I have to do it on his terms?

Even if I'd thought about telling them when I was bleeding out on that tanker, I knew now it wasn't necessary. It wasn't worth it and...and I didn't think I'd survive if my father told me it was a good thing my cover was blown and my military intelligence career was over. I didn't think I could handle seeing the tiniest flicker of disappointment in his face.

So no, I wasn't out to my parents and I wasn't coming out because my father spent a minute rethinking a hateful policy. And I wasn't out at work, assuming I still had a job, because the spirit of that policy was baked into the institution.

Eventually, I said to Shannon, "I admire the sentiment, both from you and the Commodore. The conversation you're suggesting isn't on the top of my to-do list this week."

"I don't think you want to hear this but you *can* talk to him," Shannon said. "I won't pretend I know the relationship you have with your parents but they've spent a lot of time here over the past two years. They've become a second set of parents to me and much of my family. I've heard them talk about you when they didn't know I was listening and I know they only want the best for you."

"Maybe this is the best thing for me." I ran my hand over Abby's curls. This kid was pretty cute. "So, Tom."

Shannon scooped candies into her hand as she considered me. "Yes?"

As casually as I could manage, I asked, "What's his deal?"

Her lips pursed and her brow bent to a point, she stared at me for a long moment. "By *deal,* you mean...what, exactly?"

This conversation was like stepping on a landmine. If I moved, I'd be blown to shit. If I didn't move, I'd also find myself blown to shit because the best way to get shot was to stand still. Since I was taking the hit either way, I asked, "Is he single?"

A noise sounded in her throat. Something like an irritable sigh-snarl. "One more piece of unsolicited advice for you."

I dropped my head back against the tufted headboard and closed my eyes. "What could possibly be better than the last bit?"

"Tom isn't a toy," she said. "Don't play with him."

My eyes still shut, I asked, "Why do you assume I'd do that?"

"Not an assumption," she replied. "Only advice."

I nodded, patting Abby's back as she slept. It didn't seem like a good time to mention I was horrible when it came to taking anyone's advice other than my own.

7

TOM

DRAGGING myself from my beautifully appointed South End apartment and out of the city to Boston's North Shore on a weeknight was not my idea of a good time. My weeknights were routinized down to the minute and I liked it that way. I'd meal-prepped the week but yet I was hand-carrying sushi to a knife-wielding military operative who didn't bother with shirts or remembering people he'd talked to for a few minutes five years ago.

For fuck's sake. This was not in my macros for the day.

But this was what chest hair—and lonely boys with stupid muscles—did to me. Crazy irrational things like eating outside my meal plan and abandoning my sensible bedtime.

All of this ignored the fact I hadn't notified Shannon about my second visit of the day to her home. I'd spent the afternoon debating it but as much as I adored the supreme ruler of the Walsh world, I didn't want her to know I was calling on her brother-in-law.

Not that I was calling on him. No, we weren't *seeing* each other. We'd only eye-fucked each other a bit and now we were eating dinner. Nothing to report here. I was merely skulking up the back steps to the apartment over her garage to deliver some sushi and...and that was it. We'd eat and talk, and then I'd leave. That was *it*.

Fucking chest hair and sad eyes and stupid muscles.

And Shannon didn't need to be bothered with the specifics of my life. She was busy diapering and nursing and sniffing baby heads. Unless I crawled into bed between her and Will to ask him for a cuddle, she didn't care what I was doing with my evening.

"Hello there."

I glanced up the staircase and found Wes at the landing, leaning against the doorjamb. Bare feet, hoodie, jeans. The sweatshirt hid his waistband but you could be sure I checked out that button fly. I was mildly heartbroken when I didn't find any exposed skin.

"What? No knives?" I deadpanned.

"Not unless you're into that," he replied.

"I'm not," I called, pausing two steps beneath the landing. I shot another glance at his fly and the outline behind it. Goddamn, I could not stop myself today.

"Good. Me neither," he rumbled, taking the bag from me. Then, "You have no idea how much I appreciate this. I've missed it about as much as I miss the use of my arm."

I shook my head, brushing off his thanks. "I know you've been overseas for a time but there are apps, you know. You can order anything now. On your phone."

I mimed tapping the imaginary phone in my palm, still

two steps beneath him. He granted me a half-smile then fucked me right up.

"I wasn't referring to the food, Tom."

I glanced up at him, watched his hard eyes scrape over me. He'd remembered my name. That shouldn't have meant something and I shouldn't have been the kind of person who considered that a win, but old traumas died hard.

Give me a crumb and I'd make believe it was a whole cake.

He stepped aside, motioned for me to enter the apartment. I noticed his hands then, the good one and the one partially concealed by his brace. They were fabulous hands. Big, with long, thick fingers and wide palms. All I needed in a man was a fuzzy chest, good hands, and steady employment.

If my data was in order, it appeared this guy was working with the holy trinity.

He continued, "I admit the food is a nice benefit. But I wouldn't want it getting—uh—colder? I don't know. Just get your ass inside, all right?"

I didn't know what I was getting into with this man. I didn't know where he'd been or where he was going but I knew I wanted to talk to him tonight.

And I wanted to see that chest hair again.

"FUCK ME, THAT WAS GOOD." Wes pushed away from the coffee table and leaned back against the base of the sofa, his legs folded in front of him. "Remind me about the time we met," he said, running his palm over the nape of his neck.

I busied myself with dragging the tips of my chopsticks through the dish of soy and wasabi between us. "Do I have to?"

"Yeah," he replied, laughing. "I hate that I can't remember. I never forget people."

As if that made it any better. "Mmhmm." What did it mean that I was the one-off Wes forgot? Was I both unmemorable and unremarkable, leaving him with a mental dead zone where I was concerned?

Ugh. Stop that.

I hated when my insecurities went off like a too-early alarm clock, clanging away until I chucked them out the window.

He tipped his chin up as he studied my legs. "I can't believe I forgot someone like you."

I pointed my sticks at him. "Meaning?"

His brows arched up as he stared at me another beat. "Meaning you're someone I'd like to remember."

I shook my head, not wanting to take possession of the heat behind his words. It wasn't for me. Even if he was fuzzy and employed and I was someone he'd theoretically remember, this unlikely gathering was even more unlikely to occur again. He'd leave and go wherever he went, and he'd stay there.

"It's all good," I said. "It was your sister's wedding. You had other things to notice. And I was making my way through a lot of issues back then."

"What kind of issues?"

He tipped his chin up again. Somehow, that tender gesture was enough to cut right through my bullshit and bring me to heel because I didn't think twice about saying, "Everything. Family stuff, work stuff, boy stuff."

His forehead crinkled. "What's your boy situation now?"

"There is no situation," I replied with a tight grin.

Wes drummed his fingertips against his lips as he hummed to himself. "I was fucked-up that weekend," he murmured.

"More than you are right now?"

He laughed at his brace. "Somehow, yes. It was the first time I had my heart broken. This is just my arm."

I wanted to ask. I wanted to know. I wanted a detailed accounting of who hurt him and how. Instead of requesting any of that, I asked, "And that's the only part of you fucked-up right now?"

He shrugged. "Maybe." Then, "I'm sure you were a pretty young thing at that wedding."

Talk about backhanded compliments. "What does that make me now?"

"Still pretty," he replied with a laugh. "But now you're old enough to stay on the right side of my conscience."

"That's funny," I started, eyeing his brace, "I don't get the impression your conscience calls all the shots." When he replied with a small shrug, I continued. "How did you hurt your arm?"

"I can't tell you that, and even if I could, I wouldn't. You don't need to know what I've seen, sweetheart. You don't need those horrors in that pretty head of yours."

"Oh, you're one of them," I drawled. "You know what's best for everyone. Got it. Good to know."

A smile pulled at his lips. "And what about you? Are you one of those thoroughly excessive Thoms with an h? The t-h-o-m variety?"

"I'm only basically excessive, I'm a t-o-m Tom. I have a friend who is a p-a-w-l Pawl and I admit I thought about making the switch a few years ago." Because I was more than a little masochistic, I asked, "Would it surprise you to know I've seen plenty of horrors?"

He ran his tongue along the seam of his lips, silent for a beat. "Nothing surprises me," he replied. "But it would be a big help if you could tell me who needs a one-way ticket to a watery grave rather than making me do the legwork on my own."

As much as I wanted to curl up in his lap and drown in the safety of his arms, I shook my head, waved away his words. That was the proper response. "None of that, please, 007."

"How old are you, Tom without the h?"

"Twenty-nine," I replied.

"I was right," he whispered, almost to himself. "I didn't forget you. I didn't let myself remember you."

"That's one way to revise history." I snapped one of the containers shut. "And what about you, Old Man of the Mountain?"

Wes pressed his palm to his chest. "Can't you see I'm already wounded? Jesus. Please. Allow my thirty-six-year-old ass some dignity."

I studied the dark shadows under his eyes. He was tired but that wasn't a symptom; it was his state of being.

"Will you come back?"

I stared at him, not sure I understood what he was asking. I didn't know whether I wanted him to want me. Or not want me. Or any of it. I didn't think so. I couldn't get my arms around the contradiction of being forgotten and memorable all in the same day. I decided I wasn't going to try. The sentiment was far too familiar for my liking.

"Shannon is technically on maternity leave until late April or maybe early May but she's started doing some work again. I'll be dropping by to meet with her once or twice a week until she's back in the office. More, if she needs it."

I turned my gaze to the takeout containers and started consolidating the leftovers. A few pieces of hamachi remained along with some uni and tako. I'd ordered the California rolls in an odd attempt at bratty humor but Wes had eaten all of them.

"I didn't ask you about Shannon."

His words scraped out. Rough, a bit annoyed. I liked it so much that I wanted to rub my face up his thigh and nestle myself in his lap and beg him to grumble at me some more. He didn't need to know that. "Then what are you asking?"

He laughed, shook his head as if he couldn't believe someone would make him spell himself out. And why should he? He was perfect and hot, and that fuzzy chest, for fuck's sake. *For fuck's sake, he has stupid muscles.*

"I'm asking if you'd visit *me* again," he said. "With or without the A-plus sushi. I can't get far on my own—"

"Somehow, I don't believe that," I said under my breath.

Another laugh, another head shake. "Okay, I'll grant you that," he replied. "I'm not *supposed* to go far. How about that? Do you believe it?"

"I'll accept it," I said. "And what is it you're looking to gain from me visiting you?"

He tapped his fingers against his sweatshirt. "I have several answers for that but I guess the truth is I'll get a friend. I'm in short supply at the moment."

I continued tidying the coffee table as I thought about Shannon and Will and the rest of the Walsh family, and I wondered how anyone could want for friends with that crew on hand.

But then I remembered how I spent my days surrounded by that same crew and felt exactly as Wes did. They'd do anything for me and they'd be there in a heartbeat if I needed them. Shannon was the mother-sister-fairy-godmother I'd needed but never deserved. But they didn't live in my world. They didn't share my reality.

"All right. I'll come back," I replied, hazarding a glance at Wes. A smile warmed his face and it took all my strength to keep from dragging him into my arms because anyone with that much sweet and boyish needed to be held close, held tight. And degraded a bit too. Yeah, some time on his knees would do him real good. "How about Friday?"

8

WES

BACK WHEN I was going through BUD/S, the Navy SEAL qualifying course, one of the training exercises involved hiking through the Tijuana mudflats at night. It wasn't true quicksand but it was impossible to cross that terrain without experiencing the unmistakable suction of thick, wet mud. And the urban legends were accurate—fighting the force of the mud only made it suck harder.

Being trapped at my brother's house with a slew of injuries and an order to wait indefinitely for further instructions from the CIA reminded me of those flats.

I was stuck. I couldn't go anywhere. I couldn't do anything. I couldn't fix any of the problems in my life. I was…stuck.

And it sucked so hard.

I KNEW the minute Tom's car cruised down the driveway but I resolved to stay in the apartment and wait for him to arrive at my door. I was in control here. I had a plan for this evening and that plan didn't include scampering down the stairs and fussing all over him.

No, I had my shit in order. I was chill. I'd pop open a beer, try to reach the itchy spot on my back that'd been driving me nuts all day, and wait for him to come to me.

I did none of those things.

By the time he'd killed the engine, I was waving him in from the doorway. "Come on," I called, "you'll freeze your ass off if you stay out here much longer."

Tom's response came in the form of a frown and then the chirp of his car alarm engaging. He hunched into his winter coat, one that appeared to favor style over any degree of substance, and trudged toward me with a cloth grocery bag in hand. He didn't meet my gaze.

"Hey," he said as he approached the door, his lips still pinched in a frown. With his free hand, he clutched the lapels of his coat. I couldn't imagine that protected him from much of the brutal cold or slow-falling sleet.

"Let me take that," I said, reaching for the bag when he stepped into the narrow vestibule.

That earned me an impatient scoff which was an improvement on the frown but only in the sense that pirates were an improvement on bandits. For reasons I couldn't grasp, Tom didn't appear happy to be visiting me tonight. Maybe it wasn't about me. It could've been the weather. Complaining about the weather and its associated impact on road conditions was a team sport in this region. Or work or politics or anything. If he hadn't wanted to come, he would've bailed out. It wasn't about me. Couldn't be.

"You have a broken arm or something," Tom said, holding the bag away from me. "And it's just dinner, not a sack of gold bars. I can handle this. Thanks though."

I didn't know what the fuck was going on here but I gestured toward the stairs. "I still contend you're going to freeze your ass off. Upstairs, now."

"I'm not in the mood to be daddied tonight."

I cocked my head to the side to catch his eyes. "But you'd like it some other night?"

Finally—*finally*—he dragged his gaze up the length of my body and met my stare. A quick flash of defiance sparkled in his eyes and I had the distinct sense I was kidding myself if I thought I was anywhere near in control. "I don't know how you can complain about me being cold when you aren't wearing shoes or socks."

"I've clocked twenty-eight days of extreme weather training up in Alaska, on Kodiak Island. Plus some bonus training in Scandinavia. I've also spent the better part of the past decade hanging out in some of the frostiest corners of this planet. I know something about cold. I'd choose hot, sandy beaches every day and twice on Sunday but you could lock me outside barefoot all night and I'd be no worse off come morning."

Tom gave my feet an impatient huff. "I'm not interested in testing that hypothesis."

"Then let's go upstairs."

Tom went ahead of me and I ignored all the knowing glances he tossed over his shoulder as I studied his ass like it was fine art. That I didn't touch was the true test of my endurance.

Once we reached the apartment—which was a generous name for the space above the garage—Tom shrugged out of his coat, rolled up his sleeves, and busied himself with the contents of his grocery bag. He unpacked glass containers with red lids and some with blue lids, a metal mixing bowl, and a few ingredients gathered in a mesh sack. He did it all with the finest set of forearms I'd seen in ages.

I reached for the glass containers. "I can help with—"

He slapped my hand away. "No, I have everything organized." He slanted me a look before returning to his bag, his lips still pinched in a frowny-scowly-irritable twist. "I didn't realize it was Valentine's Day. When you asked me to come back and I suggested Friday. Today. I didn't realize it was Valentine's."

"Okay," I said slowly. "So, that's…a problem?"

"Of course it is." Tom rustled through the handful of cabinets that comprised this kitchen. I refused to call it a kitchenette. That word didn't belong in my mouth. When he found a cutting board and set it on the worn countertop, he said, "I made a date with you on Valentine's."

I still didn't understand. It was possible I was missing the point because I couldn't stop salivating over his arms. And his spiffy vest. I loved three-piece suits as much as the next guy but there was something about his trim body tucked into those barely pinstriped trousers, the crisp white shirt, that vest. And the tie. Jesus Christ, that boss man tie. "If it helps in any way, I didn't know it was Valentine's Day until you mentioned it just now."

He plucked a chopping knife from his bag, eyeing me with a wary stare. "You don't feel like I've trapped you into a Valentine's date?"

I watched as he slipped off the blade cover and sliced a lime in half. "How could I?"

"Then this isn't a Valentine's date," Tom said, mostly to himself.

"If that fixes this frowny-scowly-irritable thing you have going on, then sure." Knowing he was likely to slap my hand again, I stepped closer to him and smoothed away the creases on either side of his mouth. I slipped my fingers along the sharp line of his jaw to the back of his neck. "But like you said, it *is* a date and this is Valentine's, so—"

"So, nothing," he replied, swatting my wrist. "Go away, I have a glaze to make."

"Glaze, huh?" I leaned back against the kitchen counter with my arms folded over my chest as I watched Tom stationing fresh ginger, garlic, lime, oil, and a few other small jars I didn't recognize in a line beside his bowl. I grabbed one of the jars but he yanked it away before I could read the label.

He wagged the knife at me. "Don't touch."

I pointed at the blade. "I imagine we're even now. On the knife-wielding front."

"You're welcome to think that," Tom replied.

I studied him as he chopped and measured, every movement deft and intentional. He knew what he was doing and he looked good doing it. "What's this glaze all about?"

He replied with a tiny, almost imperceptible head shake, saying, "It's nothing."

I tipped my hand toward the array of ingredients. "It looks like something."

"It's just a little sesame ginger sauce," he said. "I made some last weekend when I was meal prepping—"

"Sorry, I didn't catch that. You were what?"

"Meal prepping," he repeated. I still didn't understand but I nodded as if I did. Rule number one of spycraft was acting like you knew what was going on. "It's my Sunday routine. Meal planning, grocery shopping, and then meal prepping. I look at my calendar for the week to determine if I have lunch meetings or evening events, and organize my macros from there." I nodded again. Still didn't get it. "And I made some of this sesame ginger sauce but when I opened it before coming here, it didn't smell fresh anymore. Sometimes that happens with the ginger. It can turn after a few days, you know?"

"Yes," I agreed. What did the ginger turn into? I did not know. "I've had that experience."

He pinned me with a look that would've been a glare if not for the upward curl of his lips. "You have not."

I rolled my hand, prompting him onward. "Continue with your story. It's fascinating."

"There's nothing else to it," he replied, a laugh ringing in his words. "Can we talk about something else? You're making me nervous."

I shifted closer to Tom. "How am I doing that?"

"You're watching me mince ginger. That's weird." He nudged my belly with his elbow until I backed up. "I'm going to screw up this recipe if you're not careful."

Once the ingredients were in the mixing bowl and he'd started whisking, I asked, "So, uh, where are you from?"

"Oh my god," he muttered.

"What? You wanted to talk about something else. What's wrong with asking that?"

"Nothing. It's fine." He rolled his eyes at the sauce. "It's the least interesting thing about me but the question that gets asked the majority of the time. I was born in Connecticut, the northwestern part. Lived there as a kid. Haven't been back since."

"I'm from San Diego," I offered. "It's my favorite place in the world and I'm comfortable saying that as I've seen a fair amount of the world. Since I loved it there so much, I went to the University of California in San Diego and then went to SEAL school on Coronado Island, just over a bridge from San Diego."

He glanced up at me, that scowl still betraying itself with a hint of a smile. "Is this your way of telling me your stay here will be brief?"

The second rule of spycraft was always knowing the out—exits physical and otherwise. The only trouble was I didn't have a clear out. Staying here another month or two wasn't my idea of a good time but my body was still healing and my job was on hold and there wasn't an alternative waiting for me around the corner. And I was on a date—on

Valentine's—with a man I was interested in getting to know.

"I'm not sure," I admitted. "Though I'm guessing I'll ship out by springtime."

I *had* to ship out by springtime. Even if the Agency didn't want me anywhere near Russian interests, they'd have to send me somewhere. There had to be some low-level ops requiring a guy who spoke enough languages to get around and could talk antiquities. There was always something going on in Monaco, the Caymans, Polynesia. They'd need me soon enough. They always did.

"Mmhmm." He resumed whisking. "Good to know." Then the whisk clanked against the metal bowl and he flattened his hands on the countertop, hanging his head. "Should I just go? I mean, you're leaving in a month or six weeks or whatever. Why am I even here? I should've stayed home tonight, drinking my calories and watching serial killer documentaries under my weighted blanket."

I stepped behind him, braced my hands on either side of his, and rested my chin on his shoulder. For a moment, I held myself steady, waiting for him to refuse me. When it didn't come, I leaned in, layering my torso over his back. I tucked myself right up against his ass because how could I not?

"You're here because I asked you to be here," I said. "And you came because you wanted to."

"I came because you were sad and lonely."

"You're not wrong." A laugh rumbled out of me. "And you're not wrong about my time here being short. But listen to me, Tom. There's no reason you should drink your calories and watch serial killer documentaries alone, not when you could do it with me."

"You forgot the weighted blanket."

I looped my good arm around his waist. The scents of ginger, garlic, and lime wafted around him but there was also a dash of something warm there, like cinnamon. "I don't even know what that is but it doesn't matter. I'd love to get under a blanket with you."

"Where have you been that you don't know about weighted blankets?"

I laughed into his neck. "I've been out of the country and had my eye on other priorities. You'll have to give me a thorough demonstration."

"That's the second time you've invited yourself to my bed."

"It's about time you noticed." Then, calling upon all the restraint in the world, I peeled myself off Tom and returned to my post beside him at the counter. "If you don't give me something to do, I'm gonna keep pawing at things." *At you.* "Put me to work."

With the reluctance of a true control freak, Tom assigned me the task of clearing the coffee table, setting out silverware, and filling water glasses while he warmed the dishes he'd brought with him. He ordered me out of the kitchen area, adding, "I hope you're not too religious about mixing your regions and cultures on the plate."

Again, I was at a loss but that wasn't slowing me down. "Not at all."

"Okay, good," he murmured, setting a pair of dishes on the table. "I know the whole ginger-garlic-lime thing doesn't technically line up with the kimchi thing but I'm working on adding more fermented foods to my diet this year." He unfolded a paper towel and spread it over his lap before glancing up at me. "I think it works well with the broccoli."

"Yeah, I get it. I'm not picky, but"—I shoved all the broccoli florets to the corner of my dish, the kimchi to the other, and forked up the salmon—"where is the rice?"

He spooned the sauce over his salmon. "What rice?"

Tom gestured for me to return the fish to my plate for its saucing. I did, saying, "You're supposed to have rice with salmon and broccoli. It's required."

His brows arched up. "According to…?"

"My mother. Martha Stewart. Mess halls everywhere. Probably the United States Department of Agriculture. You know, the basic tenets of well-rounded meals."

"I don't eat grains," he replied.

"And why is that?" He glared at me for a second as if I was the one being absurd in this conversation.

"Really?" he asked. Fully absurd. "Fine." Then he pushed up to his knees and yanked his vest and shirt up, freeing it from his trousers. "You want to know why? This is why. Bread and pasta haunt my dreams but I'm shredded."

The tail of his shirt gathered in his fist, he pointed at a *pristine* set of washboard abs. Pristine verging on holy. I'd pray to those abs. Pray *for* them. A fine trail of dark hair danced down the middle like an invitation. I had to adjust my jeans to keep my cock from strangling itself behind my belt. "I see."

"I've been off sugar and starches since I started training to climb the Seven Summits. Mostly."

He continued holding his clothes which bordered on entrapment. Honestly. It was like he expected me to sit here and be a good boy while he showed off his slim, sculpted torso. Like he didn't expect me to reach out, curl my hand around his belt, and drag him over here so I could lick that belly.

I'd already extended my arm when the words he'd lobbed at me like a water balloon exploded in my head. "Wait, you're climbing the Seven Summits? For real, you're going up Everest?"

He glanced down at my hand, the one hovering over his belt buckle. His lips parted. His throat bobbed as he swallowed. And then he looked up, meeting my stare. "Not Everest. If I make it to the end of a very, very long series of climbing goals, it'll probably be Denali. But yeah, maybe. Someday."

I closed the hand frozen between us into a fist before reaching for Tom's vest and shirt and smoothing them down over his belly. "Where have you climbed so far?"

He dropped onto his bottom and stretched his legs out beside me, crossing them at the ankle. "I've hit all the base camp climbs in the American Northwest. Olympus, Baker, Hood, Rainier, Shuksan. Glacier, Forbidden, and Pikes Peak. The Inca Trail and Machu Picchu. I went to Japan last summer to climb Fuji." He chased a floret of broccoli around the dish with his fork. "I have a long way to go before I'm ready for anything bigger."

"That's awesome." I shoved a forkful of fish into my mouth. "Really awesome."

He jerked a shoulder up in the international sign of *it's not a big deal*. "It's the most random thing, actually. I'd never thought about climbing anything but then I saw this documentary—"

"You're into documentaries, then," I said, forgetting all my manners and interrupting the man.

"Yes." He speared some broccoli, dragged it through the puddle of sauce on his plate. "And podcasts and all those things old folks like yourself enjoy bagging on." He paused, presumably waiting for my rebuttal, but I only gestured for him to continue. "I saw a documentary about the environmental and economic impact of climbers on Everest and how it's a very lucrative business but much of the money spent on those expeditions isn't flowing back into the local economy. On top of that, there's a ton of garbage left behind by the expeditions and the risk of dying on the mountain is rather high."

"And naturally, your first inclination was to take up the sport." *This* I understood. "I like how you think."

"No, that's not how it went," Tom replied, a true smile splitting his face. God, he looked so young like that. Young and lovely and unscathed, as if he hadn't yet learned how shitty the world could be. "I was really intrigued by the whole thing and listened to a few podcasts and audio books. One of those books was a young adult novel—"

"And you're into young adult fiction," I said under my breath.

"—and the journey in that story was so beautiful and

engaging, and I loved how the main character saw himself as part of the mountain's ecosystem rather than a force trying to best the mountain. That really clicked for me. I'm not trying to win at life, I'm just trying to live. You know?" I started to agree because I understood this too but he kept going. "After that, I wanted to see what it was about. I wanted to be part of the mountain and see what I could learn from it." He gave another *no big deal* shrug and ate the broccoli he'd tortured for the past few minutes. "Climbing and hiking are easy enough around here. The trails are forgiving and they don't require much more than insect repellant and sturdy running shoes. It didn't take long to work up to more challenging trails."

I leaned against the base of the sofa, using the nubby fabric there to ease the itch still terrorizing the middle of my back. "What's the next big climb you have planned?"

"I haven't finalized anything yet but I'm thinking about seeing the sights in Europe this summer and squeezing in climbs during that trip. If it all works out, I'd hit up Breithorn in Switzerland and Tofana di Rozes in northern Italy."

Can I come with you? Can I show you around and watch over you? I had to gulp down some kimchi to keep myself from asking.

"It's probably silly but I've always wanted to see Rome and Paris and Versailles, and all those places," he continued. "I know the summers are the busiest but it's the best time for my schedule. The only other time we close the office is over Christmas and New Year's, and while I could take a vacation outside those blocks, I don't want to rearrange all of my current build schedules for that. At this point, we're planned out to next January."

"Are you an architect?"

He shook his head as he gathered a pile of kimchi and broccoli on his fork. "I'm the managing director of operations. It's a fancy way of saying I keep the hammers swinging and money flowing."

I didn't know why he was hell-bent on insisting everything he did was inconsequential. He only climbed mountains and ran an architecture firm and whipped up sesame sauces and wore suits like a revelation. Nothing about him was inconsequential. "Doesn't sound fancy, it sounds important."

"Everyone at the firm is important," Tom replied.

Every time he bounced that shoulder or gave me that frowny-scowly-irritable face, I felt as if someone was scooping something out of me, like a melon baller between the ribs. The odds were high it was phantom spleen pains or the beginnings of the gunshot wound infection I was past due to enjoy. That I felt those twinges whenever his dark eyes turned shy and he downplayed everything was a coincidence. "What did you do before you were managing director of operations?"

He grinned down at his plate, laughing to himself. "I was Shannon's assistant. Before that, I helped out around the office, whatever needed getting done. Walsh Associates is the only place I've—okay, what the hell are you doing?" When I didn't respond, he rolled his eyes toward the ceiling, saying, "You're wiggling again. You've been doing it since we sat down and I just need to know why you're wiggling."

"Apparently I've lost the ability to engage in any covert action." I set my fork on the plate and folded my hands in my lap. "It's complicated."

He pursed his lips and hit me with a sharp stare. "Should I show myself out?"

"Okay. All right. Here's the situation." I pointed at the brace on my arm. "There's this, which isn't great, and there are a handful of other injuries that have made it impossible for me to maintain normal exfoliating and moisturizing routines." He continued staring at me, fine creases and grooves dug into his forehead and the corners of his eyes. "What I'm saying is my back is disgustingly dry and scaly and riddled with dead skin because I can't bend this arm enough and I can't twist the other side because the muscles are still fucked-up over there. I can't reach. It's hard enough to get a damn shirt over my head, let alone get a loofah between my shoulder blades."

Tom studied me for a long moment, his gaze roving over my body. Eventually, he said, "Let me see."

I blinked at him. "See what?"

Again, he shifted to his knees but instead of flashing his belly, he brought his hand to my shoulder and pressed, urging me to lean forward. "I want to see why you can't sit still."

He rucked up my hoodie and t-shirt, and ran his palm down my spine. I shivered into his touch, shuddering out a laugh as I said, "Sorry about that."

There was another twinge between my ribs but this felt

like warmth and need rather than a gradual excavation of my soft tissue. This felt right—and that was strange. There was nothing sexy about my dry skin situation.

"Oh, holy Jesus, this is a mess. I didn't believe you," he murmured, his fingertips skating over the worst patches of it. "But you're right. You need a good scrub."

A vein of heat bloomed low in my core. "Are you offering?"

He shifted forward to meet my eyes, the shadow of a smirk pulling at his lips. "Are you asking?"

9

TOM

IF I'D GIVEN myself permission to get naked with G.I. Joe tonight, I would've coordinated my suit and socks with my underwear. On most days I coordinated everything, but this morning I'd intentionally selected hunter green boxer briefs to wear with red houndstooth socks and a navy pinstripe suit. The idea was simple: put myself together in a manner that would inhibit future taking apart.

It was true what they said about best-laid plans and mismatched undergarments because here I was, stepping into the shower behind him. There were no urgent kisses, no roving hands. None of the fanfare usually associated with stripping down to skin and getting that first eyeful. This state of undress was functional, much like a locker room or finding a man flailing in a frozen lake and dragging him out and ripping off his clothes and yours because he needed your body heat to survive.

Wes wasn't dying of hypothermia but he was in need of

a favor. And that was why I'd ordered him into the shower. He needed a favor.

I could've remained fully dressed and met Wes's exfoliation needs from outside the stall but the position of the showerhead and the volume of space this man took up would've left me soaked regardless. If anything, this was the responsible choice. The last thing anyone needed was water all over the floor.

Yeah, this made all the sense in the world.

Unfortunately, my cock had yet to receive any of those messages. The confusion was understandable. We'd spent more than an hour flirting and I hadn't stopped thinking about his fuzzy chest all week and now we were naked. Of course I was hard and throbbing and dizzy from the reality of this.

"Nice of you to join me," Wes mused. "I was beginning to think you'd gone home and left me in here to prune up alone."

"Now listen," I said, unceremoniously yanking the curtain shut behind me. "You're the one who puppy-dog-eyed your way into a community bathing experience when I'd planned for no such thing this evening. You can give me a few minutes to lay out my clothes so they don't wrinkle."

"Does it matter if your clothes wrinkle? It's like nine o'clock. Are you going somewhere after this?"

"And if I am?" I asked, devoting my attention to adjusting the dial rather than rubbing my body all over the extremely large and naked man in front of me. So, *so* big. The only saving grace was him facing away from me, blind to the heart-eyes gaze I shot at his backside. Under different circumstances, I would've ordered him to touch his toes while I licked that ass but this vintage shower stall was too narrow for anything of that nature and we weren't in here for that anyway. I wasn't here to lick anyone's ass tonight. Nope, none of that. I was here, naked and wet and wedged into a vinyl time capsule from the 1970s with some chest hair and good hands on Valentine's—for skin care.

"Then I'd like to know where you're going," he said. "Maybe I'd like to go there with you."

"Has it occurred to you that you're not invited?"

"Has it occurred to you we're showering together? That's gotta count for something as far as your Friday night plans go."

"Part of your problem is the water temperature," I said, shamelessly changing the subject. Maybe it was in keeping with the topic. I didn't know. All I knew was my cock was starving for attention. "It's way too hot. You're scorching your skin."

Wes turned his head to the side but kept his eyes cast down as he said, "I need it hot."

I ran my hands over his shoulders, down his spine, settling on his waist. "You're not going to put an end to the dry skin if you continue boiling yourself."

"You don't understand." He sighed as he flattened his hand on the wall, leaving the other—the one usually enclosed in a brace—across his belly. "Everything fucking *hurts*. All the fucking time. But the hot water..."

Hearing this from Wes was like slipping on 3D glasses. Suddenly, he wasn't a giant, rippling wall of man or an ass I wanted to taste but a warrior with wounds littering the landscape of his body. There were surgical incisions, sutures, and cuts and bruises in varied states of healing all over his back, arms, flanks. He kept his injured arm tucked close to protect himself. And I wanted to protect him too.

"It helps," I finished. "The hot water helps." He nodded, still staring at the floor. I didn't know how to interpret that. I couldn't tell if he was embarrassed or shy —though I couldn't see why he'd start with that now—but it sent tiny pinpricks stabbing at my heart. As if I needed to feel something on top of all this. "Here's what we're going to do, my friend. I'm going to use the sugar and oil mixture we whipped up in the kitchen and you're not going to play the part of the tough guy who refuses to mention anything when he's in agony while I do it. Understood?"

A noise sounded in his throat. It was rough and strained, somewhere between pain and annoyance. "Do you come by that bossy attitude honestly?"

I reached for the bowl of homemade sugar scrub waiting on the floor outside the shower. "Would it change anything if I hadn't?"

He barked out a laugh, the force of it shaking his entire body. From my vantage point, I had to imagine the bright, surprised grin on his face, the way his eyes crinkled, the clench and roll of his torso. The slight point of tongue he liked to drag across the seam of his lips. The shaft between his legs, thick and heavy for me.

"Nah, it wouldn't change anything, Tom. I'd like you just the same."

And now my cock was poking the ass I wanted to lick.

Goddamn. I wasn't getting out of this with a drop of dignity intact. "Just tell me if I'm going too hard, okay?"

Another deep-belted laugh and then— "Can't promise you that."

Since my stomach was cartwheeling in my throat, I didn't respond. Couldn't. Instead, I lifted my sugar-and-oil drenched hand to the center of his back and circled my palm over his skin, following the long, corded slopes of muscle to the ridge of his shoulders down to the base of his spine. I stopped at that point but lingered there, scrubbing his waist and flanks, taking care to avoid the wound near his elbow. It was healed but only recently, the divot where skin and tissue once existed still pink and tender.

"Is this all right?" I managed, transitioning to his biceps.

"Yeah, good," he said in a broken, rusty sort of way. "Yeah, everything's good." Somewhere in my chest, a groan broke loose and floated up to my throat, where it clanged out of me like an untuned bell. "Does that mean it's good for you too?"

"Oh my god," I panted out. "Would you be serious for a minute?"

"I'm being extremely serious," Wes replied. As I sluiced warm water down his arm, he took hold of my wrist, bringing my palm to the center of his chest. This forced me closer, my front pressing against his back, my cock nestling between his cheeks, my lips grazing his shoulder, and it forced another loud groan from me. "*Tom.* I haven't been *serious* like this in a long time."

I sifted my fingers through the glorious fuzz on his chest, tugging only enough to rip a low, purring howl from him as his back bowed and he slapped his hand against the wall. He didn't know it yet but there was nothing I loved more than when men turned to hungry, helpless beasts for me. When they whined and squirmed and begged in silence as they fucked the air until I took pity on them.

No, I wasn't bossy by nature. I hadn't taken up this assertive mantle after any thorough analysis of my inner workings. I'd heard no calling to dominance. In truth, I didn't enjoy this power dynamic for anything more than selected moments. I couldn't—and didn't want to—carry it off beyond these instances of quiet, needy surrender. But when it happened, the authority fit like a second skin.

Dragging my hand down his torso, my destination obvious, I said, "This is new for you." He shuddered out a breath as I closed my fist around his length and settled my free hand over the curve of his backside, my middle finger sliding down his cleft. His hips punched forward in an erratic cadence as I stroked him slow, much slower than he wanted. "Letting someone else take care of you, that is. You don't like being the one in need of tending, do you?"

"No, I fucking hate this," he wailed.

Resting my fist at his base, I asked, "You'd like me to stop?"

His answering growl and thrash almost did it for me. Just the friction of his body against mine and the way he hated this but he loved it too were nearly enough. But then he found his words, yelling, "*Fuuuuuuck, fuckfuckfuck,* no, don't you dare stop."

I circled my finger over his back channel, offering the barest amount of friction despite the way he clenched around me. "If you don't want me to stop, you're going to have to let me take care of you," I crooned.

"Not fair," he grumbled.

I twisted my fist down his length with as much ambivalence as I could harness, considering I was actually drooling for his dick, asking, "Why not?"

He found the rhythm, thrusting into it as I gave him much less than he wanted. "Because—because I've already met my torture quota for this quarter."

I responded with several thorough strokes and pushed a finger inside him, only enough to tease. Only enough to make my blood sizzle at the thought of pushing my cock inside him. "I'm not about to torture you, sweetheart. I just want you to earn it."

If anyone was being tortured here, it was me.

Wes's voice broke as he whispered, "*Fuckfuckfuck*" and as I'd expected, he dropped his shoulders, ducked his head, and took what I was giving—for a minute. Then he closed his hand around my forearm, tugged me around him until he was gazing down at me, and took both our shafts in his hand, pumping as idly as I had.

This time, I was the one whispering "*Fuckfuckfuck.*"

With a quick wince, Wes rested his injured arm on my shoulder and closed the wisp of distance between us. "Go ahead," he growled. "Make me earn it."

Thin rivers of water ran down the midline of his chest, pooling at the place where he held us in his wide palm. God, I *loved* hands like that. Big, rough, capable.

But I'd meant it when I told him I wasn't in the mood

for the daddy treatment. I wasn't going to be handled tonight.

I returned my hand to his ass, a finger brushing those sensitive pleats while his eyes turned dreamy and unfocused. With my other hand, I pried him off our erections, directed him to hold on to the shower wall, and resumed control of the torturous stroking. As I knew he would, he surged into my hand, groaning and cursing and growling as our crowns slipped against each other. And when I pushed inside him once more, his eyelids drifted shut as an appreciative groan rumbled out of him. His eyes still closed, he dragged his knuckles up my torso to my neck, cupping my jaw and sliding his fingers through my wet hair while the tip of his tongue traveled over the seam of his lips.

Then Wes kissed me, his lips hot and firm, his tongue exactly as demanding as I craved. He kissed me as I worked our cocks together, as tension gathered low in my belly, as everything inside me and everything around me boiled over and the only sensation I could identify was the steam wafting around us. He kissed me as I slipped another finger inside him, as he murmured "*Fuckfuckfuck,*" as I fought to hold back the release tickling my spine because I was earning this as much as he was.

"If you think I can't hold out all fucking night, you're mistaken," he growled against my lips.

I caught his lower lip between my teeth. "Then it's a good thing I have three more fingers for you."

A laugh rumbled out of Wes as he said, "If this arm wasn't fucked-up, I'd nail you to the fucking wall."

There was no hiding the way my erection throbbed

between us at his words. "Is that how it goes? You fuck me good and rude, and that's enough? Hard and fast like you're getting away with something?" I dragged my fingers over his most tender spot as a delirious noise rose up from his chest. "It's not enough for you, sweetheart. You want my fist in your ass and your balls slapping my leg and your dick begging my hand for mercy, and you want to work for it."

His mouth found mine as he erupted, a kiss that broke into a roar that twisted into a branding of tongues and teeth and lips. It was the roar, that primal, primitive noise that settled around us like an ancient cloak, that tipped me over the edge and then the unapologetic nip of his teeth on my skin that had everything inside me flooding out.

Surprising absolutely no one, this big puppy-dog-eyed man was a cuddler. His dick was still hard and spurting in my hand but the way he nestled his head on my shoulder and breathed lazy kisses onto my neck told me he was ready to settle in for a long, cozy snuggle. And that would be fine if not for the fact the snuggle stage was reserved for much later in my relationships. I saved it for men I considered my boyfriends, ones I'd celebrate holidays with and add their birthdays to my digital calendar. Ones I'd introduced to my friends and could imagine inviting to spend the night at my apartment.

It was a wonky way to live but logistics were my sweet spot.

I shifted us toward the spray, washing our hands and torsos and sending the evidence of this moment down the drain while he continued nuzzling me. I could wait a few minutes before enforcing my boundaries. I'd already crossed enough of them.

This type of vulnerable, intimate embrace didn't come naturally to me. I'd never say it out loud but I didn't know how to be affectionate, not in the traditional sense. I didn't know but I wanted it just the same. I wanted to be tucked under someone's arm while we sipped drinks with friends. I wanted to hold hands walking down the street. I wanted to lean into him while we rode a crammed Orange Line train and feel him hold me close to his chest.

Affection wasn't my first language but I desperately wanted to find someone for whom it was because I wanted to learn. I wanted the kind of confidence I channeled in these raw, uninhibited moments to extend to an act as simple as resting my hand on the small of his back while we ordered at a coffee shop. I wanted to feel as empowered in everyday situations as I did while stroking him in a shower.

But the trouble with wanting it, of being starved for it, was the ease with which I grew attached to every guy who offered me any kind of attention, even when I should've known better. Even when it should've been obvious I was nothing more than a body, a mouth, a cock. For some people, affection wasn't a language but a currency, and I'd always realized it too late—when I'd been used, forgotten, brushed aside.

"I was thinking about watching a movie," he murmured to my neck. "There's a lot on Netflix I haven't seen. Not in this language, at least."

I reached outside the shower for the towels I'd hung

there and drew one over Wes's shoulders before knotting my own around my waist. I didn't acknowledge his statement or the implied invitation. I doubted Wes was one of those guys who threw men away when he was finished with them but it didn't matter because I took care of myself now. I didn't interpret embraces as promises anymore, and I didn't assign emotional value to orgasms, not until I was certain the emotional value ran both ways. And I didn't curl up in bed to watch a movie after jerking a guy off in the shower, even on Valentine's Day.

"I don't have any popcorn but there might be some in the main house," he continued, a sweet, glowy glint in his eyes and an easy smile warming his face as he shifted the towel to his hips. "Is corn a grain? Is that on your naughty list too?"

"Corn is a starch, yes," I said, leading him out of the shower. "Let's get you moisturized. We can't have you using the furniture as a scratching post anymore."

I didn't speak while sweeping body lotion over his back, arms, and chest, but for a minute I leaned into the hand he rested on my hip. He did it with possession, his thumb stroking the tender spot like he owned it and it was his right—his *prerogative*—to hold me this way. It seared me like a marking, far more than when he'd spent all over my hand, my belly, my cock.

It was his entitled touch that reminded me his stay here was temporary and I knew better than to settle for bread crumbs. It wasn't a smart use of my time and I didn't have the emotional energy to spare.

So, I stepped back, out of his hold. "I should go."

Wes reached out his hand, tucking one finger under the towel hanging from my hips. "Go get the popcorn, you mean?"

I stared at his arms, the long-healed scars and the freckles and the golden hair. He was so damn pretty. "Home. I should go home."

"Your objection to grains is that strong, huh?" He drew his hand away from my towel and grabbed his arm brace off the lid of a hamper. His gaze was fixed on the brace as he adjusted it but I could tell the glowy glint had left his eyes. The smile was gone too and in its place was a firm, emotionless expression betrayed only by the sharp set of his jaw.

Wearing nothing more than a towel was a real inconvenience right now. I couldn't dispose of this uncomfortable moment by walking out and driving away and filing this experience under "fun night, no future." At best, I had a full minute of dressing ahead of me, two if I bothered with socks and the vest. Fucking vests. Why was I so enamored with those fucking vests? Oh, right. They showed off my narrow waist. I always knew my vanity was bound to bite me in the ass.

Two minutes to dress, another two to collect my food storage dishes—no, fuck the Pyrex. It was replaceable, even if those specific lid colors were impossible to find. Everything was replaceable. Unless, of course, leaving those things behind looked like I was preening for a follow-up invite, which I wasn't.

Goddamn, I wanted to come back. I shouldn't want it

and I couldn't want it but I did, I fucking did. I knew it but I couldn't admit it, not with words, not with actions.

Two minutes to dress, zero minutes on the Pyrex but several pained thoughts, one minute down the stairs to the driveway, another minute to the street. I could be out of here in four minutes, and thirty minutes after that I could be circling the South End for a parking spot. Sixty minutes from now, I could be at home, under my weighted blanket with a true crime doc queued on my screen.

I wanted it like that—leaving and driving and circling-circling-circling and just waiting, waiting for something I didn't know if I'd recognize when I found it. I wanted it like that and I was going to leave here in four minutes because I didn't cuddle on the first—second?—date and all those pinprick stabs to my heart were hormones and loneliness and Valentine's Day, and that was it.

"It's cool. Whatever it is," Wes said, his words tinted with indifference I didn't believe. "I just thought you might want to hang out and kill some time but you've got other things going on. Like I said, it's cool. Thanks for your help with everything." He glanced up at me, his lips folded in on each other like I didn't deserve to see his real reaction. "I mean that sincerely. My back was driving me crazy. Thank you."

"Wes, I—" I, what? I wanted to prepare a glaze while he pawed at my ingredients again? I wanted to watch that movie while substituting seaweed for popcorn? I wanted to climb into his lap and sleep with his heartbeat under my ear? "Don't let your skin get to that point again. Call me if you need, you know, help or something."

"Thanks for the offer. You know, you're welcome to stop by. I'm here most of the time. If I'm not here, I'm at the main house. If you ever want to come over and eat fish without rice, even without the burden of scrubbing dead skin off my back, you know where I am. And that's all it has to be."

"Yeah, okay, maybe," I lied, bobbing my head as I backed out of the bathroom. It wasn't okay. I wasn't built for pop-ins, for quickies, *for all it has to be.* I wasn't in the market for a friends-with-benefits fixup and I didn't do flings. "Good night."

Wes didn't respond. He closed the bathroom door behind me.

MY WEEKENDS, much like my weeknights, followed a strict routine. But this structure wasn't about aggressively controlling every inch of my life to cope with the things I couldn't control.

Not anymore, at least.

These days, the predictable Saturday morning cycle of laundry and cleaning saved me from staying up all hours on a random Thursday because I'd realized the inside of the refrigerator hadn't been washed—ever. Or discovering I had no clean socks on a Monday morning. Saturday morning housekeeping allowed me to focus on those specific chores at that specific time, and gave me a moment to unwind from the week and feed my need for order.

My Sunday afternoon cycle of grocery shopping and

meal prepping fed the same need while also helping me focus on the week ahead. Some people stumbled into work on Monday morning without previewing their calendar or any other preparation. I wasn't one of them. Life handed out more than enough surprises without adding the disaster of cooking a new meal each night to the equation.

There was a time, a couple of years back, when routines were the tool I used to punish myself. There was no real strategy or logic but self-harm wasn't a linear behavior. Ninety minutes of exercise daily, four and a half hours of sleep, eating fewer than twelve hundred calories, saving sixty percent of my take-home pay, working through illnesses and injuries and emotional black holes, all in the name of checking off boxes and staying on track. I didn't offer myself much mercy back then.

I was better now. I listened to my body and my mind. Even when I struggled against those old, creeping feelings of worthlessness and disposability, I knew them for what they were—liars. That didn't make them vanish but I knew how to talk myself out of that downward spiral.

But there was one shameful routine I hadn't managed to quit. Every few weeks, I opened my laptop and pulled up my mother's and sister's social media accounts. I hated that I did this. That I wanted to know about their lives without me. Every time I stalked them, I promised myself I wouldn't do it again.

But I couldn't help it. I went back, month after month, as if I'd find some sign I existed in their consciousness. The truth was no different now than it was fourteen years ago, when my mother informed me I was dead to her. No different than sixteen years ago, when I was sent away to a boarding school that favored hard labor, hours of forced prayer, starvation, and solitary confinement as conversion therapy methods. No different than seventeen years ago when I told her I thought I could be gay and she told me I was wrong because her god wouldn't allow the devil to send "one of them" to destroy her family.

I could look back on that without the flames of panic and shame burning me from the inside out. I could separate my mother's intolerance and my older sister's complicity from my self-worth. But I couldn't completely separate myself from them. They'd cut me off but I couldn't return the favor in full.

I'd spent years interrogating those emotions and I knew they didn't stem from a desire to reunite with my biological family. I'd abdicated all connection to them. But I wanted them to know they'd failed. All the effort they'd put into "fixing" me and reshaping me and rejecting me was in vain. They'd failed.

I visited my sister's Facebook profile first. Joy was married with two children and worked as a real estate agent. There was some irony associated with my sister choosing a career in such close proximity to mine. I didn't sell houses but I managed the process and the money that led to homes being restored before Shannon sold them for top dollar.

Joy frequently posted her listings on her profile. Since I was petty as fuck, I always scrolled through the photos, mentally critiquing the camera angles, staging, and lighting. Our listings were so much cleaner. When I was feeling cruel, I pulled up the property records to see how far below asking price her listings sold.

Her most recent post featured an old photo of her on our father's lap, her small body tucked under his arm. She always posted this photo around this time of year. It was at least twenty-five years old and exquisitely cropped. The image seemed to center on Joy but that wasn't the truth. Only the most careful observer would notice the knobby knee peeking out from under our father's hand.

That grainy bump of skin was all that remained of me in her world.

The text of the post was equally remarkable in its ability to delete me from her history.

DADDY, it's been twenty-four years without you but I remember your laugh like I heard it this morning. Sometimes, out of the blue, I think I can smell your cigars. It's been so hard without you, Daddy, but Ma and I have been strong. We've helped each other through the lowest, darkest times. In our hearts, you're still away on that business trip and we're still waiting by the window for you to come home.

You'd be proud of the woman I've become and the grandchildren I've given you and Ma. I tell Clara and CJ about you every chance I get. I know you're watching over us and lighting the path for us.

Your little girl always,

Joy

LOOKING BACK on my childhood through the lens of

adulthood, I could see my father's sudden death as the origin of my mother's religious fanaticism. She'd always possessed an abrupt sense of morality but his death was the big bang that'd weaponized her beliefs. I hadn't recognized any of that when I was a kid. All I knew was my father was gone and the rational parts of my mother had gone with him.

My father worked in printer and copier sales, and spent more time on the road than at home. My memories of him were entwined with the cities he visited and the stories he told about those places. To my child's mind, locations like Akron and South Bend, Harrisburg and Charlottesville were fascinating and exotic. They were known for interesting food and curious histories. I was a full-grown adult before I discovered Akron was known for rubber and not made of rubber.

He died in a multi-vehicle crash near Poughkeepsie. Drunk driver. A mix-up at the scene of the accident meant he was gone two days before we were notified.

My mother found solace in her faith but she also found anger, resentment, blame. She wrapped herself in the church's most exclusionary teachings as if it would protect us from the kind of tragedy that took my father. As time passed, she adopted a version of the story of his death as her proof that evil lurked in the world and it was out to destroy good people. First, it was that the driver who'd T-boned the car wasn't only drunk but also high on illicit drugs. Then he was smuggling those drugs over the border. Selling them too. Eventually, the driver was a gang member, a sleeper cell terrorist, an undocumented immigrant. At times, all of the above.

It took me years away from her home to understand it wasn't about faith or religious teachings. Faith didn't look at young people and tell them their existence was wrong. Faith didn't restrict food, shelter, and comfort to help them conquer their evil urges. Faith didn't threaten children with disease, misery, and eternal damnation because of the way they were born. Faith didn't force anyone to cut family out of photos, burn them from memories, throw them away like last week's garbage.

It was never about faith.

The next post read, "Need a good pork chop recipe for dinner! Easier the better, crockpot or instapot. This working mama has a crazy day ahead! Child friendly, please! My picky three-year-old is something else!"

A groan slipped past my lips as I scanned the replies. Pork chops and crockpots and picky toddlers. But it wasn't about that. It wasn't even about the niece and nephew I'd never met. It was the appearance of life indented by only one loss. She had all the heartfelt words for my father but nothing more than strategic cropping for me.

My stomach churned the same way it always did when I pinched this particular bruise. It always hurt and it always left me feeling sick.

Scrolling down, I stopped on a photo of Joy, her husband, her kids, and Ma in themed t-shirts at Disney World. The caption read, "We finally made it to the promised land! We are dead on our feet but it's been a fun day! So blessed!"

I had to stop with this. I knew that now and I knew it every time I typed her name into the search bar. But this was the end. It had to be. If I could walk away from sweet boys with stupid muscles, I could stop torturing myself over a family who'd cut me off like a wart in the way of their blessings.

I lowered the laptop's lid and pushed away from my desk. My brussels sprouts needed to come out of the oven.

MONDAY MORNING DIDN'T COME SOON ENOUGH.

I was a fan of Mondays. I liked fresh starts and the urgency associated with a new week. They were the perfect opportunity to put a weekend of questionable choices behind me. And I loved climbing the old stairs up to the office's attic conference room for our seven a.m. Monday meeting. I started out at Walsh Associates ten years ago as a gopher. Whatever they needed, I went to get it. I was sent to collect everything from permits to lunch to broken bricks at the junkyard. That was back when the only Walshes running this sustainable preservation architecture shop were Shannon and her brother Patrick, and our meetings took place around a shared desk while we sat in folding chairs.

As they finished school, Shannon and Patrick's younger brothers—Matt, Sam, and Riley—joined the firm. Miss Andy Asani came along shortly after and Patrick immediately fell for her. Now we had accounting managers and paralegals and office assistants. We were far more than a quaint family operation. Walsh Associates was five times bigger than it was when I spent my days juggling coffee and paint samples.

These days, we met at a custom-built table and sat in chairs that cost more than my monthly rent, and these people were the closest thing to family I knew.

Yeah, I was a fan of Mondays.

I set my coffee and laptop on the table and settled into my usual seat between Sam and Andy. Patrick sat opposite me, already scowling at his screen. He suffered from an acute case of resting grouch face. It couldn't be helped.

"I hate it when Shannon isn't here," he said.

"I know." I opened my laptop and keyed in my password. "She'll be back before you know it."

"Not soon enough," he muttered.

In addition to his resting grouch face, Patrick's tolerance for ambiguity was immeasurably short. He could manage the unexpected with his restoration projects but all hell broke loose if someone reorganized the supply closet without notifying him well in advance. He was notorious for firing administrative assistants—if they didn't walk out first—within weeks of hire. Three months without Shannon, the strategic, financial brains of this operation, was almost unbearable for him.

Soon, Riley and Matt filled the remaining seats and the meeting started. We used this time to share updates on the current slate of projects and plan for upcoming work. Patrick was tied up with a multi-home restoration on Cape Cod and commuting down to Wareham each day this week. I couldn't comprehend why anyone would subject themselves to that drive but questioning Patrick's methods was about as practical as trying to bury a ghost.

"While I'm out of the office, Andy is in charge of building issues and Tom is in charge of business issues," Patrick announced.

At that, the trio of younger brothers exchanged a series of glances, gestures, and arched brows.

"I'd be offended by this but honestly, I'd rather not be the one on the hook," Matt said.

Riley pointed at him. "Same."

"This works for me. I have no desire to handle anyone's issues," Sam added.

"I wasn't asking your permission but thanks anyway," Patrick muttered. "Can we talk about the North End situation? Where are we with the permits?" He glanced between his fiancée and his brother. "Either one of you, please."

"Permits cleared, cranes scheduled for this week," Riley said.

"We're shutting down Charter Street between Salem and Unity so we have to get this right the first time," Andy said. "If everything goes as planned, we have a forty percent chance of getting it right."

"That's horseshit," Riley replied. "At best, we have a twenty-five percent chance of getting it right. The HVAC unit we're trying to air-drop into this brownstone will be the cause of major traffic disturbances for the day. Worst-case scenario, our crane operator uses that unit like a wrecking ball and we knock down the property we're restoring."

Patrick turned a baleful glance in my direction. "You'll

be on site if this falls apart and we need to play nice with Boston Police?"

I added a note on my calendar. "I'm on it."

"I'll join you," Sam said. "This sounds like history in the making."

"We're making something," Riley replied. "History, irreparable damage, what's the difference?"

"I appreciate you supervising, Tom," Patrick said with a sigh. "What else do you have on deck this week?"

I toggled to my cash flow and credit line spreadsheets. "Just moving money and contractors around to cover all the projects Matt has teed up. We're close to maxing out our tradespeople if we continue scheduling at this pace."

I didn't fetch paint samples or collect broken bricks anymore. Now I managed restoration logistics for dozens of ongoing projects, hundreds of general contractors and building tradespeople, and more city and national historic register permits than reasonable. In the process, I moved millions of dollars around each week to keep the work flowing.

With Shannon out of the office until spring, her responsibilities fell to me. I didn't mind overseeing the paralegals but supervising Patrick's assistants Dylan and Lissa—the ones he hadn't fired yet—was not my preferred use of time. Thus far, we'd worked through issues of pens Patrick found "too inky," unilaterally silencing all mobile phones as notification chimes annoyed him as of late, and relocating a printer with an unfortunate jamming tendency to a different corner of the office.

Dylan, Lissa, and I agreed the jam was the result of user error. Patrick didn't need to know that.

"Since we won't continue scheduling at this pace," Patrick said with a pointed look at Matt, "it should be fine."

"Why not? This is working for me," Matt replied.

Sam reached for Matt's coffee, gave the cup a shake. "It's worth noting you're on your third coffee of the day and it's not even seven thirty."

Matt blinked at him. "Your point being?"

"We'd love it if you lived long enough to see your child born rather than running yourself into the ground and dying from the caffeine shivers," Andy said.

"I'm doing this because of the baby," Matt argued, his arms stretched wide. "I want my schedule clear come July and August so I don't have to worry about the baby arriving in the middle of a punch list. It makes perfect sense."

"It might make sense but we're going to max out our contractors and trades if we're not careful," I replied. "I've tried to add more capacity but we're already utilizing the best people in the city."

Sam pushed Matt's coffee out of his reach. "You're going about this all wrong. You need to be more selective. Don't say yes to every client who comes your way. Don't take on every property Shannon buys. More selective."

Sam was on the opposite end of that spectrum. He had a baby, a little boy, and now he preferred projects that *spoke to him*. At the moment, he had one property in progress. By comparison, Matt had twenty-one.

"Thanks for the advice," Matt said. "Really. I appreciate

it. I really need you telling me how to structure my restoration agenda."

Sam pursed his lips as he adjusted his cufflinks. "I'm only trying to help."

Patrick pointed a pen at Matt, one of the not-too-inky variety, saying, "If you overextend our resources and prevent me from getting the good hardwood refinishers on my properties or Gigi for my roof gardens, it will not end well for you. You can work yourself to death but do not fuck with my schedule. Understood?"

Matt jerked his shoulders up. "Fully."

"Next," Patrick snapped, stabbing at his keyboard.

"I think *we* are next, Patrick," Andy said.

He blinked up at her and the agitation in his eyes softened. "Oh, right. Yeah." He glanced at everyone else, saying, "We set a date."

Our Monday morning meetings served as the singular, sacred time in each week when everyone gathered to share updates on projects and plans for upcoming work. Without fail, the last quarter of the meeting shifted from the family business to the business of family.

"Since it's not humanly possible that you two have agreed upon a wedding date and you're more than likely talking about your next dinner party or some kind of special tasting menu pop-up event at a restaurant you like, why don't you clarify that statement," Riley said.

"Are we done?" Matt asked. "I have things to do."

Sam shook his head. "You're not getting a reaction out of me until my save-the-date arrives."

Andy slid an envelope across the table. "Consider yourself served."

Matt, Riley, Sam, and I leaned toward the hand-lettered address. No one touched it.

"Go ahead," Patrick said, shrugging as he continued banging at his keyboard. "It's legit."

"You set a...*wedding* date?" Sam asked. "For yourselves? To get married?"

"After all this time," Matt murmured. "What's it been? A year? Two?"

"I can't see how that matters to you," Patrick replied.

Riley tore into the envelope, held up an engraved wedding invitation. I snatched the card from him, studying the pertinent information. "April. *This* April," I announced. "You're getting married in two months?"

Andy closed her laptop, laced her fingers together over the lid. "Yes. Everything fell into place."

"When I get engaged, I'm not allowing any of these shenanigans," Riley said. "We're going to set a date and get married and there won't be a year and a half of wandering the world until a date appears to us in our dreams."

Sam glanced at him. "Is that engagement forthcoming?"

Riley buried his face in his hands and let out a muffled sob-laugh. "I don't fucking know."

Matt gestured toward him. "Okay, well, you should—"

Riley held up a hand. "Nope. Nope. I don't want to hear it. I don't want to talk about it. Just go about your business and let me muddle through my shambles, thank you."

"That won't be a problem for anyone," I replied.

Patrick shut his laptop with a sharp snap. "We're

finished here," he said, pushing to his feet. "Remember, Andy and Tom are in charge while I'm out of the city."

"And thank god for that," Sam muttered.

I THOUGHT about Wes all day, and the next day, and every day after.

I forced a blank smile and shrug when Andy asked over lunch whether I was seeing anyone. I met her polite prying with a promise there was nothing to report. A handy in the shower wasn't the genesis of a love match. Regardless, she promised my wedding invitation would be issued with a plus-one.

When I sat down to eat dinner on Thursday night, I laughed out loud imagining the conversation Wes and I'd have about the cherry glaze I drizzled over my brussels sprouts. With every bite, I debated jumping in my car and driving out of the city to see him.

That's all it has to be.

But I couldn't let myself do that. I couldn't be his good-time guy while he recovered. And that was all Wes wanted from me—all he'd want from anyone. If it hadn't been me, it would've been someone else. The FedEx guy, for all I knew. He hadn't chosen me. He hadn't even wanted me. I was there and I'd offered—and offered and offered and offered until he was coming in my hand.

Wes lived in a short-term world. Everything was temporary—and it was that sense of disposability that kept me in my apartment, my weighted blanket tucked up to my chin and the true stories of mass murderers on my screen, night after night.

I was being smart. This was self-care at its finest—knowing when something wasn't meant for me and walking away despite the undeniable draw. Despite stupid muscles. Despite snuggly, cuddly men hiding beneath their scars and chest hair.

This was adulting and it was awful.

10

WES

ABBY HANDED me another stuffed animal, saying, "Give loves."

"Okay," I replied, rocking the plush kangaroo despite the other twenty animals on my lap. "Like this?"

She swatted my hand with a primal shriek. "Loves," she repeated.

I glanced over her head at Will. He was busy pacing the nursery, Annabelle nestled on his chest. "What does your little pterodactyl want from me?"

"She's asking you to love her animals," he replied, as if that was obvious.

Another shriek, another swat. "Give loves."

"I'm trying." I hugged the kangaroo tight. This child was militant as fuck. To Will, I asked, "How am I supposed to do this to her satisfaction?"

"If you don't know how to love a stuffed animal, you have more problems than I thought," he said.

"I mean, isn't that obvious?" Abby snatched the

kangaroo away with a disgusted glare and scurried back to her toy box.

"It's becoming clearer," he murmured.

Yeah, there was no mistaking my many issues.

It'd been a week without Tom darkening my doorway. If nothing else, all that time spent watching the door forced me to work on my strength. What else was there to do but lift increasingly heavy objects while waiting for my only friend in the world to arrive? I was forced to rest too. I couldn't greet Tom with a yawn so I enforced a regular bedtime for myself. But I continued begging off dinners with the family. I didn't want to miss Tom if he arrived. That was my rationale. It wasn't about avoiding my family because they'd make well-intentioned but really fucking stressful comments about my recovery, career, and general well-being.

And also, the dogs and babies and people were a lot to deal with when I was very busy lifting weights and watching windows. A whole fucking lot.

So, I'd continued skipping dinner. As they had since I'd settled in the garage apartment, someone walked plates of food up to me each evening and they lingered for a bit, but I hadn't been in the mood to talk. I didn't have anything to say. I preferred it when Shannon came up. She didn't fuss over me. She'd set the dishes in the kitchen and then flop down on the sofa. Within seconds, she'd be asleep, and she stayed that way for exactly twenty minutes. I'd timed it.

Will was a far more complicated visitor. He asked every question in the known universe, scrolled through the television channels with a comment about everything he saw, and stared out the windows while providing an excess of information about his neighbors and their charming suburban lives.

Isolation worked well for me. It wasn't that bad. I could manage the mounting confusion over my next career move. I could handle the nails-on-a-chalkboard pain in my arm. The loneliness was the only piece to make me question my choices. Why did Tom leave? And why hadn't he come back to me?

Abby returned, a small blanket in tow. She draped it over my shoulders like a cape and then launched herself at my back, her arms coiled around my neck. "Loves," she cried, pounding my spine with her tiny feet. Every time she connected with the wound on my flank, bile warned in my throat.

"*Oof*. Love isn't supposed to hurt, baby koala," I said, prying her off my back. I gathered her in my arms and held her still for a moment. That was all she'd allow before twisting away and resuming her play.

"Just like Shannon. Her elbows are like swords," Will said, still pacing. "She nailed me in the face a few months ago and gave me a bloody nose."

"The wife? Or the one-year-old?"

"Abby. The wife wouldn't intentionally draw blood," he said, laughing. "You'd be so much happier if you'd burp."

I blinked up at him. "Are you…talking to me?"

Will shook his head as he started another circuit around the nursery. "Your problems are much bigger than this little girl's digestion."

Abby marched over, collected two of her animals from

me, and deposited them in her toy box. She continued until I'd been relieved of all creatures but then she started the process all over, again shrieking at me to show them affection.

"I'm trying," I pleaded. "Show me, Abby. Show me how." She grabbed the bunny out of my hands and lashed both arms around its body, rocking and cooing and strangling the shit out of it. I picked up a hot pink teddy bear and held it the same way. "Okay. See? I can do that."

She shrieked again and stole the bear from me. These girls looked like my brother but there was no mistaking the Shannon in them.

"Why did you call me up here?" I asked Will.

He glanced at me as he carried Annabelle to the changing table. "Zone defense."

"If I'm supposed to be watching your six, I can't say I'm succeeding." I sat the remaining animals in a row beside me. "Then again, it's not like I'm succeeding at much these days."

"You know how the CIA works. It's always a game of hurry up and wait with them," he said. "Give it time to blow over while they cover their asses."

"It's been six weeks," I muttered. And it wasn't going to blow over. My security clearance had been revoked and my covert status was trashed. They hadn't sent the official word yet but I was as good as done in the intelligence community. They weren't calling me in to run a mission center or advise station chiefs or support any of the National Clandestine Services teams. I wasn't going to the Caymans. They were done with me, I knew it.

"You need to ask yourself whether you want it," he said, slam-dunking a diaper into the pail beside the changing table, "or you want to move the hell on. Kaisall and I could put you to work tomorrow if you're up for it."

I flopped back onto the rug and stared at the clouds painted on the ceiling. "Sorry but my subscription to *Soldier of Fortune* has expired."

"Consider it," he said. "We're building some new teams and we could use your expertise."

Working for my brother was a punishment neither of us deserved. I had no interest in his A-Team reboot operation, especially considering those fools didn't even do deep-cover espionage. They did quick gigs where they hoped like hell their Green Beret-turned-mercenary could blend in with the locals long enough to rescue the abducted diplomat or steal the nuclear warhead that'd gone missing the last time our government overthrew a regime. They knew how to pull off small, precise, *quick* jobs. They didn't do what I did and I couldn't do what they did. Not anymore. Maybe five years ago, but not now, not after all these years in clandestine work.

"The actual last thing in the world I want is to pose as an antiquities-but-also-arms dealer again," I said. "I've run that gag a hundred times too many and I know the borderlands too well."

"That's not the work I have in mind but it doesn't seem like you're in the mood to hear anything," Will said.

He wasn't wrong about that. I wished I could attribute today's sense of despair to my career or my aching body or my father needling me to get help last week. It wasn't any of those things—it was everything. Everything was wrong and I couldn't make any of it right.

And I hadn't seen Tom since last Friday night. Clearly, everything was fucked with that, even though I'd tried so hard to keep it easy and flirty and fun. But when everything was wrong and it didn't matter how hard I tried to make it right. Easy, flirty, and fun didn't exist. Those things formed a thin, crackly layer at the surface and hid the mess beneath. And Tom knew it as well as I did. He knew and he didn't want any part of it.

Abby flung herself on my torso, giggling and shrieking in equal measure. "Jesus Christ, baby koala, you're gonna kill me," I grunted, shifting her away from my wounds. "What kind of MMA are you teaching her?"

"You gotta play with her, man," Will chided. "That's why you're here."

"And if she murders me in the process?" I asked, curling my arm around her body and holding her upside down. Her squeals of laughter forced a smile out of me.

"You'll still get a star on the wall at Langley," he replied. "They'll reevaluate their investment in your training but you'll get that star."

"Is this what Grampa does with you?" I asked Abby, still upside down and giggling. "Or is it just yoga and meditative breathing with him?" She babbled out some nonsense and I set her down on her bottom, thumbing away the happy tears streaking down her cheeks. "You have a wild child on your hands, William."

"She's very spirited," he agreed.

I'd expected Abby to body-slam me again or begin her

stuffed animal redistribution work but she laced her arms around my neck and nestled in my lap. "Shhhh," she said, her finger pressed to her lips.

"Okay," I whispered, wrapping my arms around her little body. She squeezed her eyes shut.

"Judy and the Commodore are out of the house until Monday," Will said as he resumed pacing. "Since you haven't left the garage since last week, I wasn't sure whether you heard about that."

"Don't you know how to deliver news without commentary?" I asked. "And yeah, I heard. Dad's made a point of giving me minute-by-minute rundowns of his day for the past week like I need some kind of SITREP."

He shifted Annabelle to his other arm, saying, "Then I'm sure you know Judy usually hangs out with Abby while Shannon meets with Tom."

I glared at him. "Excuse me?"

"Oh, you didn't know Shannon and Tom meet for an hour on Friday mornings? Yeah." Will consulted his watch. "I'm sure he'll be here soon."

Goddamn. I looked like a vagrant. I was wearing the same sweats and t-shirt I'd slept in and I needed a hot shower. And a plan. I really needed a plan. "Why don't you save us some time and tell me which reaction you're expecting from me."

"I noticed he's visited the garage a few times," Will said, as casual as he fucking pleased.

"Don't you have hobbies? Interests? You spend an obscene amount of time surveilling your own house." I caught a glimpse of my reflection in the window. Fuck, my beard was a mess. I needed to get myself in order. Knowing Tom, he'd take one look at my scraggly condition and take a giant step backward. "Come on, man. Read a book or something. Start a Netflix series. Have a conversation with your wife. Stop watching CCTV footage of your driveway."

"Not that I need to explain my security methods to you, but the system pings every time a vehicle breaches the perimeter," he said. "I noticed Tom didn't leave until late last Friday night."

"And *that's* why you asked me here." I glanced down at Abby, still play-sleeping in my arms. Would she freak out if I moved her? I needed to get my ass in the shower if I intended to catch Tom while he was here but I didn't want to restart the shrieking cycle. "It's not cool to use your kid as a decoy."

"I was serious about the zone defense," he said with a laugh. "If you ask nicely, I'm sure Shannon would let you crash her meeting."

"She warned me about him," I admitted. I didn't have anything good to wear. Nothing I'd want to wear around Tom. My entire wardrobe was a result of my mother's visit to an outdoor megastore after my arrival here last month. I was all stocked up on relaxed-fit jeans, flannel shirts and thick, white socks. That, and a few UC San Diego sweatshirts stolen from my brother.

Now that I thought about it, I could borrow another sweater from him. Something slimmer than the generously cut flannels my mother selected. Based on the past couple of weeks, I knew Will had a fuckload of dark blue and black quarter-zip pullovers that weren't baggy enough to double as a parachute. Black would work. If I wanted Tom's attention, I had to stop being a despondent mess. I had to get my shit together. And find a sweater that did me some favors.

"She's protective of Tom," he said. "She warned you about yourself."

I stopped mentally raiding my brother's closet. "Wait a minute. When did I become a cautionary tale?"

Will peered at me. "Dude, I don't know your life but you haven't stayed in one place since college. You don't have a permanent address beside Mom and Dad's house and your primary language changes every few months. You don't know where you'll be this time next year, and last I checked you prefer it that way. That's not Tom. He likes his roots. He's big on routines and structures. He's all about constancy and you...are not."

I tickled Abby's ribs because it was better than facing these cool, objective truths. She burst into giggles and flailed in my arms. "Yeah, I've noticed that," I said over her gleeful cries.

Will grinned at his daughter as he paced the room. "Then the question is whether you'll let the warning stop you or you'll take it and proceed."

I liked to believe I didn't run from fights but the truth was, it depended on the nature of the fight. The ones I was tasked with carrying out by government agencies were no problem. Taking on my own fights was a different story. I'd never been able to step up to the plate when I was the one on the line. In the past, I'd dodged every shot that came my way because it was easier than putting myself in a vulnerable position.

I knew this. I could acknowledge it. But I hadn't survived some ham-fisted torture in a secret prison and performed surgery on myself with a pair of pliers to dodge this shot.

That was what I told myself while I showered and dressed and returned to the main house to join Shannon's meeting with Tom.

11

TOM

I'D WORKED for Shannon Halsted—formerly Walsh—for almost ten years. In that time, we'd sat for thousands of check-in meetings. Actually thousands. I'd done the math. Anywhere between one and ten meetings per week, nearly every damn week per year, over the course of ten years. Thousands.

We'd met through the worst, the strangest, and the most unproductive circumstances. In the middle of freezing construction sites—or better yet, in freezing alleyways behind those construction sites. A random aisle in the middle of Home Depot because my boss needed to walk and talk. A hair salon while she had her bangs trimmed. I'd even accompanied her to a doctor's appointment so we could touch base in the waiting room.

But I'd never reviewed action items and issues with Shannon while the man I'd promised myself I'd stop lusting over studied me the way a lion studies a gazelle.

He was clothed this time. That was positive. Or not? It could go either way. But that goddamn tongue of his didn't know how to stop painting the seam of his lips.

True to form, Shannon offered nothing more than, "Wes will be joining us today," when I found them seated at her dining room table. She had a perfectly good home office upstairs but preferred big tables like this one where she could spread out her files, notebook, and computer. She liked having a perch from which to preside.

I didn't question Wes's presence or even acknowledge it beyond a tight smile-and-nod move. I nearly strained my neck doing it because every single muscle in my body was pulled taut and even that gesture stretched me in unpleasant ways. It would've twisted into an eternity of awkward if Shannon hadn't jumped right into business and saved me from overthinking Wes's every blink and breath.

But the pace of this meeting wasn't enough to keep me from wondering about his presence. Why was he here? What did he want and what did he hope to gain? I couldn't imagine him going into business with Shannon and her brothers but what did I know about Wes Halsted? What did I really know?

It wasn't much. I'd gathered stray details about the middle Halsted from my colleagues this past week but it was like solving a puzzle with half the pieces missing and the other half turned over, cardboard-side up. He'd started as a Navy SEAL before joining the Central Intelligence Agency. Or National Security Agency. Or some different, more covert agency for which Shannon's youngest brother

Riley—the one who traded in truth-based gossip—couldn't remember the name. I'd learned Wes had a talented tongue and that was no euphemism. He spoke multiple languages and seemed to pick up more with ease.

Part of me wished it was a euphemism.

Actually, *all* of me wished for that.

"I need a favor," Shannon announced as she closed her notebook.

I lifted my shoulders. "Name it."

She pointed her pen toward her brother-in-law. "Take Wes out for lunch. The boy hasn't been off the property in weeks and he needs a field trip."

I shifted to face him, my jaw locked and my eyebrows arched. "Is that what you want?" My words were chilly. I didn't like being manipulated. "You're a big boy, Wes. You don't need Shannon to speak for you."

Wes started to reply, a smirk already carving grooves into his perfect face, but Shannon held up her hand, stopping him. "He didn't ask me to do anything. I think he needs a visit with the outside world and since I trust you on a deep, absurd level, I knew you'd be able to handle it." She paused, waiting for some reaction. I didn't offer her one. "If there's some reason why that's an issue or a problem I don't know about between you two, I'd love to hear an explanation."

"No problems, no issues," Wes said, his gaze locked on me. "I'm up for lunch. What about you, Tom? Would that be okay? We can eat anything you want, even salmon and broccoli."

Shannon watched us staring at each other across the table and I knew she was unaware of my nonexistent relationship with Wes. Shannon was a great many things, but after all these years, I could read her like a book. And that book wanted to know why I sassed off and why Wes knew my go-to meal.

"There's a quaint spot here in Swampscott with excellent sandwiches," Shannon offered, edging her way back into the conversation. She tapped her keyboard, peered at the screen. "Though your afternoon is fairly flexible, Tom. You could show Wes one of our favorite martini lunch spots in Boston."

I swiveled toward her with a dead-eyed glare. "Thanks."

"Is that your employee morale program, Shannon? Martini lunches?" he asked, that smirk pulling at his lips until it formed a smile.

She bobbed her head. "If the vodka works, keep pouring it."

He responded with a deep laugh that warmed my skin like a blanket fresh from the dryer. "We're not in the military anymore, Toto."

"Not nearly," she said before glancing back at me. "Take the old boy out and keep him busy for a bit. He won't say it but he's starved for the real world and human companionship and all those things."

Wes hunched forward as he laced his hands on the table, his shoulders dropping. He looked shy. I liked him shy. I liked him vulnerable. The cocky SEAL thing didn't do it for me but I'd take a sweet, quiet boy any day.

"If I wasn't busy with my duties as milkmaid and chief baby cuddler, I'd tag along with you," Shannon said.

"I need some clothes," he said. "I didn't come here with anything and I really hate the underwear my mother bought."

"Then you should go without," I said, not stopping to think for a second. I wasn't going to chastise my boss for believing she had any business in a martinis-and-underwear outing. Meddling was her way, in all things. "Okay. Let's have lunch and then go shopping."

"Sounds like a fun afternoon," she added.

Wes stared at me as a smile brightened his eyes before reaching his lips. "I think it will be."

WES LEANED FORWARD, peering out the windshield as I unbuckled my seatbelt.

"Is this," he started slowly, "a...*mall*?"

"Yes, it is," I replied, settling my scarf around my neck. If I kept my hands busy, I wouldn't accidentally rub his chest or throw myself into his lap. I wouldn't drown myself in his scent or demand he rub that scruffy beard of his between my legs. And I wouldn't ask how he was doing or whether his back was itchy again, or anything like that. If I kept my hands busy, I'd remember all the reasons this wasn't safe for me. "Malls are where people buy clothes, which is what you asked to do this afternoon."

"I don't think I've been to a mall since I was a teenager." He glanced over at me, taking in my charcoal trousers, tailored shirt, robin's egg tie, and vest—another fucking vest. "Is this where you shop?"

"Not that it matters but no, it's not." I shoved my keys and phone into my coat pockets. "Shall we?"

As I reached for the door handle, Wes stilled me with an arm across my chest. "Why aren't we going somewhere you shop?"

I stared down at the hard plastic of the brace on his arm. It saved me from bathing in his pouty question and enjoying the feel of him holding me still, the rough possession hadn't dissolved since last week. "Do you need a bespoke suit?"

"I don't know." His brows furrowed, he stared at my eyes behind my glasses, my lips. When he sucked in a breath, I knew he was remembering everything. I was too. "Maybe I do."

"I don't think you need a suit," I whispered.

Wes curled the hand resting on my chest into a loose fist, gathering up my shirt and tie and edging me toward him as he leaned closer. His lips hovered over mine as he said, "Tell me what I need, Tom."

It was my turn to gasp—and shift away. "There are a few shops that will meet your needs in here and, at the off chance you can't live without a decent suit, we'll stop into Nordstrom."

Wes didn't release my shirt and tie from his hold. I could've shaken him but neither of us wanted that. No, I preferred the super-fucked-up option of refusing him while also savoring the entitlement to my body he possessed. "And that martini lunch I was promised?"

"How about The Cheesecake Factory?"

A jagged, broken laugh burst out of him. "All right, Tom. We'll play it your way." I sensed him shifting closer, his chest meeting my shoulder and the warmth of his breath on my ear. "But don't forget what happened the last time you thought you were running the game."

As if I could.

I SCOWLED at the martini across the table. I didn't have an issue with the martini, not exactly, but I refused to watch while Wes curled his tongue around the olives impaled on the cocktail stick that arrived with his martini. It was gratuitous—and intentional.

"You're sure you don't want something stronger?" he asked, stabbing the stick in the direction of my mineral water with lime.

"Certain." I ran my fingers over the damp edge of the paper napkin beneath my drink. It was fruitless as this napkin was bound to disintegrate before our meals arrived but it gave me something to do. And that was what I needed when seated across from the captor of my every waking thought.

Now finished with the olives and his show of oral acrobatics, Wes laced his fingers around the stem of his glass, asking, "Busy week at the office?"

"No more than usual," I replied, still occupied with my napkin. "Riley, that's Shannon's youngest brother, and

Andy, she's Patrick's fiancée and he's Shannon's oldest brother—"

"I know," Wes interrupted. "You don't have to draw the family tree for me. I met them all at my sister's wedding and I talked to Andy about Isfahan and Tehran for, I don't know, probably an hour."

"It's good of you to remember all those people." I shot him a tart glance. "After all this time too."

His brows arched up, a smirk firmly in place, he lifted the glass to his lips. "You're fuckin' adorable when you pout like that." After a long sip, he said, "You want a sip of this, baby? It's nice."

"No, thank you."

"All right, all right." Wes studied me as he ran his tongue over his teeth, his lips parted just enough to remind me what I was missing. "Then tell me what Andy and Riley did this week." He tipped his chin up in a manner that seemed to codify his request, making it a law I was bound to obey.

"They dropped a five-ton HVAC unit into a brownstone in the North End," I said, a laugh seeping into my words as I spoke. I still couldn't believe they'd pulled it off without incident. "It was extremely close to turning into an epic disaster but it worked out beautifully. We didn't even pay overtime fees to the crane operator because we nailed it on the first shot."

"It must've required a lot of work to make that happen," he said.

"On the day of the delivery, it was mostly a matter of prayer and crystals and begging everyone to do their jobs.

But yeah, there was a fair amount of planning ahead of time too," I said, toying with the napkin again.

"That must be why I haven't seen you since last week."

With a sigh, I rested my elbows on the table and pressed my clasped hands to my mouth. I wanted to explain but that would mean exposing my soft, vulnerable underside and I wasn't ready for him to see that. I wasn't ready for anyone to see it. And he was leaving soon enough anyway. It didn't matter.

"Did I do something?" Wes continued. "Or did I just totally misinterpret the vibe?"

I snapped my head up, meeting his gaze. I opened my mouth to refute his comment but the server arrived with our meals and fussed over our need for drinks, condiments, and anything else short of world peace until I couldn't remember a time when she wasn't glued to the end of our table.

When she finally departed, Wes lifted his glass toward me, saying, "You're adorable when you pout but you're fuck-all hot when you're annoyed. It was actually quite enjoyable for me to sit here, watching while you seethed with impatience."

After shooting a disinterested glare at the salad I had no intention of eating, I glanced away, blowing out the pained breath I'd stored somewhere between my shoulders for the past seven days. The one I'd held since stepping into that hot, hot shower with Wes. The one I'd held like a life raft while everything inside me kicked and screamed for oxygen. But I was doing the right thing, I was sitting with my discomfort and accepting it as a part of growing and healing.

Right? *Right?*

It wasn't possible I was suffocating in my own air because I was wrong. I was learning how to take care of myself. This misery and loneliness and want was supposed to teach me something. It wasn't supposed to make me want to sweep the plates away and climb over the table into Wes's lap where he'd fist my tie and bite my lip.

Sucking in a jagged breath triggered a shift somewhere inside me, somewhere hidden behind vital organs and the muscle memory of trauma. It pulsed like the first bursts of a panic attack but then it mellowed, becoming something bordering on pleasurable. I'd lived through plenty of panic attacks but none of them knew anything of pleasure and I didn't know where that left me. My internal world was rearranging itself and I seemed to be enjoying it.

So what if he's leaving? So fucking what?

"As a matter of my own information gathering," Wes continued, "will there ever be an instance where you want ketchup? What about scrambled eggs? I'm sure you eat eggs but I'm getting a distinctly soft boiled to medium poached feel from you. How about turkey burgers where you use lettuce for the bun? I'm betting you're into that. Turkey burger, probably some avocado, maybe some roasted poblano if you're feeling frisky. Ketchup wouldn't make sense in that situation but you know where I'm going with this. And I can't imagine potatoes have a place in your starch-free life but I'm looking for a clear go/no-go on the ketchup. Any response would be appreciated, Tom."

My eyes narrowed, I watched as Wes demolished his cheeseburger while going on about—I wasn't even sure what. "What the actual fuck are you talking about?"

He laughed in a way that made me want to run my hand over his belly and feel his joy. "It's nothing important." Then, his expression sobering, he asked, "Why does it look like you're solving a massive problem over there?"

"It's not important," I echoed.

He ducked his head, his eyes creased in the corners as if he was listening closely because he didn't trust my words. "Yeah?"

For the first time since finding Wes seated beside Shannon, I gave myself permission to say exactly what I wanted. "I was just thinking I won't be happy until I get you out of those jeans."

When his eyes widened and his lips parted, Wes growled. "Say that again."

"I want to tear them off you. I don't care if they rip. I'd probably be happy about it," I said.

He tipped his chin up as he regarded me from across the table, still doubting my words. That was fair. I'd given him plenty of reason to doubt me with my wild swings between hot and cold. Then he said, "Yeah. I can see how you might enjoy that."

I pointed to his martini. "Are you going to finish that?"

Wes shook his head, pressed two fingers to the base, and slid it toward me. "All yours, baby."

After fishing some cash from my wallet and dropping it on the table, I tossed back the remains of his cocktail. There was something intoxicating about this form of intimacy, almost dizzying. It was so much stronger than the liquor and, based on the growl rattling out of Wes, he knew it.

"Let's go," I said, scooting out of the booth.

Wes gave my untouched salad a frown before standing. "You're not hungry?"

Offering a curt shake of my head, I replied, "You didn't read the vibe wrong, okay?" I waved a hand at the table. "And I don't want to fuck up my macros for the day. Not when I owe you Netflix and popcorn."

Wes folded his arms over his chest, again peering at me as if I'd spoken a foreign tongue. "You owe me...Netflix. And popcorn."

"There's a new documentary I want to watch," I said. "I hope you like serial killers."

"I want to revisit this matter if you don't mind." He pointed a finger at me, those almighty arms still crossed like he was baiting me into licking him here, in the middle of this restaurant. "What do you mean, do I *like* serial killers?"

Impatient, I gestured in the direction of the mall entrance. "I'm getting your ass into something from this century then I'm taking you home and I'll explain it all there."

Wes settled his hand on the small of my back and saw more than heard my quick, gasping whimper at his touch. Smirking, he urged me forward. "I knew you needed something stronger."

I LEANED against the dressing room door, a load of clothes slung over my arm, and knocked. "How are you doing in there?"

A strangled snarl was his only response.

"What does that mean? You don't like these pieces I picked out? They don't fit?" Another snarl followed by some cursing and a grunt. "Wes. Use words."

"I need help getting this over my head. My arm—I can't —it's stuck." A second, more colorful stream of cursing. "I'm fucking stuck."

"Let me in. I'll help." The door cracked open and I slipped inside to find Wes lost in a navy blue turtleneck, only the crown of his blond head poking out and his injured arm tugging ineffectually at the hem while his other arm twisted at an awkward angle.

"Help," Wes whined from inside the sweater.

I'd sent him in here alone under the pretense of efficiency. It made sense. He'd try on the first round of options we'd chosen, I'd hunt for more, and no one, not a single soul, would notice the similarities between a shower stall and a dressing room.

But that calculus omitted a critical factor—my boy couldn't wiggle anything slim-fitting over his head without assistance.

"Okay, all right," I muttered, dropping the items I'd selected on the bench behind him. "I can't reach you up there, sweetheart, I'm going to need you to sit down." I brought my hands to his waist and backed him up until his legs hit the bench and he lowered himself down. "Very good, that's right. Now, let's straighten this out." I tugged at the wayward sleeve, adjusting until he could drop his arm around my waist. "Though it did try to strangle you, I think this is a good look for you."

Wes rested his head on my belly. "I can't even dress myself."

"It's a very slim cut." And it did look outrageously good on him. "And this fabric doesn't offer much stretch."

"I can't even dress myself," he repeated.

"Then we'll stick with button-downs and more forgiving pullovers." I ran my fingers through his hair and rubbed the back of his neck under the sweater. "Do you want to see the jeans I found?"

"I want you to keep doing that," he mumbled into my vest.

I blinked down at him, not understanding his meaning until I watched almost from outside my body as I kneaded his tense muscles. Logically, I'd known I was touching him. I'd made the conscious choice to stroke him in a manner I assumed he needed. And yet I couldn't believe I was doing this, that I was giving affection without second-guessing myself. Without ruminating over whether I was doing it right, doing it proportionally.

So, I did the only thing that made sense to me. I stopped, coughed, pushed my glasses up my nose, took a step back. "I grabbed two different sizes of these jeans because they looked narrow and your thighs are rather beefy—in a good way. Nice beefy. Good beefy. We should all be so lucky to be your brand of beefy."

Wes lifted his head, looking up at me with the same puppy gaze that had stripped me out of my clothes and sent me into the shower after him. "You might want to leave because I will legit cry if I can't get these on by myself."

I reached for the larger size and shook them out, dropping them beside him. "Go ahead and cry. I'm not leaving." I leaned back against the door, my arms folded and ankles crossed, and pointed at the jeans. "I think you'll like those. God knows they're an improvement over the grunge-era relic you're currently wearing. May I ask how they came to be in your possession?"

Yes, this was the question I needed answered while Wes pushed to his feet, unlatched his belt, and drew his zipper down. I couldn't have asked whether he wanted me to pick out some new boxers for him—*Jesus, if you love me at all, you'll let me choose this man's underwear for him*—or whether he needed more hooded sweatshirts. He seemed to favor those hoodies and it was important to me he have an adequate supply as I intended to nab one from him tonight.

"—and, look, I don't know. The wallpaper was too loud for me to argue with anything she said but somewhere along the way, my mother decided I'm the kind of guy who shops at a fish and game superstore. Maybe I told her I wanted something from there. Fuck, I don't know. I didn't have the heart—or the energy—to criticize her choices."

He bent his leg to free himself from the denim, revealing a close-fitting pair of black boxer briefs embossed with the unmistakable ridge of his cock. I dug my fingertips into my biceps to keep from launching myself at him.

His hands on his hips, Wes pinned me with a stare that would've been venomous if not for the ghost of a smile passing over his lips. "You should've eaten lunch when you had the chance."

"And why is that?"

Shaking his head as he reached for the jeans I'd set out for him, he said, "Because you're giving me a cock-hungry face right now. Fix it before I dickslap it off you."

Fighting my own smile, I replied, "I haven't a clue what you mean."

Grumbling about my bossy attitude, Wes yanked up the jeans and fastened the button fly without incident. Not a single tear shed, unless we included my cock in that tally in which case it was absolutely weeping at the sight of his long, powerful legs and sweet ass. That second-skin turtleneck too.

Smoothing his hands down his thighs, he asked, "What do you think?"

"I think"—I gulped down my first response, which went something like *I want to bury my face in between your legs*—"I think they're a remarkable improvement. How do they feel?"

He glanced down, his shoulders lifting as he studied the fabric. "I can live with this."

"Sit down," I ordered. "To see if they're comfortable."

Wes obliged my command but he wasn't leaving it unmatched. "Come here," he rasped, shifting back on the bench and spreading his legs.

I went to him. I stepped into the wide arc of his thighs and ringed my arms around his neck. His hand found the tender spot behind my knee and scraped up, up, *up* until his thumb traced the seat of my trousers and the head of my cock, until his palm cupped my ass. Until I was a heartbeat on legs.

I gave him one of those pouts he enjoyed so much. "Yes?"

He patted his thigh. "Come a little closer."

I dropped a knee onto the bench but that wasn't enough for Wes. With his hold on my ass, he jerked me onto his lap, onto the thick, swollen ridge of him trapped beneath the denim. I took advantage of this position, grinding myself against his length like I didn't care about privacy or propriety or the promises I'd forgotten over lunch. In response, his grip on my ass turned vicious, as if he intended to keep a piece of me for himself.

"Where," Wes started, his voice strained, "did you get this beast of a dick?"

"I come by it honestly."

He pressed his lips to my jaw, nipping just enough to make my cock pulse with every bite. "I'd like to come on it until I'm so dehydrated I need to be hooked up to an IV."

I hummed as I thought this over. As I granted myself permission to have a short-lived fling without regret and without losing myself in the process. "How long would it take to get you to that point?"

"Three or four days," he said, his lips sipping at mine. "You up for it?"

"Some of us have to work on Monday, sweetheart. We don't all have the next month or two until shipping out."

Three lines formed between his brows, along with brackets on either side of his mouth. "Since we're on the topic, I should mention my entire life is up in the air. I can't get into the particulars because the government doesn't love when their operators illegally divulge classified information but suffice it to say, my next steps are much foggier than I'd suggested last week." He spared me a glance as he swept his palm over my ass. "Not that the current ambiguity of my career should change anything for you."

But it did. Oh, it did.

I gazed at his beard, feeling my boundaries collecting themselves and realigning into something new but close enough to the original that I couldn't pick out the changes at first glance. They were there like grains of sand, only obvious when I looked for them. But I didn't want to sweep the sand away or set myself back to rights.

"You're wearing these jeans out of here," I said, snapping the tag at his waist before moving on to the turtleneck. "The sweater too. And I'm going to walk a few paces behind you and plan all the ways I'm going to defile you tonight."

Wes dragged his tongue over his lips and then he kissed me, hard and fast at first but then deep and deliberate, like sucking caramel off a spoon. I fisted my hands in his hair and rocked against him without shame, without reservation, and it was everything. Absolutely everything.

I wasn't settling for bread crumbs—I was snatching the whole damn loaf or cookie or wherever it was bread crumbs came from. I wasn't settling. I was taking and I was doing it with the awareness this wouldn't last but I'd survive it nonetheless.

Wes rested his forehead against mine, huffing out a

gentle laugh. When he didn't explain himself, I asked, "What was that for?"

"I was just thinking it's really cute you're under the impression you'll be the one doing the defiling."

Yes. I'd need that stolen hoodie to keep me warm when he was gone.

12

WES

SOMEHOW—AND I wasn't entirely certain about this turn of events—Tom and I spent the rest of the afternoon trolling dressing rooms without completely mauling each other. There was a little mauling but that was to be expected. Nothing egregious. Nothing that couldn't be handled without adjusting ourselves as we left those dressing rooms and wiping the grins off our faces while we did it.

After leaving the mall, Tom drove us to what I could only describe as an abandoned gas station with a van parked in front of a leaning line of chain-link fence which barely lived up to its purpose of cordoning off the old pumps. There was no sign on the van or any other indication food was available for purchase but that didn't stop Tom from declaring, "This is my favorite taco truck."

I jabbed a finger in the direction of the faded maroon van. "That's a *taco truck*?" I scowled at the generator seated on cracked pavement and its duct-taped rigging. "You're sure that isn't a give-no-fucks, out-in-broad-daylight meth lab?"

Exasperated by my very reasonable questions, Tom swiped at his phone for a minute. Then, "I don't know, Wes. Maybe that's on the secret menu." He dropped his phone into the cup holder. "After all the crying and whining you did about being hungry—"

"Pardon you, I neither cried nor whined."

"—I figured you'd eat first and make ridiculous judgments later," he continued.

I leaned back, crossing my arms. "Forgive me for having questions about all this, considering you and your spiffy red-soled shoes measure your steamed salmon portions down to the milligram. It's a shock, babe, to hear you enjoy tacos from a van at a gas station."

He picked up his phone again, tapping at it while he asked, "Are you finished?"

"No, not until you explain how van tacos fit into your grain-free, macro-dictated, Denali-climbing lifestyle."

Still busy with his device, he said, "Skip the tortilla and it fits just fine. And everyone gets a cheat day." He killed the engine and pocketed his keys, glancing at me as he reached for the door handle. "Come on, would you? We have better things to do than sit here, arguing about whatever this is. I promise you, I'll never put anything in your mouth that doesn't belong there."

Since that was a valid point, I followed him to the back of the van where we found a woman as old as the trees simultaneously stirring spoons in two separate crockpots while a teenage boy with big-ass headphones over his ears mashed avocados. Tom ordered for both of us, swinging a glance in my direction while he did it like he was daring me to challenge him.

I didn't. I enjoyed this side of him, the wide stance, the firm shoulders, the "No, I've got this, put your money away, Wes" side. The one concerned with care as much as control. I didn't keep with any hard and fast rules about who or how or when but it was fair to say I was comfortable being the one who exercised it. But more than that, opportunity for me to allow someone else to make decisions, even about things as trite as tacos and jeans, didn't come around too often. Men didn't look at me and expect I'd roll over and show them my belly.

I hadn't figured out what Tom expected from me yet.

Once we were back in the car, he started the engine but made no move to drive anywhere, saying, "Given that it's Friday evening and Boston experiences approximately six hours of rush-hour traffic as a matter of city pride, all of which is compounded by the fact we're on the North Shore and I live in the South End, we're looking at least ninety minutes to my place."

"Fuck that," I replied. "It was, what? Twenty minutes here from Shannon and Will's house?"

He glanced at the road. "Maybe a little more, yeah."

Control didn't belong to either of us—we could push and pull and shove and bite. We could share it. "Then that's where we're going."

With a thoughtful pout that made me want to bite his lip, Tom asked, "Should we grab some tacos for Will? Shannon wouldn't touch this but it would be—"

"Again, fuck that." I shook my head like I hoped to fling that idea into incoming traffic. "He can get his own tacos. We're not his delivery service. And we have something about serial killers to watch, which isn't the kind of statement I imagined myself making tonight but here we are, parked beside a taco truck that's served as a meth lab at least once in its history and is probably currently laundering money. I've stopped trying to make sense of it." I peeked inside the bag. I had to admit everything smelled amazing. "It's a good thing you haven't been abducted or robbed."

He flung a hand toward the van. "By the little old lady with the cataracts and the gnarled arthritis hands? Do I really seem that defenseless to you?"

"It's not you I worry about," I replied, still poking in the bag. "It's the money launderers. Gramma Guacamole might not be the criminal mastermind but those cataracts make it easy for her to turn a blind eye to the cash washing operation."

Tom shifted into drive, muttering to himself, "Oh my god."

"Holler to the heavens all you want, honey. I'm just saying this shit is real and pervasive." I snagged a bit of carnitas from inside the foil wrapping and popped it in my mouth. "You're right. This is good."

"BEFORE WE GO UP THERE, I think we should talk through some logistics and expectations."

"I'm fully versed in the logistics," I replied.

"How did I know you'd say that?" he said under his breath. "I meant PrEP and condoms and those logistics."

"Ah, well," I started, running a hand over my throat, "I'm good with condoms."

"And I think we should talk about expectations." Tom coughed, glanced out his window, shot a cautious glance in my direction. "I know you said things are up in the air for you but they're bound to come down at some point, right? I'm just saying, I'm not laboring under any pretense of us starting a long-term relationship but I do expect you to call me tomorrow."

"Won't it be rather odd for me to call you when we're sharing a bed or are you referring to a role-play situation? I'm down either way but since we're discussing the logistics, we should logistic the fuck out of this, don't you think?"

"You want me to spend the night? I didn't bring an overnight bag."

An impatient rattle sounded in my throat as I dropped my head against the window. "I don't give a fuck about overnight bags and neither should you because I want you to jog your hot ass up the stairs, get rid of your clothes, and decide where you want to choke on my dick. Okay? That's what I want."

"And what will you be doing during this fairy-tale sequence of events?"

I lifted the paper bag. "I will be enjoying these tacos."

"That's not even close to how it's going to happen," he argued, his index finger raised like he was about to recite the pillars of a strategic plan to me. "Last week should've served as an indication I'm not going to kneel at your feet."

"Naked," I added. Keeping a straight face was becoming increasingly difficult. "Kneel at my feet *naked*."

"Not going to happen."

I nodded toward the garage. "Then why don't you tell me how you'd like this to go."

Again with the index finger, Tom said, "We'll go upstairs. You'll be allowed to admire my ass because after all the squat challenges I've completed, I've earned that admiration. We eat and watch something that doesn't need to be followed closely and then you'll spend some time on your knees. After that, well, I don't know. I'll have to decide whether you look better bent over the sofa or the bed, and go from there. Eventually, we're going to watch that documentary."

"I'd admire your ass without the squats," I said. "I'd call you tomorrow too. And even with my life up in the air, I intend to treat you like I'm lucky to have your company and attention. I'm not about to abuse that, okay?"

He dropped his hand to his leg, slowly drumming his fingers there as he gazed blankly at the garage. "Okay."

"And, listen, for what it's worth, I look great everywhere," I said. "Bend me over a sofa, a bed, a stack of milk crates, the dugout at Fenway, anywhere you can think of. There's nothing either of us can do about it. I was born this way and I have to tell you, it's a curse as much as it is a blessing. But you"—I traced the line of his jaw, up his temple, over the arm of those trendy glasses, into his midnight-dark hair—"you would look so much better. You, with that flawless golden skin and those long, long, *long*, lean muscles. You, with that granite-carved belly and those dimples at the base of your spine like the start of a treasure trail. You, with that beautifully filthy mouth and the mind to match. It's you, Tom, with all your order and precision and clearly defined expectations, as if you'll be able to control this, control us. I think you know you won't be able to but that's not stopping you from giving it hell. That's why you didn't turn up all week. You were trying to find some control." I leaned in, dragging my knuckles from the knot of his tie to the buckle of his belt. "Don't bother with that, baby."

I felt his sharp intake of breath and the following gulp. Then, "Okay, let's go upstairs now."

WE BOLTED UP the stairs but it was too far, too long, and I stopped every few seconds to drag Tom into my arms, grind up against him while I squeezed his ass.

We slammed into each other on the landing, kissing, biting, touching everything we could find.

We fought to get each other's coat off, fought to get closer.

We tumbled into the apartment, kicked the door shut behind us, sagged against the first solid surface we could find.

We toed shoes off while shuffling across the living room.

We ripped clothes from each other, caring nothing for

seams, buttons, zippers. No two people had ever enjoyed being naked as much as we did in this moment.

We wrestled our way into the darkened bedroom but stopped a few steps from the bed, our chests heaving as hot, urgent breath rushed out of us.

"I want the lights on," I said, my lips on his neck. "I want to see you."

Tom rolled his body against mine, sending his cock sliding over mine in the most glorious agony I'd ever experienced. "Then turn the lights on."

"I'm fucking starving for you," I said as I stepped back to hit the light switch. "Prepare yourself."

He reached out, threading his fingers through the patch of hair on my chest and *fucking pulled* while his shaft tangled with mine again. "I'm not the one in need of preparation."

I backed him onto the bed and chased him up to the bank of pillows before layering myself over him. He wasted not a single second in rocking his hips up, moving our shafts together while he trailed a hand down my back and between my cheeks. For my part, I matched his thrusts and hooked my arm under his knee and opened him wide for me, wide enough to lick every inch of him as soon as I found the strength to back away from this heaven.

Tom slipped two fingers inside me as the thick head of his crown stubbed over mine and I babbled a string of obscenities into his chest while I gnashed my teeth against his nipple. I wasn't positive but I might've called him a cock-sucking ass genie which didn't make a ton of sense as there'd been no cock sucking as of yet but I was mostly embarrassed about the ass genie bit. That wasn't my best work.

"Are you close?" he ground out between thrusts. "Can you come like this?"

"Have I exhausted you already?"

"Not nearly," he replied. "But I want you to come before I fuck you and then after."

A small corner of my brain revolted at the idea of forcing that much structure onto sex but the rest of my brain was obsessed with how amazing everything felt. "Is that what you want?"

"Let me take care of you," he murmured, his lips on my neck, my earlobe. "Let me soften you up before I flip you over and fuck you so hard you feel it in your throat. Then I'll suck your cock until you forget how to form words. Let me do that for you, baby. Give me this big, big body and all these stupid muscles. Give it all to me. Let me have it, let me have you."

Tom skimmed his hand down my side, the backs of his fingers and knuckles, and that touch was enough to set me off, my length pulsing against his as I erupted.

And I was still spurting all over us when he shifted to his knees, saying, "I'll be right back."

I wasn't certain how I felt about being left alone with a puddle of fluid on my belly and a need for something more thrumming in my blood but Tom wasn't gone long enough for me to generate an opinion in one direction or another.

"Are you comfortable on your belly?" He nodded toward the gunshot wound as he tore open the condom packet.

"Obviously, I don't want to do anything that puts strain on your arm or—"

"Come here." I watched as he rolled down the condom and then beckoned him toward me. He obeyed, crawling up the bed until I was caged beneath him. "You did this. You take care of it."

He followed my gaze to the wet spot on my belly and bowed his head, sweeping his tongue over my skin in luscious swirls. He made slow work of it, taking his time licking everywhere but my rapidly lengthening cock.

"More," I demanded, and he complied, sucking me *deep deep deep*. But it wasn't as simple as a cock and mouth. He was busy edging my thighs apart, rolling my sac in his palm, pushing two, then three fingers inside me and working me where I needed it.

He pulled off, his lips shiny as he asked, "Ready?"

I nodded, a sharp quip on my tongue about him being a good boy and waiting his turn, but the words evaporated in my throat as he shoved into me. I couldn't believe the thick, unyielding throb of him. Every inch of me burned for him, for more.

"I'm officially obsessed with your ass," Tom said as he held himself still, his eyes closed and his lips parted. "Fucking obsessed."

He rested his palms on my thighs, his thumbs circling the tender inner skin as he rocked inside me. I met every thrust with a growl and a vicious snap of my hips. "You should be. My ass is incredible."

Leaning forward, he pressed the heel of his palm to the center of my chest, anchoring me in place as he pounded me. He could've taken the iron spike that was my cock in hand or teased my balls but held me there, staring into my eyes as he took complete possession of me.

With that knowledge setting my skin on fire, I fell apart. I came with an unholy shudder and shout that kicked Tom over the edge too, moaning, "You fucking ass genie, what did you just do to me?"

It wasn't supposed to be funny at all but I burst out laughing just the same and there we were, laughing and fucking and coming and holding each other like this, *this* was the only way we'd ever have sex again.

NATURALLY, we showered together the next morning. I still needed help with my back and Tom needed me teasing his ass. It worked out beautifully for all involved, save for the small issue of Tom running empty on fresh clothes. In our haste to attack each other last night, we'd failed to bring any of our new purchases inside with us, leaving him to choose between his day-old suit and my oversized jeans and flannels.

"Walk of shame chic it is," he said, shaking out his trousers.

"I don't know what you usually do on Saturdays but my schedule is wide open and I like your face."

"Your schedule isn't the only thing wide open, honey," he said, shooting a pointed glance at my naked body.

"I'm air drying," I said in explanation, not bothering to close my legs or cover myself with my towel. He liked looking at me and I liked being seen. "Can we get back to the day ahead, please?"

"I do have some plans today," Tom said as he tucked in his shirt. "If you're all right with visiting my place, you're welcome to come along."

I sat up, buzzing the towel over my wet hair. "Yes, please."

We dressed in comfortable silence and, at Tom's insistence, we gave the apartment a quick clean-up to address last night's energetic arrival. Since I knew Will and Shannon would be in the kitchen with the babies and I wanted them to know I was taking off, we made a quick detour to the main house.

Everything was right with the world. Happy, fuzzy hormones made my body feel like sun-warmed sand. I felt righteously used and degraded in a real nice way. My man was a dirty sex maniac and I loved it. Things were finally on the up.

But then we bumbled into the kitchen with our sex-rosied cheeks and hands tangled together, and my fucking parents were sitting at the table with Abby and Annabelle on either side of them.

"Oh my god," I wheezed, dropping Tom's hand and taking an enormous step away from him. "Weren't you two supposed to be in Vermont?"

"Good morning, Wesley," my mother called, her attention trained on Annabelle. Maybe they hadn't noticed. "What has you up and out at this hour?"

"No but seriously, what happened with Vermont? That

was real, right? Vermont was real? That happened?" I sputtered.

"Last I checked, Vermont continues to exist, yes," my father replied as he cut something on Abby's plate into small pieces. It looked like a waffle. Maybe a pancake.

"And you were supposed to *be there,*" I continued. "In Vermont. The state that does exist."

"Ice dams," my mother said with the kind of *oh darn them ice dams!* tone that made me think I was supposed to understand anything about this conversation. "All over the place too. It was a mess."

I was quaking. My entire body, quaking. Shaking from the inside out. I couldn't do this right now. I couldn't talk about sex or identity or anything like that with my nieces in the middle of everything and my father sawing away at a pancake and my mother playing peek-a-boo with Annabelle's little feet. I couldn't. *I couldn't.* Not now, not today.

"We decided it was better to turn around and come back but we picked up some syrup and maple candy on the way," my mother continued. "I want you to take some maple candy, Tom. It's such a fun little treat."

Oh my fucking god. I was so busy with all the soul-deep quaking and the collapse of my grip on this reality, I'd forgotten about Tom. I glanced over but instead of standing beside me, Tom was lurking near the door, extremely interested in his phone.

"Thank you, Mrs. Halsted. It's very kind of you to think of me," he replied. "I'd love some maple candy."

"It's right over there on the counter, next to those jugs

of syrup," she said, laughing a bit to herself. "Is there a better name for them? I've spent my entire adult life around sailors and I can't seem to say jugs without giggling."

"I'm going out," I announced, louder and more forceful than this conversation required. "I'll be gone for the day."

My father, still working on that pancake, raised a hand with a tiny pink knife snared between his fingers, saying, "Enjoy yourself."

Tom collected his candy and marched straight out to his car, never once acknowledging my presence as I trailed behind him. I required several minutes to come down from the human earthquake situation and when I did, I found I wasn't drowning in those happy hormones anymore. I wasn't light or loose. It wasn't until I sucked in a deep breath that I felt the tight cording of my shoulders, the pressure on my chest, the burn in my throat.

And the ice dam beside me.

But fuck, I'd earned that ice.

"So," Tom started, glimpsing in my direction as he stopped at a traffic light, "which part of this are you hiding from your family?"

All the buoyancy I'd experienced before walking into that kitchen was gone and I was not buoyant, not floating, not even treading water. I was at the bottom of the ocean, gazing up at the world above and wondering why everything was so fucking difficult.

"I'm sorry," I said, trying to shape remorse from the tense air between us and failing because it was only air and

I was only a man and this was heavier than either of those states.

Tom pursed his lips, dipped his chin. "Okay."

We were both aware that wasn't an acceptance of my apology. "I'm not out with my parents."

He stared ahead, offering no outward reaction, which succeeded in killing me a bit. "Okay."

"Or the military," I rushed to add, as if that made it better. It wasn't simply my parents but the entire military-industrial complex too and this was clearly an improvement on the situation. "I mean, it was illegal—*I* was illegal—when I joined. It hasn't been that long since that order was repealed."

"And yet you still did it," Tom murmured, frowning at the traffic ahead.

I held out my hands and let them fall into my lap. "Of course I did. I understand the point you're making but I always knew I'd join the Navy and I believed better days were to come. And I believed it wouldn't be that difficult to keep my personal life separate as a matter of smart teamwork. I don't know how your office works but in my line of work, there's no space for anyone's love life in a war zone."

"Okay."

I shoved my fingers through my hair. "But it's not okay. That's obvious, Tom."

"I'm just trying to understand," he replied. "That's all. I'm trying to understand the motivation behind this choice."

"It's just—it's complicated," I said, sighing through

another round of hair pulling. "There's the military, and my father, who is the military, basically, and it's complicated."

"Families are really fuckin' complicated," Tom said softly. "I get that part. Believe me, I do."

Assuming that was an invitation, I asked, "What's your family situation like?"

"We are not talking about my family right now," he said in the most aggressively emotionless tone I'd ever heard. It wasn't an invitation. "And I believe you when you say it's not a step you're ready to take. I'm not about to tell you how or when or what to do."

That drew a snicker from me. "You tell me what to do all the time and you enjoy it."

Tom didn't share my humor, still staring at the road ahead, his lips pursed in a grim line. "Every family is different and the internal mechanics are, as you said, complicated. I understand and accept these things without question. But"—he shot me a quick *I really fucking mean this* glance—"I am not your dirty little secret. If that's how—"

"It's not," I interrupted. "Whatever it is you're going to say, it's not. No."

We were silent for several miles, during which time I debated the likelihood I'd survive if I simply opened the car door and performed a basic tuck-and-roll maneuver onto the highway. I figured the fall wouldn't kill me but the oncoming traffic just might, and that seemed like a better way to go than asphyxiation-by-cold-shoulder.

Then, as Tom merged onto an exit ramp, he asked, "What are your trivia strengths?"

I peered at him, pausing for a long moment. "My-my *trivia* strengths? Trivia as in...what?"

"I usually circle up with friends on Saturdays for game nights and dinner parties. Tonight, we're going to a pub for trivia and I'd like to know you'll be useful for more than your pretty face because I play to win. So, what are your trivia strengths?"

"I've been to every continent, I know how to pickle any fruit or vegetable and my undergraduate coursework was in anthropology." I didn't know what the hell just happened here and I was honestly afraid to ask. "The rest is classified above top secret."

"I have a lot of questions about the pickling which we'll save for later," Tom said. "How much of that anthropology degree do you still recall?"

"I can tell you almost everything there is to know about the Yanomami people in the Amazonian borderlands and the lost colony of Roanoke, I can explain the difference between the Minoans and the Mycenaeans, and I can pick real artifacts and antiquities from the fakes at fifty paces. I'm fluent in a half dozen languages, conversational in another half dozen. I know where to eat in Aleppo and where to drink in Sarajevo and where to people-watch in Odesa." Glancing at the back seat, I continued, "I can also build a serviceable bomb with the junk you've got back there."

"I do not have *junk*," Tom replied. "And while it's wonderful to know that, we aren't likely to get any questions about bomb building tonight."

"If it comes up, you know who to ask. It's not a good

idea for me to talk about it but if you needed to know eight ways to kill someone and make it look like an accident or natural causes, I have that quadrant covered too."

"Assassination techniques, bomb building...this stuff rarely comes up in trivia categories," he said. "But thank you. It's good to know we're covered on all of *that*." He took a breath before adding, "Wes, please know I'm not asking you to make any enormous life decisions right now but I am saying I won't be with someone if they can't be open about their relationship."

And there it was. That was the line. If I wanted this, if I wanted him, I had to find my way across it. "All I can promise is I'm working on it. I'm working on myself. I don't want to live like this and I don't want it to spill over onto you in any way."

He drove for several minutes without responding. I revisited my previous contemplation of jumping out of the car.

Eventually, he said, "Okay. I get it. Growth and healing take time. No one understands that as well as I do."

I was thrilled I could stay inside the vehicle and in his presence but I couldn't stop myself from peering at him and wondering what the hell he meant about knowing something of healing?

13

TOM

DESPITE THE FACT Wes wasn't out to his parents—how did I always find myself in perfect situations made imperfect by life and reality?—I took him to trivia. Introduced him to my friends. Marveled at the way his big paws grasped his pint of beer. Admired his depth of knowledge in the liberal arts. He'd warned me about that in advance but it still shocked me when he showed up with the skills.

And I fell for him a bit too. When he ran his hand down my back while we waited for our table, when he pulled out my chair for me. When he engaged Max in a detailed discussion of the leading rugby teams and then when he let Bryce vent about issues with his mother's hospice care and a little more when he indulged Flinn's questions about the Navy. When he draped his arm over the back of my chair and leaned into me while giving Pawl and Joseph recommendations for their trip to Croatia this summer. When he hugged them all goodbye and said he'd see everyone again soon, even promising Max he'd join his intramural softball team as soon as his arm was cleared for such activity, and he seemed to mean all of it. When he hunched close to me as we jogged against the howling wind toward the T station and when he buzzed his hands up and down my arms when we finally made it inside.

I fell for him a little more when he tucked me against his chest while we waited for the train, his chin on my head and his heartbeat steady under my ear. And I fell even farther when he closed his hand around mine, a lopsided grin on his face and that glorious entitlement shining in his eyes as we walked from the station to my apartment.

And then I fell the rest of the way when he layered his body over mine and trapped me against my apartment door while I fumbled with my keys, saying, "If I don't get you out of these clothes and on your back in the next minute, I'm going to die."

It wasn't the statement about wanting me naked or the foreshadowed promise of fun and games while naked that checked the last of my boxes as far as this man was concerned. It was the way he wanted to fuck me straight through the door but slipped a steadying hand inside my coat, flat on my belly and not moving lower to prevent me from pitching forward and hitting the floor when I got this door open. He didn't know it but he was one of the good ones, the thoughtful ones, the *I'm going to be cautious with you* ones.

He didn't know it at all and if pushed on the matter, I was certain he'd deny it in at least four different languages. And that was why I didn't have to mention it to him.

"Please don't die," I murmured. "Not on my account."

The bolt disengaged. I turned the knob. We stepped inside. And that was when we lost our minds.

The hand Wes had anchored on my belly to prevent an ugly fall fisted in my thin sweater as he freed me of my outerwear. The keys skated across the hardwood floor and he slammed the door shut. Still holding me by the sweater, he swung me around and jerked me flat against his torso. We stumbled over the collection of winter boots I kept seated beside the door and took out the coat rack and my antique umbrella stand in the process. An awful clanging noise filled my dark apartment but we didn't care. I looped an arm around his neck as we treaded over that mess, bringing him down to meet my lips while I ripped his coat open and rucked up his shirt.

Groaning, I ran my palm down his torso. "I get so stupid when I see this."

He leaned in, scraping his teeth over my neck while he worked my belt loose. "This sexy librarian look of yours murdered me tonight. I couldn't stop thinking about sitting you on my lap and teasing you sick. About dragging you into the bathroom and getting my mouth on you. Just fucking *murdered* me, Tom."

As I pulled his shirt over his head, his elbow shot out and two small crashes sounded behind him. "I'm gonna make you clean that up."

"You'd like that, wouldn't you?" My belt snapped out of the loops and flew across the room. Another tiny crash. "Seeing me on my hands and knees?"

"I'm not sure." I cupped the thickness behind his jeans. "I'll have to see it to decide."

A snarl rang from his throat and he lashed an arm around my waist as he backed me across the room. The force of my body hitting the wall sent a picture frame sliding to the floor. It seemed to land with a rough thud but that could've been my heart bashing against my ribs. Then Wes slid to the floor.

He rested his hands on my trouser-clad thighs as he ran closed lips over the outline of my shaft. It shouldn't have felt as good as it did, like he was massaging the achiest part of me with nothing more than a pair of firm lips. I shoved my fingers in that gloriously thick blond hair of his, twisting those strands enough to remind him who was in charge here.

And since we'd never agree on matters of control, Wes traded lips for teeth. It wasn't a bite so much as a very intentional scrape of his teeth along my shaft from base to tip and the pressure was unreal. That, and the wool fabric of my trousers plus my boxer briefs beneath combined into a slow rolling wave of sensation. He pulled his teeth over my head, nothing more than a sharp flick, and my whole body shuddered.

Wes beamed up at me with self-satisfied grin.

I raked my nails over his scalp, scratching exactly as hard as he wanted. "Yes, baby, you did good. And you look gorgeous down there. But save those sweet smiles for when you're gagging on my cock and you can't see through your tears, okay?"

He ran his tongue along the seam of his lips, his brows arching up as he flipped open the button at my waist and drew my zipper down. "I hope you'll remember this conversation when I'm plowing you into the mattress and rearranging your organs."

I gestured to where my fly gaped open. "Less talking, more gagging."

Peeling my boxers down, he shot a glance at my sweater. "Get that out of my way."

Only because he curled his palm around my shaft and stroked me like he had a debt to repay did I comply. And only because he was quick to take me into his mouth, not wasting time on teasing kisses or tentative licks did I resist forcing myself into the back of his throat—at first. And it was only the precious sighs and hums he uttered while his eyes watered and saliva streaked down his jaw reminding me to savor every depraved second of this because it wouldn't last. But the way his hips punched the air, grinding into nothing but helpless to stop searching for an outlet for all the need arcing between us had me cupping the back of his neck and whispering, "That's right. That's exactly *right*."

In the end, it was the way Wes banded his arm across my backside as if he needed to snuggle while he worked me over with his mouth that did it, that wrested my control and served it to him in hot, urgent pulses.

And once again, his need for snuggles surprised no one. That it stole my release out from underneath me was the surprise, that I needed it as much as he did was the surprise. That I'd ran away from it a few days ago and now I *craved* it from a man who'd charmed my friend group and couldn't come out to his parents and wouldn't be around in a few months and I'd fallen for nonetheless.

This surprised everyone.

Wes tended to me, kissing and licking and murmuring sweet words to my body while I fought to drag oxygen into my lungs and, you know, stand. I was a breathless, quivering mess but I reached down, cupping his jaw and thumbing away the shine around his lips, the tears on his lashes. I wanted to try my hand at this affection thing. "You are so beautiful."

He nuzzled his cheek into my palm. "You taste like a memory I'd forgotten."

I ran my other hand down the back of his neck, digging my fingers into the muscles coiled between his shoulders. "What does that mean?"

"It means—it means I just want to pick you up right now and carry you into the bedroom and be extremely rude to you," he said, wincing and groaning in frustration as he struggled to lift his injured arm higher than my mid-thigh. "*Fuck,* I fucking hate this."

"Don't get too broken up about it. I wasn't letting you pick me up anyway." I drove my thumbs into the soft tissue at the crest of his shoulders as if I could take him apart, knot by knot, and smooth him out again. As if I could make it all better. "Just get up here, all right? I have a date with your dick and I'd like to capitalize on the fact I'm still delirious from that thing you did with your tongue."

Wes pushed to his feet, leaned into me with his chest and shoulders but kept his hands by his side. "I've been thinking about feeling this ass in my hands as I boosted you up and bit your neck all week."

"Then we come up with something new for you to want,

something better. Or the same thing with a few differences. We write a new playbook. It doesn't matter what you can't do, Wes. I don't care about that." I flattened one hand over his heart, the other over his zipper. "This is all I need from you."

I couldn't believe the admissions of want and possession I'd made but instead of allowing it to saturate my consciousness, I gave him a thorough squeeze which turned into an uncoordinated dance of us thrusting-jerking-spinning across my small living area, bumping into every piece of furniture in the process, resulting in another terrible crash beside us. When I saw it was one of the lamps I'd found at an estate sale near Holyoke with Shannon, I whimpered into Wes's chest. "We cannot break anything else. I know they're just things but I kind of love these things and I've spent years collecting them. That lamp was one of my favorites."

"I'll buy you some new lamps tomorrow, baby," he replied.

"That was a *special* lamp. From a special place. And it took me an entire summer to find that exact one," I replied.

"I don't care how long it takes or what it costs, I'll find you the lamp you want."

I dropped my forehead to his chest again. "I didn't know it until now but that is definitely my kink."

"Bedroom?"

I took his hands in mine. "Bedroom."

Any remaining articles of clothing were yanked, kicked, ripped off. My careful, magazine-inspired arrangement of the weighted blanket folded over the foot of the bed, the velvet quilt over the down comforter, and the layers of pillows against the headboard was destroyed with one authoritative snatch from Wes. It all went flying and—*god save me from this thunderous man*—another muffled thud sounded near the corner. But there was no time to find the origin of that thud or even chastise him for all his violent flinging because he nailed me to the mattress, his knees pressed to the backs of my thighs, his hand splayed between my shoulder blades, and my belly flat on the cool sheets.

Wes ran a hand between my legs, up, *up,* until his fingers followed the line of my crease. Back and forth, sliding down only enough to offer a glancing brush over the place I need him most. It was arrogant, really, the way he touched me. Him and his goddamn entitlement. If I could've shifted to catch a look at his face, I was certain I'd find him smirking. Or better yet, threading that wolf's tongue of his along the seam of his lips.

God, it killed me when he did that. Killed me dead because it was never an exaggerated exercise in lip-licking but a gentle, purposeful parting of his lips while his tongue danced over the sharp edge of his teeth, telegraphing his desire.

"I like how you're humping the bed. It's cute. A good look for you," Wes mused. "I could sit here and watch all night and one of these nights, I will. I'll just fucking watch you. And then I'll jerk off on your ass and you'll be such a mess I'll have no choice but to send you off to the shower. We both know what you like in the shower, don't we?"

I flexed my hamstring muscles beneath one of the knees

he was using to pin me down. He was strong but I was by no means weak. I could topple him if I wanted, reverse our positions. I didn't. I wanted him to take me exactly like this even if I hadn't known it until right now.

It was the rough scratch of his beard I felt first, that scruff moving down my spine like a tickle that only gathered in intensity, holding the pleasure of it just beyond my reach. Then it was his shaft on the inside of my thigh, the sound of plastic and foil, the cold wet of lube between my cheeks. And then he settled his knees between my legs and shot an arm beneath me, jerking my hips up, off the sheets that hadn't provided me nearly enough friction.

"I don't want to go slow," Wes warned, tapping his crown over my back channel. "I'm not in the mood for anything that could be characterized as tender, gentle lovemaking."

His hold on me was unforgiving but I managed to cant my hips toward him, a small, deliberate shift to illustrate my willingness. "And you think I am?"

Wes paused as if he meant to speak but the moment passed as he teased and I wiggled for more contact. Then, he whispered, "Stop me if it's not okay. Okay?"

My belly swooped at his softly spoken words. *I'm going to be cautious with you.* I was still nodding when he was halfway sheathed inside me and a low, guttural noise broke across my lips. Or maybe the noise came from Wes and it was deep enough to feel like it was mine. I didn't know and it didn't much matter.

Wes pulled back, pushed in again, and now we shared a groan that seemed to open and stretch around us like a fathomless sea of pressure and fullness and heat and lust and falling, falling, *falling*. With every thrust, every scrape of his teeth over my back, every primitive growl sounding in my ear, the floor disappeared and I fell for him a little more.

But it wasn't as simple as sex boiling fondness into love. It wasn't that at all and I wasn't convinced it was *love* love, the kind that crossed continents and spanned decades. It was close to love, like a spark that could bring flame to a candle or ignite a forest but I didn't know how brightly or how long it would burn yet. This was choosing something —some*one*—just for me regardless of the risks and being strong and safe enough inside myself to run headlong into him and all his issues. It was opening up my home, my friends, my body to him and watching with brazen glee as he staked out his claim to all of it.

And it was the sex too. It was the caution—and the complete disregard for such things if his punishing hold on my hips and the way he pounded into me were any indication. He wanted to protect me but he also wanted to rip my body in half while he did it and I loved everything about that, especially the part where I wanted to be ripped and protected all at once. I wanted him kneeling and begging and sobbing for relief and I wanted to help him into sweaters and scrub his back too.

"Baby," Wes crooned, shifting me down to the mattress, separating himself from me. "Come sit on my cock now, baby."

There was pain in his voice but he wasn't letting me see it as he shifted to lean back against the headboard. No, he merely patted his thighs, beckoned for me to climb aboard, and waited with his thick shaft angled toward the ceiling but I didn't miss the tentative hand he passed over his wounded flank.

"We can take a minute." I said this as I crawled into his lap and took his cock in hand but I meant it. I stroked him down to the root. "It's not like this is going anywhere."

He made an impatient gesture toward his parted legs. "I told you to sit on my cock."

And I intended to—but not before grabbing a few pillows off the floor and resolving the matter of his wound bothering him. "You're more comfortable like this? It's easier for you this way?"

He watched as I arranged the pillows behind him and at his side, tucking them in enough to give him some support. His brows lowered in defiance, he rumbled, "I'm fine."

"I'm sure you are but that's not going to stop me from reminding you we only want the good kinds of hurt tonight. Understood?"

He doused his shaft in more lube and ringed his fingers around the base, shooting a scowl in my direction that seemed to announce *you're not the boss of me.* "Get over here," he ordered. "*Now.*"

Because Wes enjoyed waiting as much as he enjoyed discovering he couldn't get a turtleneck over his head without help, he wrapped his hand around me and *led me by the dick* to his lap.

I would've resented that move if I hadn't loved it more. If it hadn't doubled the heat thrumming in my veins and turned me into the neediest, sluttiest boy in Boston tonight. Though part of me did resent it and I resented the order and structure Wes was draining from my life. I didn't get led around by the dick by anyone. I didn't whimper and babble on incoherently while inching down anyone's shaft and I didn't shake—*fucking shake*—when fully seated and then wonder whether the entirety of my body was collapsing in on itself or crystalizing into something new, something *better*, something like the way I'd always imagined myself but hadn't managed to actualize.

"Oh, that's good, that's good," Wes growled, watching with unabashed awe in his eyes as he disappeared into me.

He held me with a firm, unmoving grip while I fought to find a rhythm that didn't falter every time his broad head shuttled against my favorite spots or the vulgar thickness of him abused me in the best ways. But I did, I shuddered and gasped and just kept fucking shaking as he thrust up and I slammed down, as he restrained me with one hand on my cock and the other on my hip the way he had after that first time in the shower.

I leaned forward a bit, looped an arm around his neck to gain stability as my head loosened into fuzzy bliss and my muscles couldn't decide whether to brace for impact or sink into it. Needing more, just a little more, I reached between us, covering Wes's hand with mine and urging him to stroke me.

"No," he replied, his head thrown back and the long column of his neck exposed. "I'm not letting you jerk off while I fuck you. Not happening."

"Then do something," I ground out.

"No," Wes repeated, and that was it. *No.* I was full and stretched beyond belief, hovering in a dreamy, drunken space where my skin conducted electricity and every rock of my hips antagonized my instincts for *more, harder, now* and I could do this with him all night, all weekend, *always,* but I had to do it with nothing more than the clamp of his iron fist around my desperate, aching shaft.

"Wes, do something *now*."

He squeezed my hip harder but ignored the grip he had on my cock as he bucked up into me, stealing my breath and sending a shiver through my body. "Oh, honey. I am."

This kind of sex was medieval. We should've been fucking atop a bearskin rug or on a stone floor. It was dark and dirty and more than a little tortured. And I wasn't sure, but it was possible I'd never want it any other way.

With that thought renovating every notion I'd ever had about the kind of sex I needed in my life, I rested my cheek on Wes's shoulder, sanded my fingers through his chest hair, licked his nipple until I heard his breath catch, and then I bit him as if I meant to leave my brand on him.

"What the—oh my Jesus fucking Christ, Tom, what did you—oh fuck, I'm"—a snarl sounded in his throat and then he hammered into me as if he was leaving a brand of his own. He pressed his thumb into my hip, holding me steady, *holding holding holding* as he clenched his jaw and his body turned to granite beneath me. He punched up into me once more and I almost forgot about my cock throbbing in his hand because the sight of him sweating and panting and thrashing in my bed was too right. It knocked something loose in my head, forcing dizzy stars behind my eyes and a clench in my chest, and when he twisted the tight clasp of his fist down my shaft, it was all over. I imploded and crystalized and fell into a tiny coma.

The events following that one glorious stroke were lost to me. I didn't know what I said, what Wes said, or how I wound up lying on my back with my head on the pillow and Wes's big body wrapped around mine. But I knew how I felt during those blacked-out moments. There was the inevitable bliss of coming twice in an hour and the happy-sedated vibe that softened the world down to rounded edges and pastel colors. There was the surge of clingy hormones demanding I wrap my legs around Wes's waist and nuzzle my face into his neck and keep him close. And there was another piece, one that came to me as if spoken in a language I didn't understand and had to piece together with gestures and motions. I wasn't sure but it seemed like I felt—it was silly to even think this and my interpretation was probably off—*adored.*

Wes pressed a kiss to my temple before climbing off the bed. "I'll be right back," he promised with a quick slap to my thigh.

I heard the toilet flush, the faucet running in the bathroom, the open and close of my linen closet. I debated getting up and stripping off the sheets but at least eighty percent of my body was very much comatose and the remainder was striding in that direction. More than that, I didn't want to break the swell of endorphin-drenched quiet around me, inside me. I could curl up against Wes, allow him to tuck me tight into his notches and grooves, and I could stay there all night. I could—

Hands rolled me to my side. I was too drowsy and boneless to question it. "Here we go," Wes murmured, passing a warm, wet cloth over my torso, between my legs. "Now scoot over."

When I didn't move—what'd he asked me to do again?—he shifted me to my back and settled the down comforter over me. Pillows came next and though I didn't open my eyes to verify, I was certain the quilt and the weighted blanket followed. He climbed in beside me, fitting himself to my body.

Surprising no one at all, it wasn't as complicated as I'd imagined to snuggle after sex.

THE NEXT MORNING, I crossed my arms over my chest and leaned against the bedroom doorframe as I surveyed the remains of my living room. The living room I'd furnished in slow, deliberate additions over the past six years. It hadn't mattered to me whether the space sat mostly empty or asymmetrically assembled because just like me, it was a work in progress. I hadn't wanted to buy a sofa or art or side tables I didn't love simply because I was in need. No, I'd been content sitting on the floor, staring at blank walls, and using boxes or overturned milk crates as tables. I'd forced myself to wait for the right things rather than settle for the right-now things.

Behind me, I heard Wes yawning, stretching, and mumbling about searching for a pair of pajama bottoms. I heard a loud footfall, a muttered *dammit,* and then the moment of uncoordinated hopping one did while trying to pull on pants when exceedingly loose limbed. Then I sensed him over my shoulder and leaned back against his chest. He kissed the top of my head, saying, "Looks like we have a lot of shopping to do today. Let's hit the showers, babe."

I grimaced at the shattered lamp. I still remembered the abundance of joy I'd felt bringing it home and sitting it atop the side table like a crown jewel. "That's not necessary."

"Yeah, it is," he said, sweeping his hand at the crime scene before us. "I am getting you a new lamp and, from the looks of it, some houseplants too." He frowned at the shards of pottery and the spray of soil and pebbles across the floor. "Shit, sorry about that."

I shook my head. "It's fine."

"It's not but we'll make it fine," he added, banding his arm over my chest. "After we clean up this mess and find some replacements."

"We don't have to do that. Seriously. I like driving all over New England to find a candlestick holder and puttering around antique and vintage shops and then popping into mainstream stores too. It's my process and I'm very particular and you don't have to—"

"Oh, yeah. We're fuckin' doing this," Wes interrupted. "Boy, I am gonna antique your ass off."

"*What?*"

"Maybe I want to drive all over New England with you," he said. "I already know about your particularities and processes. I want to see the puttering." He shrugged and nuzzled his scruffy beard into my neck. "And I want to be with you. I want to see your favorite places and hear about the things you love. And I have a million questions about your friends. Max needs to leave that dirtbag boyfriend, by the way. I might need to make that guy's body disappear when I get a minute later this week."

"No murders," I warned.

"But I thought you liked murders."

"I like documentaries about the psychology of serial killers. The events that led them to kill and kill in the ways which they did. I like the investigations and the stories of the people doing the police work. I like learning about all that fucked-up stuff but I don't like the part where people are killed. I don't want you murdering anyone."

"It wouldn't look like murder," he argued. "That's part of my skill."

"Wesley Halsted. No murders."

Shaking his head, he asked, "You said this is a recurring thing, the trivia? Because they're awesome. We're doing this again next weekend, right?"

There was another fall, a secret one on top of all the big and small ones and invisible ones I'd taken last night. This one was harder, the kind of fall that stole your breath and sent your heart into your throat and your stomach down to your toes and made your blood pound so hard you couldn't hear anything else.

And I didn't believe I'd be able to hide this one.

14

SHANNON

Shannon: I didn't get a chance to ask you about Patrick when we checked in last Friday. Is he doing all right?
Tom: He's as well as Patrick ever is.
Shannon: In other words, he's growly and grumpy and pickling himself in malcontent for no apparent reason?
Tom: Essentially, yes.
Shannon: He doesn't want to say it but he's loving that project on the Cape. Something about it being an old sea captain's house works for him big time.
Tom: I agree with that and I also believe being out of the office is working well. He's not around to lose his mind about pens or printers or whatever else seems to bother him. He calls Andy about 90 times a day and she walks around with an earpiece in because of it but she knew what she was getting into with him.
Shannon: Accurate though it's kind of like a cute, forced separation before the wedding.
Tom: And what a wedding it will be.

Shannon: Are you still salty about her paper flower bouquet? Because you should really let it go. There are plenty of other things to worry about than Andy having some books carved up.

Tom: As a matter of fact, I was not being salty about the bouquet.

Shannon: If you say so.

Tom: It's sacrilege! One doesn't show their love for a book by mutilating it.

Shannon: Can we talk about Sam now? Or should we go deep on the paper flowers again?

Tom: Sam is his usual fickle self. He's fine. He'd be better if he could commit to some projects and let me schedule the rest of his year but like I said, fickle.

Shannon: Nothing new there. And Matt?

Tom: You know all about Matt.

Shannon: Yeah, I do. I got an earful from my sister-in-law last weekend at brunch. Lauren isn't loving his newfound work ethic.

Tom: He's the reason there are no available tradespeople in the tri-state area. I want to be troubled by that but his projects are finishing on schedule and under budget and they're selling for very pretty pennies. So what if he gives himself an ulcer in the process? He'll recover.

Shannon: He's not great at knowing his limits. Remember when he went running in a blizzard and Nick had to hook him up to an IV?

Tom: There's a bottle of whiskey somewhere in that story too.

Shannon: Isn't there always? These are my brothers we're talking about.

Tom: Fair point.

Shannon: And how are you doing?

Tom: Me? All good.

Shannon: Yeah? Nothing to report?

Tom: Not a ton, no. Obviously, I'm eager for you to return. I'm fine managing my team but looking after your legal assistants and Patrick's people is...special. But it's all good. We're doing well.

Shannon: Okay so is there a point at which we're going to discuss this?

Tom: Discuss what?

Shannon: You damn well know what I'm talking about.

Tom: Oh, the Broadmoor property? Yeah, I've run that down several times now with different agencies and it doesn't appear there are any living descendants with a claim on the property so I figure we can go forward without concern for a title dispute.

Shannon: That's great news and I'm actually appreciative of that update but it's not the topic I have in mind.

Tom: Well, don't keep me in suspense.

Shannon: You've been quietly collecting my brother-in-law from the house every Friday afternoon and returning him late Sunday night. The reason we're having this exchange about my brothers and their ability to function while I'm on leave is because you cut our meeting last Friday short.

Tom: And your concern is...I'm leaving the office early on Fridays?

Shannon: Oh my fucking god, Tom.

Shannon: No. No! My concern is not about the hours you spend in the office, which are extraordinary, but that you've taken to dating my brother-in-law without so much as a peep in my direction.

Shannon: ...or a thank you, seeing as I was the one who sent you two on an excursion together.

Tom: If you want to think you're the reason this happened, then... okay. Go for it.

Shannon: So, you admit something has happened.

Tom: Yes. I'll admit that.

Shannon: And you admit you'd like it to continue happening.

Tom: I...I am enjoying the moment.

Shannon: I was like you once.

Tom: I love you but shut up.

Shannon: No, really, I was in your grossly expensive shoes once and I remember telling myself it was just for fun, just while he was on leave, just...whatever. It was whatever and I wouldn't let myself think about anything more than that.

Tom: Yes. I remember that as well. It was such a treat to arrange your travel to all those random locations and then fend off questions from Patrick and Sam about your whereabouts.

Shannon: It's funny how Matt and Riley never wondered where I went.

Tom: They did, they just let Patrick and Sam function as the lead interrogators.

Shannon: Let me ask you something. About your new friend.

Tom: I am going to regret every part of this conversation, aren't I?

Shannon: Don't be so dramatic.

Shannon: Is he bossy? I mean, seriously, *seriously* bossy?

Tom: So much. But also not at all. Does that make sense? He's always barking out orders and being more assertive than reasonable but he follows my lead and waits for my permission. He also breaks into my apartment like it's no big deal.

Shannon: The breaking in! I cannot believe I'd forgotten about that, yes! What is it with the breaking in?

Tom: It's the thrill of it. I'm sure. He's just so satisfied with himself when I come home and he's there, kicked back on the sofa like a happy little pirate.

Shannon: I know exactly the expression you're talking about. I've always wondered whether it's a SEAL thing, a Halsted thing, or a this-is-just-who-Will-is thing.

Tom: I can tell you it's not just Will.

Shannon: I'm sure you know you're welcome to stay at the house together. You don't have to flee the premises. I can't imagine you're enjoying the commute.

Tom: While that is very kind and thoughtful, have you even seen the accommodations you've provided him? Because they're not what I'd expect of Shannon Walsh-Halsted.

Shannon: Wait just a hot second, my friend. We offered him every guest room in the main house but he wanted the garage apartment. I personally argued with him about it and insisted I was uncomfortable with him staying up there because the insultation is nonexistent, it's damp and drafty, and it's filled with the most bizarre collection of hand-me-down furniture in the world. It's depressing but he didn't want to be anywhere else.

Tom: You need to demo that whole bathroom, like, immediately. The shower is unforgivable.

Shannon: So, you've seen the shower?

Tom: We like my place better.

Shannon: Fair. Totally fair.

Shannon: I take it things are okay? With you and Wes?

Tom: Yes. Things are going well.

Shannon: So, here's my hang-up, I'm not going to initiate a conversation about engaging in *adult activities* with the Halsted boys but I won't walk away if you initiate.

Tom: We're not doing this. Their breaking and entering antics are one thing, how they want their asses licked is another.

Shannon: Hmm. Yeah. I hadn't thought about that segment of *adult activities* though I am a tiny bit curious whether he's…you know…rowdy.

Tom: Rowdy as fuck.

Shannon: I knew it!

Tom: He broke one of my estate sale lamps.

Shannon: Wait…how? What the ever-loving hell is going on that you're breaking LAMPS during sex?

Tom: There was a struggle. A consensual struggle. He took out a lamp, a few picture frames, and a pot of succulents. Dented the shit out of my umbrella stand.

Shannon: Will has destroyed so many nice pairs of my tights in consensual struggles but he seems to find some pleasure in ordering new ones. That makes it into a self-perpetuating cycle.

Tom: Wes took me lamp shopping and convinced me that I needed a new rug and some art for the bedroom too.

Shannon: Are we still talking about home furnishings? Because that statement was on the edge.

Tom: I have all the confidence in the world that you'll figure it out.

Shannon: I'm really happy you're enjoying this moment.

Tom: Thank you. I'm happy you feel comfortable inquiring whether your brother-in-law is a wild animal in bed and living with the knowledge that yes, yes, he absolutely is.

Shannon: I listen to my sisters-in-law gushing about sex with my brothers and the injuries they sustain and the all-natural lube solutions they employ. I've learned to have these conversations at an arm's length.

Tom: I know you well enough to spot an opening to discuss dick size from a mile away and I'm not taking it. This side show is closed.

Shannon: Can't say I didn't try.

Tom: You're nothing if not a whole lot of try, honey.

Shannon: Oh, suck my dick.

Tom: Sorry, busy with your brother-in-law's.

Shannon: Okay, now the side show is closed.

15

TOM

THE WEEKEND after ransacking my apartment, we resolved to take it easy. We grocery shopped. We went to the gym. We ordered takeout and binged a new Netflix docuseries under the weighted blanket. We talked about everything—save for the thin-ice topics of our families and his work—and it was the kind of weekend I'd always dreamed of, the kind I didn't believe could be mine. But it was mine and I was keeping it as mine, at least for now.

The weekend after that, we kicked ass at the game night hosted by Joseph and Pawl. The next morning, we held hands while waiting in line for brunch and then we kissed on the street corner. We snuggled after sex, before sex, and any time in between. We couldn't stop touching each other.

By the time our fourth weekend together rolled around, I was comfortable enough with this arrangement to introduce Wes to my meal prepping, housecleaning, and laundry routines. We also destroyed some bedsheets but shopping for linens with him was more fun than I'd expected.

We invited our friends over for a dinner party at my place the following weekend. I didn't know when I switched to thinking of them as our friends rather than mine, but change was the sort of thing that happened to you when you weren't paying attention. At some point in that evening, Wes let slip his efficacy with languages. It was true—the boy had quite a talented tongue. From there, it was decided the next party we hosted would be a full immersion event where we only spoke the chosen language and ate dishes from the culture.

And the weekend after that, when it seemed winter had made up its mind and spring was here to stay, we drove out to western Massachusetts to hike Mount Greylock. It was difficult enough to make it meaningful for me and prevent Wes from suspecting I didn't want him overexerting himself. He was well on his way to a full recovery and physical therapy was working miracles for him but I wasn't taking any chances.

I'd prepared myself for Wes to leave come spring, but spring couldn't decide if it was coming this year, and Wes hadn't left. We'd simply kept going as if not subjected to an expiration date. We cooked and argued about serial killers and hosted dinners and game nights, always crushing other couples with our trivia prowess. We checked out the farmers market but immediately decided we hated it, opting instead for lazy, overpriced brunches with bottomless Bloody Marys. We tangled our legs under a blanket on the sofa while he watched some nutty program about knives and I worked on my spreadsheets. He teased me about my precious red-soled Louboutins and I chided him for his assumption everything was a front for money laundering.

Certainly not everyone was laundering money.

We spent every weekend together and plenty of weeknights but his ongoing physical therapy sessions in Shannon's home gym kept him from fully moving in. We'd never discussed these arrangements but every time I arrived to find Wes inside my apartment—my boy didn't bother with archaic things like keys or permission—I wondered what my home had been without him. I couldn't seem to remember.

I'd succeeded in nabbing two of his UC San Diego hoodies and simply ignored the fact he'd nabbed them from Will. It wasn't Will's hoodie I wore with boxers or pajama pants or nothing at all, it was my boyfriend's. It smelled like him and it felt like him, and I didn't care about its true provenance.

We discussed the ancient—and some modern—land-based religions belonging to many indigenous people and the mythologies associated with mountains throughout the world. We debated the tension between the desire to conquer these landforms and the need to protect them from climbers and explorers as they were sacred, holy grounds. We talked *around* a summer climbing trip to Europe which was to say we planned everything down to the colors of the scooters we intended to rent in Positano—red for me, blue for Wes—but made no actual plans because we both knew the day would come when he had to go reprise his role as Jason Bourne or Jack Ryan or whichever badass hot-guy secret agent he was supposed to be this month. And now we were so much closer to that day than I'd realized, I wanted to cry.

This weekend, with winter back in all its icy glory, we chose to get lost in new documentaries and under blankets. There was no order or rhythm to the seasons' on-again, off-again dance and it was that absence of equilibrium that struck me early Sunday morning while I scrolled through my calendar for the week.

"You've been sleeping with me for six weeks," I announced.

Wes hooked his arm around my waist, dragging me back to his side. "And I'd like to continue sleeping," he rumbled into my flank.

Six weeks. Six weeks! Didn't he care? Didn't it matter to him? Wasn't this significant in a *what the hell are we doing and can we do it forever* way? And—and what of his work? Was it a waiting game, a matter of days and minutes until the call came through and he left for a shadowy, dangerous place liable to send him back to me with another broken arm, another gouge out of his torso, more pieces of his precious body surrendered to—to what? And for why? Why did they get to keep him and I didn't? He was strong and whole again, finally able to use his injured arm for simple tasks and bear his weight on it without tremendous pain. It hurt me to think about him going through anything like that again. It hurt me to think all I'd have left of him was a secondhand hoodie.

His face still pressed to my side, Wes said, "Tell me your worst things."

"Worst things?" I repeated, suddenly weary. There was a

reason I'd avoided this line of thought. "What kind of worst?"

He rolled away, bending his arm and propping his head on his palm to smile up at me. "When I was a kid, I convinced my mother I was allergic to gardenias."

I was so confused. What were we talking about? "And that's your worst thing because why?"

"Because my family has a running joke that I was such a terrible toddler, my mother routinely called me an asshole and I enjoyed living up to that name. Because I'm not allergic, I just don't like the smell. She dug up ten gardenia bushes back home in San Diego and gave them away to people who promised to replant them. They're one of her favorites."

I ran my fingers through his hair. "I can't say I disagree with her. It is an asshole move."

"For what it's worth, I send her gardenias every year on her birthday. Fortunately, I haven't been within five thousand miles of her or those flowers in the past handful of years." He edged his fingers under the waistband of my boxers, smiling like I wouldn't flip him on his back as a punishment for this teasing. "I want one of yours."

Given the fingers distracting me, it took a solid minute of thought to find anything comparable to his gardenia story. "When I was Shannon's assistant, I used to get her breakfast in the morning because she'd forget to eat and then we'd all suffer. But she only liked muffins from one specific bakery. When they went out of business seven or eight years ago, I bought all their remaining bags and put muffins from Costco in them each morning. She hasn't noticed the difference yet."

Instead of shoving his hand fully into my boxers as I would've appreciated, Wes tugged me down to his pillow and circled his arm around my shoulders. "You, sir, are just as bad as I am."

"If that's what you want to believe, sure," I said. "Tell me another."

He skimmed his fingers over the space between my shoulder blades, circling and swirling as he hummed in thought. "I refuse to split a dessert with anyone at a restaurant."

"Why?" I asked, laughing.

"Because if I wanted to get inside four mouths, I'd have an orgy." The light pass of his fingers on my back intensified as if he intended to unravel my knots and smooth me out. That wouldn't happen. My knots were as much a part of me as thorns were part of a rose, as scars were part of Wes. But he was welcome to try. "And what's the point of getting only two or three bites of cake? That's outrageous."

"But I never want a whole slice," I said, still laughing. "I need someone to share it with. You wouldn't split some cake with me?"

"Baby, please. Of course I'd split cake with you. I know where your mouth has been and, with any luck, I know where it'll be going after that cake."

With my fingers hooked around the sides of his boxers, I pushed them down his legs. "You're cute."

"I really am. I'm also naked, it seems, and it's only fair for you to join me in that," he shot back, again delving beneath my waistband. "Give me another while I help you with this matter."

Since I didn't want him straining his arm, I shimmied out of my undies before he could do it for me and moved my bare length against his. It earned me a delicious growl. "When I moved in here, the first floor unit was being sublet to the grossest guy in the world. Everything about him was terrible. Loud, aggressive, constantly rude and hostile. If he was coming in when I was going out, I'd wait until he was gone. I never wanted to be in the hall with him. He was never more than one bender away from committing a hate crime."

"This needs to end with you killing him," he murmured as he worked his fingertips into the deepest of my knots.

I flattened my hand on the small of his back, forcing his shaft against mine. "Sometimes I think you're serious when you say these things."

"That's because I am," he said. "If you didn't kill him, please tell me how this carnival of awful ended because I will leave this bed to kill him now if he's still living downstairs."

"You're doing nothing of the sort," I said through a sigh. "One of the city inspectors we often work with knew someone high up in the local DEA office. The inspector passed along a tip about that guy illegally selling weed out of his apartment. He got evicted."

"Doesn't count. That's not a worst thing. I would've killed the guy."

"Once again, that seems excessive," I said.

"Not when he scared you like that, it isn't," he replied.

"You would not have *killed* him, Wes."

"Fine," he conceded. "But I would've made sure he had several heartfelt chats with his god."

"Give me some more of your worst."

"I flunked out of sniper school. I'd wanted to be a sniper since I'd heard the word. It was all I'd ever wanted. But I'm a lousy shot and the Navy liked my language skills and sent me off to PSYOPS and advanced interrogation training."

"You just admitted you're a master manipulator. Which part of that is your worst thing?"

"You're cute and funny and I love when you stroke me with your cock," he replied. "But, yeah. I grieved the loss of my sniper dreams. I had to reimagine my future as a SEAL. Had to change how I saw myself. I didn't know who I was if I wasn't a sniper."

"You make it sound like that was the only time you had to figure yourself out."

He blinked away. We weren't talking about that this morning. We just weren't talking about it.

"Tell me more of yours," he ordered.

"I judge people for the most ridiculous, irrelevant things," I said.

"Obviously, I'm going to need an example."

I glanced at the ceiling as I searched for the least ridiculous, irrelevant instance to share. I couldn't come out swinging at people who bought couture leashes for their dogs or kept their holiday wreaths up until spring. "Okay. Excessive shows of college pride, especially on vehicles. The Georgetown sticker on the rear windshield and the Georgetown license plate frame and the GTOWN personalized license plate. Yeah, we get it, you went to Georgetown. Fabulous."

"Another," Wes said.

"Complicated coffee orders. I'm all for being particular but if it takes five full minutes, some scratch paper, and the assistance of a store manager to explain how you want *coffee*, you're doing it wrong. And I don't mean the coffee, I mean life. You're doing life wrong."

"More, I want more. I love Judgy Tom."

It was the judgy he loved, not the Tom. I knew that. I knew it, my flopping belly knew it, my pathetic, hopeful heart knew it. "People who post on social media that they'll be offline. No one is going to notice if you don't share a couple outfit-of-the-day pics, Todd. No one is sending out a search party if you don't post your workout stats one week. No one cares if you don't reblog every new social or political outrage for a few days. It's fine, we'll all be fine." I held up a hand, stopping Wes from demanding more from my snarky vault. "It's your turn."

He blinked down at the mattress before saying, "At the same time, I'm both unnaturally fixated on earning my parents' approval and blowing off their expectations to do whatever the fuck I want. I went to UC San Diego because Will went there and they were so proud of Will for it but then I decided to study anthropology because fuck all those useful programs. I joined the Navy and the SEAL Teams because my father believed the best men in the world were the ones under his command but then I took the first offer I got to join a special intelligence community program because I wanted to be different from my father and Will. I wanted to be more." He gestured to his injured arm. "And I'm pleased to announce that's earned me some fine titanium."

My heart ached for him. For the young man who feared losing his parents' approval so much he rejected the possibility of earning it. "Tell me, Wes, what do you do to take care of yourself?"

The levity sparkling in his eyes dimmed. "What are we talking about right now?"

I pressed a hand to his sternum. "We're talking about doing the things that are right for you but might not make sense to anyone else. I'll give you an example. I'm cautious about the people I surround myself with because I've made harmful choices in the past. I've ignored every sign and symptom of those choices being unhealthy for me but I'm trying to do better now, which means limits—or ends—to anything that doesn't meet my needs."

Wes dropped his hand to the blankets with a quiet, "Oh."

"It's uncomfortable enforcing limits and boundaries but I think it would help," I said. "And I think the first limits you should establish are ones with yourself."

Another quiet, "Oh."

"I care about you. I want the best things for you," I said. *And I think I love you.* "And I'll help any way I can."

He nodded but didn't say anything for several long minutes in which I contemplated drawing him deeper into my arms, leaving the bed, checking my phone, initiating sex, and asking if he was all right. I did none of those things, instead studying him for any outward overflow of emotions. I found none.

"It's your turn," he finally said, a touch of sullenness in his voice.

It seemed like as good a time as any to share this bit of my history. "I was arrested for breaking and entering."

Wes peered at me as if I'd told him the oceans and sky traded places. Eventually, he asked, "What happened?"

I pressed my palm to my chest, rubbing the tension that never went away. It was always there, drawing my shoulders up, twisting the muscles beneath my breastbone, keeping my breath quick and starved. The hunched, frantic hopelessness of it never went away. "I was homeless."

As if needing confirmation I currently lived in this apartment, he glanced around, asking, "What? When?"

"It was a long time ago. I was a teenager."

"But-but why? What happened?"

I edged a shoulder up. "It was cold. One of the coldest nights in a month of brutally cold nights and there was nowhere else—"

"No, baby, what happened that you lost your home?"

I met his eyes. "I was kicked out of the house when I failed conversion camp."

16

WES

I COULDN'T BREATHE. There was fire in my chest and I could hear my pulse and I couldn't file this information away without simultaneously shattering something. I managed to say, "Are you all right?"

"Yeah," Tom replied easily. "I mean, no. Not at all. It's mental Chernobyl, the whole package. But I'm okay. You wouldn't be here and we wouldn't be having this conversation if I wasn't."

I nearly choked on his glib tone. "Is that right?"

"Yeah, I'm very selective about the people I bring home. If they don't brandish a weapon within the first five minutes of meeting me, they're not getting buzzed up here again. I suppose it's different when they repeatedly break in but that doesn't mean I wouldn't show you the door."

"Be serious," I chided.

"Ugh, fine." He adjusted the pillow and layered his chest against mine. I urged him closer, wanting every bit of him touching every bit of me. "I don't talk about the conversion thing. I don't want pity or coddling or the 'Oh, I have no idea what you've been through but I've heard terrible things on *60 Minutes* and therefore I can slather you in sympathy after consuming some tragedy porn.'"

"I don't want your tragedy porn and I don't want to slather you in sympathy," I said. "I want to—" *I want to love you. I want to hold you as tight as I can and protect you and shield you from the world and I want to* love *you.* "I want to bury the people who did that to you."

"Oh, great, we're back to that," he muttered. "Is there some kind of transitional program for special operatives who only know how to solve problems with deadly force? Because I cannot have you running around killing people, Wes. Or suggesting you're going to kill people."

I stared over his shoulder, unfocused. "That depends on whether it's time for me to transition."

"You make it sound like it's not your decision to make," he said.

"It's not," I replied.

"Of course it is," he argued. "If I believed I wasn't the one in control of my choices and my destiny, this life would be a shitshow."

"But how can you say that?" I shot back. "You were—you were sent to fucking conversion camp, Tom. You were—oh my god, I can't even think about what you experienced there and—"

"I'm past that now," he interrupted. "It happened and it was the worst thing I've ever been through and I've done the work to know *I* am not wrong. But I don't want my identity to be tied up with trauma. I get to decide who and what I am, not my history."

After several moments when the only sound between us was our breathing, I said, "Can I ask what happened after your arrest?"

He laughed. A good, warm laugh I felt as his body shook against mine. "Shannon Walsh. There was some program where new lawyers could work off their loans or something by doing pro bono public defense work. She was assigned to my case had the charges tossed out in a hot second. Then she brought me home with her."

He almost sounded cavalier about the great and small tragedies of his childhood, like they hadn't stolen the most essential things from him. I didn't know how he did it. I didn't know how he put one shiny wingtip in front of the other. When I allowed myself to think about it, I was paralyzed by my father's history of institutionalizing homophobia. I couldn't breathe under the weight of it. And yet Tom had faced a galaxy of awful. "Ah. Now it all makes sense," I ground out.

"She's the auntie everyone deserves," he said. "She has a way of collecting strays."

I tugged the corner of my lower lip between my teeth. "So does my brother."

Tom tipped his head back, a slow grin pulling at his mouth as he gazed at me. "Is that what we are? Strays?"

I ran my tongue over my teeth as I studied him. "We're whatever we want to be," I said. "Whatever we want, Tom."

WE COMPARED schedules on the drive out of the city and along the coast, and I realized I was thankful to be stuck here. Thankful for all the misery and all the confusion, thankful for the days spent hating myself for fucking up my mission and falling down this hole. I was thankful because I didn't feel stuck anymore, I didn't feel lost. I felt rooted and right, two things I hadn't experienced since ever.

I hated the way I lost my cover and killed my covert career, I was still crushed about what happened to Veronica, and I didn't enjoy being on the hook for kicking off an international incident. All of those things were true and valid, and they didn't exclude the possibility it was time for that portion of my life to end. I didn't know anything with certainty and the mere thought of leaving the only job I knew how to do was overwhelming but I couldn't picture myself actually leaving Tom. Every time I imagined the call coming in from the CIA with orders for a new op, I imagined relief—I was capable and qualified and essential again —followed by acute, paralyzing pain. I couldn't do it, I couldn't go—and I didn't want to. The validation of being called up only got me so far and the hunger for a new challenge granted me a bit more mileage but the rest was unrelenting opposition to the notion of saying goodbye.

I'd done this enough to know leaving for a mission didn't mean leaving forever. To date, I'd returned from one hundred percent of my missions, and many operatives had similar track records. Losing a spleen and gaining some titanium screws wasn't the end of the world, even if I still resented the motherfucker who'd turned my arm into a pincushion. But I wasn't alone anymore, I wasn't the only one who stood to get hurt. For somewhere in this weird winter that wouldn't stop, I fell for Tom.

It was the last thing I'd planned to do during my confinement to Will's guest quarters and here in Boston, of all the frigid, un-surf-able places, but none of that seemed to matter anymore.

Sure, I'd need a job and there were months of physical therapy ahead of me but I wasn't destitute. I had money saved up. I could comfortably spend some time getting my arm back in fighting shape and then—well, no, probably not *fighting* shape—but I could take it slow. Even if the intelligence community didn't want me engaged in covert work, they could deploy me as a headhunter on college campuses. There were more than enough universities in the area, and CIA, NSA, and FBI were always looking for fresh meat. I could do that, I could be a nightcrawler. And I'd learn to cook too. I'd take classes or something like that. I'd learn how to make all of Tom's favorite things and maybe convince the boy to deviate from his salmon-and-broccoli habit. And we'd climb mountains together. Switzerland and Italy this summer, maybe Mexico or Tanzania in the winter. Yeah, I could do all of these things and it would be amazing. We'd sit down for one of Tom's famous logistics conversations and figure it out. We'd just figure it all out.

Maybe it could be that easy.

"Are you even listening to me right now?" Tom asked as he turned down the driveway.

"You're attending planning board meetings in two different towns this week plus a wonky historical preservation society gathering you doubt I'd enjoy, and that's on top of all the early morning shit you have scheduled," I said. "Long story short, you'll see me on Friday and that's fine because I can't be trusted to let you sleep when you'll clearly need it though you might be able to sneak away from the office for lunch."

Tom came to a stop in front of the garage. "Okay, so you were listening."

"Don't sound too disappointed, babe. You'll catch me one of these days."

"No, I've resigned myself to the fact you're a highly trained government operative with a brain like an Access database and you not only hear but also remember everything, except for me, the first time we met."

I slapped a hand over my heart. "Will I ever live that down?"

Tom took my hand, brought my palm to the weekend scruff he'd taken to growing. It felt amazing on my neck, my chest, between my thighs. "I had a crush on you that weekend."

"It only lasted the weekend?"

He gave an indecisive shrug. "I kept trying to put myself in the same spots as you and catch your attention but you weren't giving it."

"I'll give it now," I said, slipping my palm to the back of his neck and pulling him closer. "I'll give you all my attention now. As much as you want, for as long as you want it."

His eyes had a dreamy, glowy quality to them when he asked, "Do you mean that?"

I bobbed my head in agreement, ready to promise him

everything I had to give and a few things I didn't, and brought his lips to mine. "I—"

Headlights slashed through the dark interior of Tom's car, briefly blinding us both and breaking the moment. I kept my palm on his neck and placed the other on his chest as I swiveled in my seat to find the origin. A black Suburban with tinted windows rolled up beside us and at the same moment, my brother appeared in the doorway to the main house, his hands in his pockets.

A car door slammed shut and Jordan Kaisall joined Will at the door. They shook hands before shifting to face us. They'd planned this.

"*Fuck,*" I whispered.

"What's wrong?"

It wasn't going to be that easy.

"TO WHAT DO I owe the pleasure of this visit?" I asked Kaisall as we followed Will through the house.

He started up the stairs, one hand braced on the railing as he forced his opposite leg to comply. I hadn't been there and I didn't know the particulars but I knew Jordan Kaisall's SEAL career ended on his first mission. I'd always viewed his busted leg with the small store of shrugging, side-eyed patience I kept on hand for people who couldn't handle the reality of this work but now it looked more like a fucked-up party favor. Now it looked like I had a party favor of my own.

"You're a special case," Jordan called over his shoulder as I trailed his gradual ascent.

My brother had his own career-ending injury too. It wasn't obvious from looking at him, not the way it was with Jordan and his pronounced limp, but a helicopter crash, some shrapnel, and a few other extraordinary circumstances left him with a world of nerve damage in his shoulder. Surgery had resolved most of it and I was positive he could've returned to the SEAL Teams if he'd wanted, but that injury was the end of his time there. He was done and he wanted out, and while I'd fed his decision more of my shrugging, side-eyed patience, I saw it differently now. I saw the impact of having someone waiting for you on the other side.

"I must be real special for you to come all the way up here," I said. "Do you drive? Train? Ferry? A bit of each and some hang gliding just for fun?"

"Anything more than fifty miles, Kaisall takes his jet," Will said from the landing.

When we joined Will, Jordan's face was red and his chest heaved from the exertion. I should've glanced away and given the man a moment to collect himself but the reminder of my not-so-distant struggles to get a sweater over my head without assistance ran down my spine like ice water. "That's a rather large carbon footprint for you, sir."

Waving me off with some muttered noises about me being a pain in his ass, Jordan led the way into Will's home office though calling this place a *home office* was a failure of the language. This room was what would happen if Pottery

Barn had a merchandising agreement with James Bond's R&D team. Bookshelves and locked cabinets swallowed up one wall. Another wall was composed entirely of screens, all displaying maps, satellite images, CCTV arrays, with a narrow desk and chair tucked under the bank. A leather sofa with some linen and twill pillow he couldn't have selected by himself. Another desk with three computer monitors, a keyboard, and not a single scrap of paper in sight, not even a stray Post-it, extended out from a wall unit that looked an awful lot like a secret firearm safe.

"It's always fun to catch up but you're due on a secured line in five minutes," Jordan replied, shutting the office door behind him.

That heavy *snick* sent a shiver through my shoulders. It was too weighty to be the sound of any ordinary door closing but more than likely an armored door, the sort that refused entrance or exit without fingerprints and retina scans and forty other biometric conditions.

I swung a glance between them. "This is"—I gestured to Jordan—"you know what's coming. That's why you're here. You know what's going on and it's bad. You wouldn't be here otherwise. How bad? Dishonorable discharge bad? Judge Advocate General bad?" Jesus Christ, I really didn't want to go to military prison. I really did not want that on the table. "War crimes bad? Is that why you brought the jet? What—"

"Quiet down," Will ordered, wagging *get your shit together* hands at me. "You can't listen if you're busy inventing worst-case scenarios."

"Jordan fucking flew here so you two could hold my

hands through a call you didn't dare tell me about until right now. If it's not the worst-case scenario, you guys need to work on your staging because this setup is weak."

Jordan stepped in front of Will, saying, "They're not sending you to the Hague or any other criminal proceeding but they have to put this multi-agency program to bed as quickly and soundlessly as possible. You know what happens anytime covert work makes headline news. There are questions and inquiries and hearings. Programs get shuttered."

"I'm aware of that," I snapped. "The last three programs I've been in have been shut down. They reorganize under a new name and then carry on business as usual. I know how Washington works, Jordan. I don't need that lesson from you."

"And somehow, you know all of this but didn't know it was time to get the fuck out before your cover was blown," Will said. He had his arms crossed over his chest, his hands bunched into fists as if he was working hard at restraining himself. He probably was. If there weren't babies down the hall and my parents in the kitchen and a wife who'd tear a stripe off his ass for it, he'd knock his brand of sense into me the old-fashioned way. "For fuck's sake, you didn't even know which agency you were working for. They don't give a fuck about you. They're not going to shuffle you into a new program, Wes. They're going to leave you out in the cold. It's a damn good thing Jordan was the one to provide your exfil because you know what would've happened if one of these agencies had done the job? It would've ended the only way it ever ends for exposed operatives."

"Oh, great. We've reached the portion of the performance where Will says, 'I told you so,'" I drawled. "And it's only taken"—I made an exaggerated show of studying my watch—"four minutes. This might be your personal best."

"They're not going to tell you this but they're recalling all the assets operating in this program's portfolio," Jordan said, ignoring the steam coming out of my brother's ears. "Like you said, they'll turn some into assets for other programs and other agencies. Some will be turfed. They've already burned a few too but my sources suggest that was coming regardless."

"You wouldn't be here if they were turning me over to the SEAL Teams or an intelligence agency, so I'm being released. That's why you're here. Because I'm done. Because my partner is dead and my arm is too fucked-up for active duty as a SEAL and I missed *one* surveillance camera and now I'm fucking done."

It was funny to think how much I'd embraced this idea no more than an hour ago and now I was prepared to raise hell over it. This wasn't a path I'd chosen because I was ready for a detour, it was the open-handed slap I'd cowered against since waking up in Nova Scotia.

Funny. Yeah, that was one word for it. I didn't recognize any of the emotions I'd contemplated on the drive up here. I didn't want this. I didn't want a shove out the door when I'd sacrificed the past fifteen years of my life, my identity, my vital organs to this work. I'd given up everything and I had nothing to show for it. I was thirty-six years old and my CV was a Sharpie's paradise of redactions and I was starting over. It didn't matter whether I could translate insurgent chatter or lure college students away from the sweet, sterile life of finance or law in favor of hard targets and surveillance teams and interrogation resistance techniques. Nothing mattered. Not the years or miles or injuries or false personas. Not the threats I'd neutralized or the crises I'd helped avert. And it didn't matter whether anyone was waiting for me on the other side. In so many ways, I was as alone now as I was on that tanker. My arm wasn't in a million pieces anymore and I wasn't bleeding to death but I was lost and so fucking angry all over again.

Will snapped his fingers, pointing to a chair in front of his computer screen. "We don't leave the deputy director waiting."

"Super cool how you two have invited yourselves to listen in while I get fired," I said, flopping into the chair and scowling at the screen.

"Do me a favor, would you? Find some discipline," Will ordered. "Don't be a dickhead to your commanding officer. They might be releasing you into civilian life and you might not like the predictable way in which this is going down but that's no reason to be a dickhead."

"Would you like to tattoo 'I told you so' down my arm? Would that make you feel better?" I asked him. "Or would you rather brand it on my chest? Just tell me which you'd prefer and we'll get it done."

Jordan, aiming hard at a casual tone from his perch on the sofa, said, "Strange thing I noticed on the flight up here, Halsted. Background profiles on the signals intelligence contractors we're looking at came back and one of the lead analysts has a connection to your sister."

Will shifted enough to face Jordan while still keeping an eye on me, as if I'd try to flee the armored room filled with weaponry and a pair of former SEALs. "He's connected to Lauren how?"

He made a looping gesture with his hand as he said, "Not entirely clear from the material Shaw sent me but he has history with one of her employees. A teacher, I think it was. Audrey something. They go back all the way to high school."

Will made an impatient noise. "I don't like any of that."

"I don't share your misplaced or exaggerated concerns," Jordan said as the screen in front of me flashed a *please hold* sign and a loud beep sounded from the speakers. "I just thought it was a strange coincidence."

My brother gestured for Jordan to shut up and Jordan gestured for Will to calm down and I did my best to behave though I wanted to tell this deputy director about the problems I had with him and his decisions.

The call was short and direct. My cover was blown and thus I was no longer able to conduct covert work in this or any other intelligence program. There was some noise about me failing to follow protocol—fucked-up noise but they had to invent some, so there it was—and not being able to place me in any overt Agency position despite my background and skills. Naval Command had issued an honorable discharge order and the deputy director's tone made it clear I was to interpret that as an undeserved gift. I'd receive more information on that portion of my separation soon but as far as the Agency was concerned, we were finished.

There were many significant differences between being a SEAL and being a spy but the most pronounced, at least right now, was the way they ended things. The SEALs loved their formality and structure and processes. They didn't even let you die without getting the full process. The intelligence community was just done with you. Here today, gone tomorrow. No ceremony, no process. No "thanks for giving us the entirety of your life for all these years, hope you land on your feet!"

"That wasn't as bad as I'd anticipated," Jordan mused from the sofa. "The rumors I'd heard leaned harder into the protocol issues."

"And to think you flew all the way up here for a disappointing show," I replied. "Sorry to break your heart."

Missing my sarcasm entirely, he waved me off. "I'm here because we want to talk about what comes next." He glanced to my brother and the thin fibers of dignity I'd maintained through all of this disintegrated in my hands. "We have a job for you."

I brought my hands to my face, the balls of my palms pressed hard to my eyes. "Oh my fucking god."

Will and Jordan took turns rattling off their talking points while I mentally toggled through a highlight reel of my final days in Russia. I'd misread the information. I'd ignored the signs. I'd fucked up. I'd fucked up and my partner was dead, my career was over, and—and fuck, what was I going to do now? Who was I if I wasn't a SEAL, a spy, an operative? Who was I without those cloaks and shields?

I put my head down on the desk while they continued with their crisply rehearsed pitch. They wanted me to work with them, they were expanding, blah blah fucking blah.

It was juvenile of me but I didn't like being lumped in with Will and Jordan. I didn't want to be part of their crew. I didn't like thinking of myself as someone who'd also experienced a career-ending injury and there was no way in hell I'd sign up for a gig like theirs. The last thing I needed was a Pottery Barn office. No, I wanted the dream scenario I'd constructed on the drive home. The college campuses and the blazers with those kitschy felted elbows and soccer in the quad while I wove a charming tapestry of the clandestine life. Cooking lessons for my man. Climbing trips to Europe and Mexico and Africa. Not...whatever the fuck this was.

When I couldn't take it anymore, I pushed to my feet and announced, "Excuse me, gentlemen. This has been lovely but I need to go walk into the ocean."

With their insistent calls bouncing off my back, I stepped out of my brother's mini-mission control center and into the hall, my heart whomping against bone and muscle in pathetic, self-piteous thuds. It was dark and cold now, evening having surrendered to night while closed up inside that office and I hated this place all over again. I hated the winter and the frosty dryness in the air and the implied house arrest and all the people who wanted the best for me and the best was doing everything their way. I hated it all and I was so fucking done, I could taste the finality in the back of my throat.

"Wes! Oh, thank god," Shannon called from the opposite end of the hall, near the girls' bedrooms. "You're here and that's perfect because I need help. Please, just a couple of minutes."

"I'm not"—I didn't know what I'd meant to deny but I suddenly found I didn't have the energy for it. All I wanted to do was curl up under blankets and pillows and sleep. But I also wanted to punch a lot of holes in walls and I wanted to break a few things. And then walk into the ocean and let it carry me to a place where none of this bullshit existed in my life. "Okay. Cool. Whatever."

"Thank you," she said, beckoning me to her end of the hall. "I need you to sit with Abby for a bit while I handle a situation with Annabelle." She pointed toward her oldest daughter's room. "She's busy with her toys. Just keep an eye on her, okay?"

"I think I can manage that," I said as Shannon let out a relieved breath, her hand clutched to her neck. "What's going on? What's the big emergency?"

"There's an explosive situation in Annabelle's room that requires undivided attention," she said. "If I didn't think this one"—she nodded toward Abby—"would teach herself to climb walls and swing from the light fixture if I turned my back on her for a second, I'd be okay on my own. But—"

"It's fine," I interrupted, far too tired for this much conversation. "I got it."

After another round of thanks and warnings to keep Abby grounded, Shannon departed to diffuse the situation with Annabelle. I flopped onto the floor, watching while she engaged in another complicated game involving socks and her play-kitchen spatula. She sang a song I couldn't decipher and that was life right now. A song I didn't understand.

I folded my legs in front of me and dropped my head in my hands because I couldn't process this or any of the truths that'd loomed over my head like a guillotine for the past few months.

Abby appeared by my side, her arms around my neck and her head bent to my shoulder. "Give loves," she said, flinging herself into my lap. "Give loves."

It wasn't that easy.

17

TOM

THIS MONDAY'S attic meeting went off the rails within ten minutes. There was no specific reason for this derailment but this squad had a way of growing rusty and fragile when down a member or two. Shannon's first maternity leave hadn't seemed as long as this one, and with Patrick spending his days on Cape Cod recently, the vibe in the office was slowly oxidizing.

Simply because they'd been storing up reasons to argue with each other, Matt and Sam crashed into a bloody debate as to whether their primary obligation was sustainable design or historical preservation—spoiler alert after a decade in this shop: that debate had no end. Since Riley knew this, he turned his attention to the breakfast burrito he'd stashed in his backpack. Patrick rested his arms on the table and dropped his chin onto his clasped hands, listening and occasionally opening his mouth to comment but stopping himself to rub his temples or shoot baleful glances at Andy. For her part, Andy ignored the entire conversation, preoccupied with wedding business. From the looks of it, she was selecting flowers for the ceremony and reception.

I stared at my screen, toggling between spreadsheets. The numbers and workflows made sense to my conflict-averse heart. I'd known the Walsh family long enough to know they yelled their feelings and I knew how to hang with it now. Back when I'd started out here, I'd struggled with it *hard*. For a million different reasons, raised voices and arguments made me anxious, and it activated my people-pleasing instincts. It was fucked-up but that was why I'd been sensational as an assistant.

I hadn't realized that then. No, I'd figured I was uniquely qualified to read Shannon's mind and keep this office running smoothly. Helping her be awesome was my gift. When she'd made noises about taking college courses in the evenings, I'd dismissed her. Shannon didn't say anything just to be nice but I hadn't even finished high school. I didn't see anything wrong with fetching her coffee and paint swatches for the rest of my life.

The best I could do didn't have to be great. I hadn't believed I was worthy of anything great.

It took several years and an out-of-the-blue decision to take up mountain climbing to find my competence and value. I wasn't certain I'd found it all, but I knew I was more than the person who made Shannon awesome.

And this morning, with the skin beneath my shirt and tie still tender from Wes's scruffy beard, I knew I was more than this firm. I'd never worked anywhere else and the prospect of leaving these loud, abrasive, amazing people who were the closest thing I had to a family was panic-inspiring, but I could. I could leave Walsh Associates, I could leave Boston. I could join Wes wherever his career took him.

What a wild idea.

We could get an apartment together if we moved to a big city, maybe a house if we moved to a less urban area. Chicago would be fun. Maybe Washington, D.C. Wes loved warmer climates so maybe Austin or Atlanta? It could be anywhere. We could go anywhere. We'd explore our new city and develop a short list of favorite brunch locations. We'd find trivia spots and make friends. We'd have dinner parties. We'd go on vacations and celebrate holidays. We'd disagree over glassware and linens, and other blissfully domestic issues. We'd share all these experiences and make something just for us.

Another wild idea? When we moved, maybe I'd send my family an update. Nothing more than a cute postcard announcing my new address but it would be enough to send a clear message to them. They'd know I was living well and living with a man, despite their vigorous efforts to the contrary. They'd know I'd survived everything they'd forced upon me and everything they'd done to me. They'd know and even if they burned that postcard while cursing my name, they wouldn't be able to burn the truth.

A teeny tiny part of me wondered whether they'd acknowledge my postcard, my existence. All these years, I'd held out the thinnest sliver of hope for my sister. That she'd be the one to reach out and acknowledge me. We didn't have to be friends or even family—we hadn't been that in ages—but we could know each other again. I could congratulate her on her wedding, the birth of her children. She could send me and Wes a holiday card. That would be enough.

It was wild—and fully fictional. Wes hadn't suggested anything of this sort. He probably hadn't imagined us together beyond the summer—if that long. He hadn't even hinted where life might take him next and from the looks of last night's surprise meeting with his brother and Jordan Kaisall, I had to believe his life was bound to get much more complicated very soon. What if he was sent to some remote place and I couldn't find a job? What if Wes didn't want me to go because Wes preferred his freedom and independence? That didn't seem outrageous, given everything else I'd learned about him.

And moving somewhere with Wes would necessitate him having a conversation with his family. Wes wasn't doing that any time soon and I wasn't going to hide in plain sight as his *roommate*. So, no. This wasn't happening. I wasn't going anywhere.

Even if Wes stayed in Boston, *we* weren't going anywhere. There was no way for us to go forward, regardless of whether Wes relocated to Chicago or the middle of the Amazonian rainforest. It had nothing to do with jobs or anything aside from the fact I wasn't willing to be anyone's secret and Wes couldn't hold my hand in the presence of his parents.

I still couldn't get over the hot slap of shame I'd felt in that moment. It didn't take much to remind me of the time when I wasn't deserving of anything at all—not a family, not a home, not even an existence. I might've shed some of the skin of abuse and abandonment years ago but trauma stuck around. It lived inside blood and bones and guts, and it didn't go away.

It took me years to grow into the idea of deserving great things but it came with the unintended consequence of expecting great things from others. I wanted my sister to take responsibility for standing by, silent, while I was rejected. I wanted my mother to apologize for everything. And I wanted Wes to resolve his issues with his parents so we could be together without hiding anything.

I knew I was worthy of all these things but I still didn't know whether it was wrong to hope for them.

18

WES

SINCE I COULDN'T SLAM the door behind me—sleeping babies and all—I stamped my boots on the doormat. It read House Halsted in the *Game of Thrones* typeface. My brother was really leaning into his cheeky suburban life.

Unreasonably annoyed about that doormat and furious about everything else in my life, I stomped up the driveway and toward the town center. I didn't know where I was going but I had to get out of that house. It was good of Will and Shannon to put up with me this long and I could admit I enjoyed hanging out with Abby and Annabelle, but I couldn't stay here another minute. I needed a break, I needed some new scenery, I needed—Tom. That was it. I needed Tom.

I knew how to breathe when I was with him.

All the problems piled on top of me were less oppressive. The future was brighter. I wasn't prepared to say the birds sang more sweetly or sunbeams felt warmer but things were good with Tom. *I* was good when I was with him. I was still smarting and salty as fuck from the way things went down with the CIA and not too thrilled with the Navy either but I could see beyond those issues with Tom. I could set everything aside—the busted arm, the living arrangements, the lack of transferrable skills, the conversation I couldn't bring myself to have with my parents—and indulge in the grossly underrated glory of coupledom before taking on the business of sorting out my new civilian life.

I'd had no idea relationships could be like this. I thought it was learning to ignore the other person's obnoxious habits and mediocre sex. No one ever told me relationship sex could be phenomenal or that friends and brunches and game night gatherings would become essential elements of our coupled existence. I hadn't understood the way two people could combine into *we* and *us*, and how that *we* contained exponentially more than we possessed independently.

Hell, I'd spent the last two years *married* and this was news to me. Yeah, sure, it was spy-married but I'd heard operatives insist they knew their mission partners better than their significant others. I'd assumed that was accurate. Now I felt bad for them. Veronica had been an incredible partner and I'd trusted her with my life but two years with her was nothing compared to two months with Tom.

Two months. Fuck me. It seemed like I'd pointed a meat cleaver at him only yesterday, and today I couldn't wait until the workday was through to see him.

Two months was a relationship eternity for me.

I'd never...well, I'd never. My life had been organized

around deployments and missions for as long as I could remember, and that structure allowed me to keep a filing cabinet of fuck buddies at military outposts around the world. There was a time when I'd believed I wanted it that way. I'd had it all figured out. There was nothing I'd wanted more than exciting new missions and an untethered, unlimited life.

We was a storm that altered geographies and redefined borders, that redefined me.

IT WAS BARELY NOON by the time I reached Beacon Hill and the row of brownstones on a narrow cobblestone street where Tom's office was located. I knew from experience he didn't stop to eat—if he even managed that—until after one in the afternoon, which meant it was too early to drop by and surprise him for a lunch date with a side of life coaching now that I was unemployed.

I'd thought about catching a train into the city last night and asking Tom to put me back together after my discussion with the deputy director—and then Will and Jordan—but I didn't relish always being the one in need of fixing in this relationship. As long as Tom had known me, he'd been engaged in some amount of problem solving and reassembly, and while my appreciation for his efforts was bottomless, I didn't enjoy being on this rung of the ladder. I didn't resent Tom for being ahead of me but didn't want him climbing down to lend me a hand time and time again.

I didn't go to him with the shards of my life last night

and that was for the best. I was still angry as fuck and right there on the edge of picking a fight with anything that looked at me sideways, but when I'd awoken this morning I hadn't felt as gut-punch needy as when I'd crawled into bed. That was an improvement.

To kill time and some of the hyper energy I'd accumulated this morning, I wandered around Boston Common, the Public Garden, and the gold-domed Massachusetts State House. Rows of old townhouses bordered the park, the kind Tom's firm restored.

I could see myself falling hard for this city if I had a view of the Common from my bedroom. Then again, I doubted Tom and I could afford a townhouse like these. Probably not unless I got a kickass job, which seemed unlikely at the moment. Not that we'd discussed living together or buying a parkside townhouse or the possibility of me bringing my up-in-the-air situation down to the ground.

We hadn't discussed any of it but it seemed to exist in a pocket of possibility not unlike us trying a new sushi place tomorrow evening, inviting friends over for a Lego building game night next week, getting tickets for a show next month, going to Europe this summer. If we could do those things, we could just as easily get a townhouse or a condo together. We could do anything we wanted. Now that the CIA wasn't anxiously awaiting my return, I had all the flexibility in the world. Might as well enjoy it with someone I loved.

And I did, I loved Tom.

With that thought shimmering in my blood like a secret

prize created especially for me, the toe of my boot caught on the sidewalk's uneven stones and I stumbled, reaching out for anything as I hurtled to the ground.

The impact skinned my palms, wrenched my bad arm enough to make me curse cobblestones, and left my knees throbbing. But more than that, I was appalled. I wasn't clumsy. I didn't trip over knobby old sidewalks. My nerves and coordination were things of Navy legend. If I hadn't made the cut at SEAL school, there would've been a comfortable home for me in the circus.

I collected myself and continued on toward Tom's office as if I hadn't taken an epic fall but now I was rattled. For the most part, I didn't share the superstitions most SEALs came up with although it was difficult to accept I'd merely tripped on an uneven sidewalk, difficult to see it was an accident rather than a harbinger. It sounded outrageous as I turned it over in my mind yet I couldn't stop thinking about the time I'd tracked a chemical weapons dealer halfway across Europe and had him in my sight only for a chunk of gravel to sputter out from under a garbage truck's tire and crack my windshield. I'd known in my gut at that moment it was a sign, the mission was fucked, I had to get out—and it was a damn good thing I'd known because I backed off just in time to spot a trio of snipers taking aim from rooftops lining the street. The same sense had hit me before a roadside bombing in Afghanistan, a shitty situation with a turned operative in Belarus, and shoddy intel from local sources in Syria that would've ended with a livestreamed beheading.

I had that sense right now. The oily swish in my stomach, the key-turn tightening in my shoulders, the cold wash of awareness down my spine. I couldn't trace this feeling back to anything rational as I couldn't define the way the frequencies around me shifted. I knew only that they *had* shifted and I was walking into a tenuous moment.

But that didn't make a lick of sense. I wanted to laugh at myself because why the hell would there be any danger in visiting Tom for lunch? It was *Tom*. I'd shown up on his doorstep a time or ten and it'd never been a problem. I knew he took his job seriously but surprising him during the day wasn't on par with evading snipers. It just wasn't.

I paused on the narrow street, craning my neck to stare up at the tidy windows making up the face of the Walsh Associates offices. Staring, thinking, debating whether it was best to go back to Will's house and beat myself up in his home gym.

Pushing away all the weird vibes, I climbed the steps to the front door and up to Tom's office. After all the stories he'd told me about this place, I could've found my way around blindfolded. He hadn't mentioned it was swanky as hell. No wonder he was obsessive about his suits and shoes and everything. He had to be, working here.

I rounded a corner and found Tom and Andy, the one with all the hair, seated with their backs to me at a small meeting table inside his office, hunched over several magazines. Their positions granted me a minute to observe him in his element.

"I understand you like this vibe," he said, pointing at one spread. "I'm sure it will be gorgeous in its gushing abundance. However, as you are asking my opinion, I have to tell you these arrangements look like flower vomit."

"I'm not talking about the gushing abundance," Andy replied, laughing. "I'm more interested in how these use random silver containers like soup tureens and teapots rather than glass vases. How it's a little Hogwartsy."

"Oh, then, yeah," he conceded.

"There will be no gushing, no flower vomit. I'm thinking some clean, simple arrangements in antique sugar bowls and putting the candles in tall cylindrical glass vases to make it look like they're floating. Like in the Great Hall because that's precious and I love it."

Tom pressed a relieved hand to his chest. "And I love that for you."

I leaned against the doorframe, saying, "I also love that for you."

He whirled around, his hand still on his chest, and his face split into the most perfect smile and I knew right then my sixth sense had misfired. For the first time in months, I knew—*I believed*—everything was going to be all right.

"Oh my god, it's so good to see you." Gesturing to Andy, Tom said, "Wes, I'm sure you remember—"

"Andy. Congratulations on the engagement." I reached out, offering my hand.

"Thank you," she replied.

I tipped my chin up at Tom as he pushed out of his chair. "Any chance I can take you to lunch?"

"Did you hear my stomach rumbling from the North Shore?" he asked, wrapping me in a quick squeeze. "Yes, of course you can take me to lunch."

While he busied himself with collecting his phone and shrugging into his coat, I asked Andy, "Would you like to join us?"

I prayed the answer was no. She was wonderful and it would be fine but I'd come here to see Tom and I wanted him all to myself.

"If you'd asked me an hour ago, I would've said yes, but since then I've consumed two bowls of soup and a kale Caesar the size of this table," she replied. "And I'm heading out early this afternoon to sample cakes with Patrick so I should get back to work anyway. Thank you though."

Thank god.

I followed Tom out of the office and back onto the street, letting him select our destination. As we headed in the direction of some café he insisted I'd adore, I asked, "What were you looking at with Andy?"

"Well," he started as if I'd inquired into a topic of massive significance, "she came in with a lineup of five different tablescapes and I have to be honest with you, I was alarmed."

"Alarmed?" I repeated.

"Very much so. They were lovely and opulent but garish nightmares, which is the exact opposite of what I'd expect from Andy. I've known her for five years and everything about her is classic, elegant, understated. But she comes in with these tablescapes and centerpieces and it's insanity. I'd sooner die than have flower-vomit centerpieces at my wedding."

Tom continued talking about Andy's plans and how they finally arrived on the same page but the record player in my head kept skipping on the words "my wedding," each pass sending bile up my throat. I knew that wasn't a turn of phrase; it was obvious he'd devoted real thought to the details of his wedding day and—and oh my fucking god, he wanted to get married.

Marriage had never once entered my mind. It'd never seemed like an option for me but more than that, I'd never felt the desire to get married. I supported that choice for anyone who wanted it but I wasn't one of those people—and it appeared Tom was.

Right? Or was I reading between lines that hadn't been written?

"Hey, so, you want to get married?" I asked.

Tom caught me by the sleeve and spun me around to face him, effectively causing a ripple of pedestrian displacement on the narrow sidewalk. His lips were parted and his eyes wide and this was the wrong moment to shove my hands into his hair and kiss him but I did it anyway.

Against my lips, he whispered, "What did you just ask me?"

Shit. I stepped back, dropped my hands to my sides. "I meant, like, hypothetically. You want to get married, hypothetically, at some point in the future to someone? I mean, you want to be married to someone? Someday?"

I wasn't positive but it looked like he mouthed *Wow* as he slowly shook his head at me.

Because I couldn't stop myself or stop the constant repeat of "my wedding" in my head, I kept going. "Hypothetically, that is. Not necessarily now or me or anything but ever? You know, do you want to go to the Solomon Islands? Like that. Hypothetical."

He studied me as if he was searching for my malfunction while people streamed around us. And that was fair because I couldn't control the words spilling out of my mouth and there was a cold sweat breaking out on my forehead and my stomach was twisting itself into an acidic knot. Tom wanted to get married and all I wanted was to put my head in his lap and turn back the clock to yesterday morning when everything was undecided and nothing was awful.

Eventually, he said, "Let's go inside. I get the sense I'm going to need a drink to occupy my mouth and some food to push around while you talk."

If I'd thought things were uncomfortable on the sidewalk, silently staring up at a menu board while standing a shoulder's width apart for five solid minutes bested it by a thousand percent. But I couldn't explain why it was uncomfortable. Yeah, I'd created a fine trap for myself in the way I'd asked Tom about his desire to get married and I'd compounded the damage by repeating the word *hypothetically* until it served as nothing more than a loud indication this topic stressed the shit out of me.

Because everything was going to be complicated today, the only available seats were at the end of a long community table. Goddamn, I should've heeded the warning I'd received when I fell earlier.

Tom curled his hands around his iced mint tea, his gaze steady on the tabletop as he said, "Yes, I want to get married. I've always wanted that. I want to make a home and a family. Perhaps not children of my own but a Yorkie or a cocker spaniel with a saucy name like Winnie Pancakes or Lord Chesterfield." He paused to sip his tea and jerk a shoulder up, his standard *it's no big deal* gesture. "A cute niece or nephew would be great to spoil and that would prevent me from worrying about the right schools and orthodontics and teaching kids about internet safety or god knows what else. And, yes, I want a wedding. A big, elaborate party and a custom tuxedo and I want an amazing blowout event with my closest friends and surrogate family."

Instinct had me bringing my hand to my mouth. I didn't know whether I was saving myself from saying something irretrievable or steeling myself against a lurch of panic-vomit.

His brows peaked as he smiled down at his tea. "And you don't think you want any of it."

The panic answered for me, saying, "I *know* I don't. I know I can't. I couldn't get married without coming out to my parents and I can't do that."

Still smiling at his tea with a hollow sort of serenity, he said, "I know you think that. I also know you're living a fractional life and it's bullshit. Your parents are supportive. They love you. They'd never turn you away or even bat a disapproving eye. I think you know that. If you don't, you should."

I flattened my hands on the table in an effort to calm the heart clanging in my chest, the dread swirling in my stomach, the blood whooshing and whooshing in my head. It didn't help. Nothing helped. I should've gone back to

Will's house. Should've listened to my intuition when it fired a clear, obvious signal.

"You know your parents are good people," Tom continued. "They love you without condition."

"My father enforced Don't Ask, Don't Tell. He exited sailors from SEAL training for admitting or even suggesting they were gay. I watched it happen, Tom. I heard the conversations he had with naval commanders about it. I remember being a kid, being a teenager, and knowing which sailor wouldn't be coming to any more of the Commodore's barbeques because he'd been spotted at *one of those* bars and now his SEAL career was over. My father is as old-school as it comes. Yes, they're good people. They're loving people. But what you don't understand is—"

"And it's still bullshit," he interrupted. "If you want to know what a bad reaction from parents looks like, take a look at my experience. Extreme, perhaps, but I was homeless because my family wouldn't allow me under their roof. Because their faith said it was wrong, that I was wrong, and they chose their faith over me without question. The truth is, Wes, you'll never be homeless. Not now and not twenty years ago if you'd come out to your family then. You'd never be hungry, never have to break into empty homes to sleep, never wonder what you'd have to sell in order to get by. I know this is real for you but you'll never see photos of your sister's wedding on social media and know your invitation wasn't lost in the mail. You'll never be shut out or scrubbed from your family's memory. They're the best kind of people, your family, and it's long past time you stop inventing reasons to avoid being the person you are. That's what it is, by the way. You can't tell your parents because that would require you to fully commit to being that person when you've found every imaginable loophole to avoid it up until now."

It wasn't until Tom stopped speaking that I became aware of the attention we'd garnered from the community table. Fingers stopped flying over keyboards, mobile phones were put down, food was ignored, and six strangers were bearing witness to this tragic moment of my life. I shifted to cordon off our conversation but there was no pretending these people weren't hearing everything.

"You're right, my family wouldn't show me the door," I conceded, hoping that turned down the volume on his gently spoken censure. "You're right about that though it doesn't mean I won't have my own version of awful to contend with."

With a flippant wave of his hand, he said, "If the response to you telling them who you are is awful, then you learn their love was conditional anyway and there's no value in love like that. There's no reason to honor family ties if they're contingent upon sexual preference, gender identity, body shape, political views, any of it. You're gay and if your parents can't keep on loving and accepting you, you shouldn't keep on loving and accepting them. You should build a life independent of them and shield yourself from that poison."

"That must be why you stalk your sister's social media," I said. "Because you're shielding yourself from that poison. Right?"

"Don't," he whispered.

"Don't what? Don't point out the holes in your argument? Don't try to explain how my family issues are just as real and valid as yours? What is it, Tom? What is it you want to control now? Because we both know you can't sleep at night if you don't have a stranglehold on everything around you."

"You don't know who you are," he whisper-yelled. "You just like playing make-believe gay. Because your justification for staying closeted is threadbare at best. Your parents, the adorable, loving sitcom parents everyone wishes they had, won't give a second thought your preferences and you damn well know it. You just haven't accepted yourself yet and you're hiding behind your parents."

"That's so fucking inaccurate." I curled my hands around the edge of the table to keep from slamming my fist down. "Have you considered for one minute that you don't know everything? Is it possible that you're not the authority on everyone's lives? Is it? I mean, you're the one still starved for your family's approval after all."

"Are you serious? You're telling me I'm the one who needs family approval? All you want is your parents' approval and—"

"This isn't about them," I hissed. "It's about me and—"

"Yeah, that's my goddamn point," Tom replied. "You're so busy wrapping yourself up in the Shawl of Disapproving Parents and playing the part of the estranged son that you've failed to read the room."

"So, what? Is this some sort of ultimatum? You want me to come out to my parents. You want to get married." I held up my hand, ticking off each point as I spoke. "What else is there? What am I missing?"

"Does it matter?" he snapped. "You're not interested in either."

"You don't know what the fuck I'm interested in because you've been busy airing your grievances about me for the past half hour."

Tom sat back, pushed his glasses up his nose, and crossed his arms over his chest. "All right, Wes. Tell me where you stand. Do you want to get married?"

19

TOM

I DIDN'T EVEN RECOGNIZE Wes right now.

Worse than that, I didn't recognize myself.

His gaze darted around the table, his lips parted and his smirk nowhere to be seen. Then he frowned at my iced tea, saying, "I've spent more time thinking about what I'm eating for dinner tonight than I have marriage but since you're insisting I make a stand on this issue, no, I don't see myself getting married."

And I didn't see myself keeping any of my harshest thoughts to myself this afternoon. "It's time I see this for what it is—a crush. A flirtation. Like you said at the beginning, we're just two people having fun together while you're here. I never should've let myself believe it was anything else."

A muscle ticked in his jaw as he said, "You need to stop with that noise."

He was annoyed. He was hurt. He wasn't the only one.

"We want different things," I continued. "I want honesty and commitments and—"

"Oh my god," he muttered. "Just because I'm not prepared to get married at some point in the next lunar cycle, you're—what? You're done with me?"

"Why should I put energy into a relationship that will expire before the eggs in my refrigerator? You're leaving eventually and this has turned into a waste of my damn time, Wes." For a second, it seemed he was on the verge of tears. He blinked, he glanced away, he rubbed a hand over his brow. But then he looked back at me, as hard and angry as he'd been since sitting down. No tears. No real distress from him. He was mad about not getting his way with that insufferable argument about his parents. I couldn't find a shred of sympathy for him. So I kept pushing. "I don't bring fuck buddies to trivia."

"If I'd known trivia was the precursor to picking out a china pattern, I would've reconsidered that move," he said.

"It's not about the trivia," I snapped. "It's what trivia represents. I'm careful about the people I invite into my world. I'm selective. And I should've selected better."

"That fucking hurts," Wes replied. "Do you hear yourself right now? Do you hear what you're saying? Because it's brutal and I don't think I've earned it."

Wes was right. These words were sharpened to a point and I wasn't about to soften them. But the purpose wasn't harming him. It was shaking some truth and awareness into him. It was forcing him to see the consequence of living a partial life, always protected by a plastic shell that would eventually suffocate him—and forcing him to see how he wasn't the only one gasping for air.

"I know that's how it feels. I know how much it hurts to hear this. But you should know, Wes. You should know about living with a version of yourself that scrunches down. The version that sacrifices pieces of yourself. The version that knows you need to do it because there's no other way to get through. To survive. Because that's all there is for us. Survival. They say it gets better and they're right but what do we surrender in the process? Survival means treading water, keeping it together, burying yourself alive so you don't die trying to survive, smuggling the precious pieces of your soul through the obstacle courses of shame and hate and confusion and indignity and fucking abandonment. And when it *is* better, when you're not treading water and you're not holding your breath, you have to teach yourself to breathe, to exhale. You have to be with yourself, Wes. You have to take stock of what's left and figure out who you are after all that survival. What's left after years of being someone else? *Who* is left? It's not easy. You have to unpack it all and decide which pieces belong to you and which belong to the person you pretended to be in the name of self-preservation, and rediscover the pieces you buried so deep you barely recognize them anymore. You have to meet the salvageable pieces of you and put them together in a way that makes sense, and you have to learn to walk and talk and think all over again. And you have to release the person you pretended to be. You need to let him go and allow yourself to be the person you are, even when it's really fucking scary to smash the façade that served as your home, your life raft. And I can't be with you if you'd rather suffocate than allow yourself to inhale."

In the too swift, too forceful tone of someone unprepared to notice, let alone unpack, their baggage, Wes argued, "That's not me."

"How is it not? All you do is pretend, Wes. If you weren't here, if you weren't forced to spend the past few months recovering, you'd still be pretending."

"Your experiences aren't mine," he said.

"No, of course not. How could they possibly be when I've spent a decade finding myself and you've spent that time running away."

"I've been a little busy with the global war on terror," he murmured. "Sorry I haven't dedicated enough time to cultivating more self-awareness. I'll hop on Instagram this afternoon and solve my problems one pastel-colored square at a time, okay?"

"It's so much simpler for you to pretend," I whispered. "That's all this is, right? You're pretending to be a boyfriend. You never had any intention of doing this for more than the minute you were here. You were just—you were just playing a game with me, weren't you?"

"I was going to take a cooking class," Wes cried, shaking his hands at me like that meant something. "And I was going to do this for a lot longer than a minute."

"That's lovely but you've made it clear you're not willing to live openly," I replied. "This isn't about your parents. It's about you and how you haven't decided who you are." I shoved my phone in my pocket and grabbed my coat.

Carrying on this conversation wasn't going to improve matters. Beyond that issue, it was also becoming self-injurious to hear this. I couldn't do it any longer. "That's the difference between us. I've known and I've paid the price for it, and I haven't run away from myself. I deserve someone who does the same."

"You're—what? You're leaving?" Wes asked as I stood. "Because I'm not ready for the precise sequence of events you've planned but never thought to share with me? I can tell you right now this conversation would've taken a different course if I'd known you were holding me to a relationship growth chart instead of springing it on me like this."

I shrugged into my coat and took an excess of care to arrange my scarf. My life might be a fresh mess but that didn't mean I needed to look like one too. "You're upset because I'm saying things you're not ready to hear—"

"Yeah, Tom, marriage is kind of a big step," he argued.

"This isn't about marriage." I had to dig for the calm, even tone I used when Patrick went full-on ballistic grouch. It was that or show Wes how he'd ripped me open. If not for the aggressively slim cut of this suit, I was certain my internal organs would've spilled onto the floor and I'd be nothing more than skin and skeleton. "This is about you not being absent from your own life. You're missing in action and you aren't ready to recognize the shell you've forced yourself to live in, the shadow life you've forced yourself to lead. This is about us being in wildly different places, and yes, I've ignored that but I can't ignore it any longer. You're not ready to make changes and you're bound to leave soon—"

"And what if I wasn't?" Wes asked, kicking the chair I'd vacated.

The audience we'd acquired sent up a gasp and turned their collective gaze toward the chair before pinging back to me. I almost stopped to explain Wes wasn't violent—not socially, as it was—and they needn't concern themselves. But this was overwhelming for me. I couldn't handle this kind of confrontation and the fact it was happening in public filled me with a kind of shame I'd sworn off.

"Then…then you're still in a different place than I am," I said eventually, shaking my head. There was no sense speaking in hypotheticals, as I'd learned on the sidewalk earlier. "And it's clear you have no intention of catching up to me."

"Wow, you are really fucking stubborn, aren't you?"

"I'm telling you what I need," I replied, working hard to keep a quiver out of my voice. "It's not outrageous for me to explain to you the things I need for emotional safety and love and the validation of my personhood. It is outrageous, however, for you to think you can sustain a relationship with someone while ignoring those needs. Think about that. Think about your outsized response to me saying I do want to get married and I also want to marry someone who is out to his adorable, loving family. Think about why all of this is so uncomfortable to you."

When Wes didn't respond, I turned and exited the café. I left him there but an enormous part of me expected —*hoped*—he'd follow. Chase after me, run up and ring his arms around me, begging for another chance. Or he'd beat me back to the office and I'd find him sitting in my desk chair and he'd drag me into his arms. Swear he was wrong and I was right because I was obviously right. Promise we'd figure this out. Promise we'd make this right. Promise this wasn't the end.

But he didn't follow.

That spoke as loudly as anything else he'd said.

20

WES

I SLUMPED BACK in my chair, blinking and gaping as if I'd been hit by a flashbang grenade. The force was the exact same. I was disoriented and shaken, and couldn't hear myself think. It would've helped if all the people staring down the table at me went back to texting and typing and living their happy little lives.

What the fuck just happened? What the actual fuck happened here? I wasn't certain but it seemed like I was dumped. And provided a detailed summary of my issues and flaws in the process.

What happened now? What was I supposed to do? I wanted to cry and yell and throw things, and run after him and swear to be better and do better and also tell him he was being demanding and stubborn as fuck. He was wrong. He didn't know my parents or my world. He didn't know the first thing about military life. He *didn't know*. And I would've told him that but he was too busy running the fuck away because it was so much easier to exclude things from his life than it was to adapt.

I was his rice, the starchy carbs in his way, and I was a fool if I thought he'd change his mind about my place in his life.

I stared down the street in the direction he'd gone. There were hundreds of reasons why Tom was wrong about everything and I embraced each one of them. He was being impossible to please and I was…I was doing the best I could with my circumstances. Right? Right. That was it. I was *trying* here and he was making outrageous demands. If I didn't want to get married right this fucking minute, I wasn't worth his time? What a crock of horseshit. And I liked pretending? I *wanted* it this way? Oh, that was unreal.

I wasn't sure how long I watched that street but the lunch crowd was gone when I glanced back at the café. I hadn't touched my food. Big, fluffy snowflakes fell from the gray clouds and formed a thick crust on tree branches and parked cars.

Again, it was cold and dark, and I was alone. Stuck once again.

21

TOM

AVOIDING SHANNON WALSH-HALSTED WAS IMPOSSIBLE. Many tried, none succeeded. She scented shifts in mood and energy as if she'd been a bloodhound in a past life. Back-to-back late season snowstorms saved me from driving up to her house for our check-in meetings on Friday but she didn't have to see me in person to know something was off. She knew the same way she knew everything—she felt it.

Those storms fucked up my contractor scheduling and project timelines and that disaster allowed me to plow the bitter sting of Wes's stubborn bullshit into furious, focused work. I kept my head down and ignored all of Shannon's inquiries by complaining about Patrick refusing to work with the carpenters I'd staffed on his Cape Cod restorations.

I didn't want to talk about Wes or his stubborn bullshit but I really didn't want to talk about it with Shannon. I loved her, I really did, but she was his sister-in-law. He lived at her house, at least for now. I wasn't putting her in the position of choosing sides. It wouldn't be fair to her, but more than that I didn't think I could bear to watch while someone decided I wasn't their priority. Logically, I knew I was a priority to Shannon. It wasn't an exaggeration to say she saved my life. But it would break my heart to make her choose.

I didn't want to talk *to* Wes either. Not unless he approached me with a promise to enumerate all the ways in which he was wrong and planned to make it right. That was my hard line on the matter and I was allowing none of my people-pleasing instincts to get in the way of that.

A younger, more frantic, fragile version of me would've gone to Shannon's house using the pretense of business and I would've lingered long enough to put eyes on Wes. I would've played it aloof and uninterested, and I would've let him take me to the garage apartment where he'd make promises to try. I would've accepted that too. I would've tolerated the half-baked gesture of *trying*, even though I knew it would amount to nothing more than some good intentions.

I would've taken those crumbs and convinced myself they constituted a feast.

When it was dark and late, and I was accompanied by little more than routines and my precise portions of fish and vegetables, I wasn't convinced I was the older, wiser man I imagined myself to be. My expectations of Wes felt needlessly complex and my response to him petty and small. Even through the rosiest of lenses, we were ages away from any conversation of marriage. It was in those moments I craved the crumbs most, even knowing they'd hurt me all over again.

For all of my work and boundaries and self-awareness, I was still angry and hurt. I'd allowed myself to believe in Wes, believe in us. My bitterness was a wizened old goblin who escorted me everywhere, scowling and sneering at everything in his path. The sun shined too bright, the laughter of children was too loud, humanity was too kind. He gorged himself on resentment and rejected pleasure like it was the next plague. He wanted nothing to do with trivia nights or any other meetup my friends organized. He was content only when occupied with spreadsheets, sweating at the gym, or grousing over my sister's social media. Nowhere did my bitterness grow more acrid than seated at the round table in the attic of the Walsh Associates offices.

The happy, coupled-up love radiating from each point on the circumference had my goblin jumping on the table, kicking over coffee cups and slamming laptops. The simple fact these people all shared their lives with loved ones who could talk about the future and didn't require them to hide any portion of themselves tasted like burnt popcorn. At the mention of Andy and Patrick's wedding, my goblin flopped down onto the tabletop with a pathetic, pained snarl.

"If you'll excuse me," I said, swiping my things from the table. "I have to be across town in ten minutes."

Patrick called after me about signing off on a purchase and sale agreement as I jogged down the stairs but I didn't respond. Even if my world was composed of paper cuts and lemon juice, I'd get it done.

I always did.

22

WES

THERE WAS no fucking way I was apologizing.

Not a fucking one.

That was my final decision and I wasn't going back on it. It didn't matter how Tom played it. I wasn't in the wrong here. Not at all. And I didn't care if he thought he was avoiding me by staying away from Will's house. I was the one avoiding him.

I could be at his front door in forty-five minutes.

I drummed my fingers on the table. My pregnant sister and her husband were talking about something and I was putting on a decent show of paying attention but the last thing I cared about was the house they were building ahead of the arrival of their first child. Or restoring, or something. I didn't care. I didn't care about anything right now.

Why would I? Tom was out of the picture. The CIA was done with me, along with the rest of the intelligence community. Even Will and Shannon needed a reprieve from my moping, as evidenced by them shipping me off to my sister Lauren's loft for the night.

I didn't need any of them. Not a single one. They could all go fuck themselves for all I cared. And they were wrong. About everything. Tom and the CIA and the whole damn world. They were all really fucking wrong. Except for Abby. That kid was cool. She always let me have the good green crayon when we colored while watching *Daniel Tiger's Neighborhood,* she served me the best socks when she grilled them, and she flung her little body at me and halfway choked me to death like she knew what I was going through.

Maybe she did. Kids were perceptive like that, even if they didn't understand the total fucking disaster that was adult relationships. Good for them.

I could be there sooner if I hailed a taxi.

I didn't say anything to Will or Shannon but even without a formal announcement, it was obvious both knew the thing with Tom was finished. I appreciated them giving me a wide berth in that area, even though Will deposited me at the commuter rail station this morning with orders to visit Lauren—or anyone else I needed to see in Boston.

I didn't have much experience with heartbreak but it was obvious mine came with anonymity. My heartbreak wasn't a fit twenty-nine-year-old with sky-high expectations, he was a nameless, faceless theory of a person. He was *in Boston.* For all of my brother's fixing, he wasn't going to fix this fuckup. He would've done it by now. He wouldn't have watched while I rage-shoveled a blizzard's worth of snow from his driveway—*twice*—and then dulled all my aches with Daniel Tiger if he'd meant to step in and put my heart back together.

Everyone had a line. Tom, Will, my father. They all had them.

What would he say if I knocked at his door tonight? What would I *say?*

Except for me. If I had a line, I hadn't found it yet. I was too busy hopscotching over everyone else's.

After I'd forced a satisfactory quantity of cake into my mouth and praised it as if I possessed the capacity to enjoy anything, I refused Matt and Lauren's repeated offers to drive me back to Will's house. They only agreed to allow me out the door unescorted when I mentioned meeting up with a friend for drinks.

My brother-in-law allotted an obscene amount of time to providing me with directions to a bar I had no intention of visiting but I nodded along while he spoke. There was no need to ruin his night by telling him I'd be able to find my way around this city with a hood over my head and my hands bound. I managed a wink in my sister's direction as she ate the remains of that cake straight off the platter.

Once I reached the ground floor of their building and made my way to the street, I started walking. The night was young as far as city nights went and it didn't take long for me to fold into crowds. I'd always been able to blend in, pick up the local accents, assimilate. I'd always been able to shed myself and become anyone else—and I'd believed that made me stronger. *Better*. Of course I'd believed it. Hell, my pedigree read like a master class of multiple personalities. It was my *job* to be someone else.

The truth was a riddle translated across too many languages to make sense. It didn't mean what I thought it'd meant anymore because somewhere in that original translation, Tom had it right. I'd spent all this time reconfiguring myself to stay safe and now I couldn't distinguish the make-believe from reality. I didn't know which pieces were byproducts of the job, which grew out of fear of my father's disapproval, and which belonged to me. I knew this but I wasn't ready to dismantle the make-believe because what would I do when I discovered nothing belonged to me?

I stopped on the sidewalk across from Tom's blue brownstone, my hands shoved in my pockets. His lights were on but the curtains were drawn and I couldn't see inside. Maybe he was curled up on the sofa, watching serial killer documentaries without me. Maybe he'd moved on with his life and was busy hosting game night. He'd do that, he'd move on. He had no reason to mourn our relationship. He wasn't sprawled on any nursery floors, wishing Daniel Tiger could throw together an episode about coping with breakups. Tom was better than all that.

I stood there for an hour before turning in the direction of the train station.

23

TOM

IT WAS ALMOST NINE O'CLOCK, the office dark and empty. I was exhausted but I didn't want to go home. I couldn't. Couldn't gather the energy to peel myself out of this chair. Couldn't leave the slow process of drowning in this shallow pond of work. Couldn't walk to the T station without a light breeze knocking me to the ground. And I couldn't open the door to my empty apartment where I'd reheat a sad Pyrex dish of vegetables and fish and just be fucking alone—again.

No, the better option was hammering away at the email on my screen. Seeing that I was vulnerable and ranty, this was the ideal moment to draft an email to my sister. I knew it was a disaster wrapped in a tragedy and sealed with cyanide but I was filled with all these emotions, most of all a wailing, venomous hurt that wouldn't quit. And I needed to direct it somewhere. What better time to reach out to my sister than now, when Wes was as good as gone.

That part hurt. It cut deep, if I was being honest.

Knowing my way around abandonment didn't make it better. The past two weeks since leaving Wes in the café had brought me right back to the worst moments of my childhood and flashed all the times I'd been discarded up on the big screen in my mind. Even when I separated out the massive issue of being forced from my home *as a child,* I was left with a series of shitty relationships with people who regarded me as temporary and disposable.

For once, I wanted to be important enough to keep.

I could admit I still had trust issues too. For sure. I hadn't exaggerated when I'd told Wes I was selective about the people in my life. I had Shannon, the fiercest surrogate mother anyone could ask for, and I had the rest of the Walshes by association. My friends were the product of rigorous vetting. There was no room for toxicity.

And, for these perfect months, I'd had Wes. I'd lived the daydream and allowed myself to imagine a world where I finally, finally got what I wanted. But the trouble with me wanting it that badly was missing all the clues that Wes hadn't wanted any of it.

That much was clear. His silence spoke volumes. If he wanted to correct my misunderstanding, he could've done it by now. It'd been two full weeks without a word from him but the worst part was I was certain to see him at the wedding this weekend and there was nothing I could do about it.

I poured a lifetime of anger into that email, purging all the blame and pain and resentment I had inside me. It went on for pages upon pages, listing every injustice I'd suffered, every moment of my stolen childhood, every dehumanizing experience along the way. I called out her complicity in this, every opportunity she'd had to speak up for me, to help.

A knock sounded at my door. I blinked up, my eyes bleary after glaring at my screen. Riley Walsh leaned against the doorjamb. "Hey," he said. "Alex is covering for someone at the hospital tonight. She won't be home until tomorrow."

"Okay," I said, still blinking.

"Come on," he said, plucking my coat from the hanger on the back of the door. He held it toward me. "Let's get some food. Beers too. Food and beers always help. Especially on Mondays."

"Why?" I rasped.

He lifted his shoulders. "You shouldn't be all alone like this. It's not gonna help."

I glanced down at my screen. The hurt, betrayed part of me wanted to send that email. Fire it off, give Joy a piece of my mind without apology. The terrified perfectionist in me who hated conflict and feared the fall out wanted to save it in my drafts folder and tweak it until I could recite the missive backward and forward.

"Whatever it is," Riley started, jerking his chin toward my screen, "it can wait until morning."

The last unbruised sliver of me knew he was right. I could rage and blame all I wanted. I could call her out and scream about everything, and it would change nothing. I couldn't change Joy any more than I could change my mother—or Wes. They didn't want it. They didn't believe they needed it. They didn't believe I was worth it and I couldn't do a damn thing to change them. I'd changed myself—my thoughts, my habits, my reactions—and that was all I could do.

But I was dog-bite angry and just as hurt, and I hit Send.

"Since that's done..." Riley stepped up to my desk and pushed my laptop shut with one finger. "What are you in the mood for? I could do tacos, burgers, sushi—"

"Not sushi," I snapped.

"Burgers it is," he replied. "There's a place right off Tremont. You'll like it."

The best thing about Riley Walsh was he knew when to shut up. He didn't ask questions. Didn't probe. He just knew when life sucked and he didn't pretend it was going to suck less any time soon. Shannon was my surrogate mother but Riley was my brother and, as far as I was concerned, those two were proof choice mattered more than blood ever could.

24

WES

I PAUSED AT THE THRESHOLD, my backpack hanging from my shoulder, and I stared into the darkened room. A night-light in the shape of a mermaid glowed back at me from the far corner. I moved closer to the crib, careful to keep my steps soundless. I couldn't pull off this dark-of-night escape if I woke the baby koala in the process.

Abby was flat on her back with her arms stretched over her head. She had no idea of the world's troubles or the complexity of being alive. She knew nothing of heartache or sadness or the unrelenting need to break away and be her own person without anyone around to comment on it. Her existence consisted of eating, sleeping, hollering for comfort. At least we had that much in common.

"You're leaving," I heard over my shoulder.

I pivoted, found Shannon shrouded in shadows. She was tucked into a rocking chair, Annabelle in her arms and a gauzy baby blanket draped over her shoulder. "I, uh, I didn't think anyone would be in here." I glanced back at the crib. "Other than the person who is supposed to be here."

"Abby was fussy," Shannon replied. "It was easier to rock Abby and nurse Annabelle at the same time than wake up Will to divide and conquer." She hit me with a brutal glare. "You're leaving and you weren't going to tell us."

"I have to go," I said, helpless to offer any better explanation.

She gazed down at Annabelle, ran a finger over her plump cheek. My sister-in-law didn't spare me another glance. I curled my hand around the backpack strap. I needed to get moving but something about this exchange kept me rooted in place. Eventually, she said, "What about Tom?"

I shook my head once. "Tom will be fine."

She glanced up, her stare hot enough to burn holes right through my clothes and skin and bones. She pointed to the ottoman in front of her. I went there and sat without question. "Tom doesn't know you're leaving."

All statement. No question.

I shook my head again. Goddamn, I was such a chicken-shit bastard. "He knew I wasn't staying."

Shannon arched an eyebrow up. "That is not good enough for me. You come here, you reach out to him, you let him fall in love with you, and now you're leaving like a thief in the fucking night. That's not good enough for him and you know damn well it isn't good enough for me."

"It's not good enough for me either," I whisper-yelled, my palm flat on my chest to keep my heart from tearing its way out. "What would you have me do, Shannon? Should I go to work for Will? That would be nice and tidy, wouldn't it? I can live in your garage apartment for the next five years while Tom waits for me to come out to my parents and I wait for him to stop rushing me."

"Listen to me, Wes, and listen good. I know your parents. I know your father. I know him as well as I know my siblings and there is no way in hell he'd do anything but embrace you just as you are. I believe that in my bones."

For a second, I thought about telling Shannon the truth about men like me, my brother, my father. The things we'd done, the things we'd seen. But this kind and frankly terrifying woman didn't need to hear these realities. They wouldn't change her beliefs about the Commodore.

"You know one side," I conceded. "I know another. Let's leave it there."

"I will not," she replied. "I won't leave it there. You could stay, Wes. You could stay here as long as you want and you could work things out with your parents and—"

"Yeah, I could," I interrupted. "But I need to go. I need to figure some things out on my own."

"And then you'll come back." Another statement. "You'll come back here, Wes."

I shrugged. "We'll see what happens, where I land."

She stared at me for a long beat and then shifted Annabelle to her other side. "What do you need?"

"Nothing," I answered, nodding toward the pack slung over my shoulder. "I'm all good, Shannon. Thank you for worrying."

"I am not referring to your ability to cross the globe with little more than your street smarts." She huffed out a breath. "I meant—you know—a warmer coat or pain medication for your arm or legally gotten money or a key to Tom's apartment because that's where you should be right now." She eyed me, all that maternal contempt in one stare. "I have all of the above if you need them, though I'm aware you can do just fine without keys."

I laced my fingers together, gazed at the rug beneath my feet. I'd planned to whisper my goodbyes and press a kiss to that precious baby's head and be gone. I hadn't expected this detour. I hadn't mentally prepared for this detour. Hadn't gathered up the words necessary to separate myself from the people who forced me back to health and the babies I'd grown to adore. And I was nowhere near prepared to pass up entrance to my love's home.

I dug deep to find the strength I'd relied on for so many years and came up lacking. "Shannon," I said through a sigh, "I…I have to go."

"I also know he'll be at the gym at five-fifteen which is"—she shot a glance at the mermaid clock on the opposite wall—"not that far from now."

I dropped my head into my hand. "Shannon, *please.*"

"Please tell you where to find his gym? Or please give you the key to his apartment?" she asked. "Because you can't possibly be asking me to make this sneaky exit any easier on you. There are a lot of people I care about in this world. A lot of people I'll do anything to protect. But you need to know Tom is a special one. He's been through too much, lost too much. I'm not going to sit by and let you hurt him."

"This isn't about Tom. It's me. I don't want to be here anymore," I said softly. "I can't—I can't be here. I need to figure out my life. I need to figure out who I am if I'm not a spy or sailor because I don't know. So, yeah, I could go to his apartment right now. I could crash his Tuesday morning workout. But none of that solves any of my real problems."

She reached out, dropped her hand onto my forearm. "I understand, but believe me when I tell you the answer is not disappearing in the middle of the night," she said. "I tell you this from experience. My sister, she needed to be somewhere else and she needed to be there for a long time. And as much as I hated it, I understood her need to leave. But I've never understood her need to leave without saying goodbye. Without showing me her face and making me believe she'd be all right when she got where she was going and letting me tell her she could always come home and I'd always go to her if she needed me. I spent entire years of my life being hurt and angry by that choice. Even now, I love her *around* that choice because that sting never goes away. Don't do that to him, Wes. Please don't do that. Don't make him find a way to love you around it."

"If I don't say goodbye, it's not over," I replied, still staring at the rug. "If I leave and put my life in order, there's a chance things could be different for us. There's a chance, Shannon, and I need the chance more than I need to take the polite route."

That earned me another bone-burning stare before she

said, "What if you *are* who he needs? You, just as you exist in this moment. What if you're already there and you're running away to fix problems you've inflated in your mind? What if you're throwing away something good and real? And what if leaving now, like this, eliminates any possibility of him ever taking you back? Have you considered that?"

"Have I considered that?" I repeated. "Have I considered that? Huh. I guess you're right. If only I stopped to assess the situation and evaluate the options. It's too bad I've been trained in advanced spycraft and special ops and spent the past decade executing top secret covert affairs which all required split-second decision-making. If only I knew how to function in fluid situations, maybe then I'd be able to crack this one."

"Your sarcasm can suck my dick," she said.

"I've considered all the possibilities you've identified and it's time for me to go." I patted her hand, still on my forearm, and gave her a watery smile. "I'll let you know where I land."

Her grip on me tightened. "Wes, please," she said. "I swear to you, there's a better way."

I bobbed my head and sucked in a breath, desperate to clear the tears stinging the corners of my eyes. "I'm sure it seems like that," I replied. "Thank you for letting me stay here."

"Anytime," she said, the word heavy as it passed her lips. "You're welcome here anytime and for as long as you want to stay."

I pushed up from the ottoman and stepped to the side

of the rocker. I bent down, pressed my lips to the crown of Annabelle's head and then Shannon's cheek. "I know."

I didn't wait for her response, instead striding from the room and down the hall before I could think better of my decision. If I stopped to think this over one more time, I wasn't sure what I might do.

25

WILL

I LEANED back in my desk chair, tapping my knuckles against my lips as I toggled through surveillance footage. I didn't enjoy watching Wes leave my home but I wasn't about to stop him. In a sense, it was long overdue. Keeping him under my roof for this long was a remarkable feat made possible only by his involvement with Tom. If not for Tom, Wes would've bounced before the end of February.

I toggled to the next screen, calling up the local traffic camera feeds. If I had to guess, Wes was headed to the commuter rail station. Trains were the most effective way to disappear quickly and do it without leaving a trail. And Wes was nothing if not efficient in his getaways, even without a secret police force on his heels.

He'd hop on the commuter rail and ride it to Boston's North Station but he wouldn't stay in the city. Not for long. He'd take his time moving south. I was certain that was where he was going and I was letting him go.

For now.

MY OFFICE DOOR banged open and— "Your brother broke Tom."

I glanced up from the report on my screen to find my wife standing in the doorway, her hands on her hips and murder on her face. "He did what?"

"He broke Tom," she yelled, enunciating every word.

"In the three days since he's been gone? Or at some other point?"

"Both. *Both.* Whatever happened before he ran out of here on Tuesday morning and every day since then."

"And you determined this during your meeting with Tom this morning?" I asked.

Shannon flailed her arms out. "If you think I needed to see him with dark circles and bloodshot eyes and looking fully disheveled, wearing a tie that doesn't coordinate with his shirt and socks, to know he's broken, then yes, Will, I determined that during our Friday morning meeting. The truth is, I've known this for the past two weeks, before Wes left. I don't know what went down between them but I can hear it in Tom's emails and I can sense it in the way he flags documents for my signature."

I knew I'd regret asking, but— "You can sense it in the way he flags documents?"

She cocked her hip and folded her arms over her chest. "Yes, Will. I can. That's how well I know him."

I held my hands out, let them fall to my lap. "What would you suggest I do, peanut?"

Tears filled her eyes. "I want you to do *something*. I want you to fix it."

It took one breath to spring out of my seat and round the desk, and take her in my arms.

Several things were true at this moment. One, Shannon had a wagonload of worries right now. At Annabelle's most recent checkup, the pediatrician voiced concerns about her being a touch underweight. That meant Shannon didn't go more than ninety minutes without nursing the baby, which left her completely exhausted. Patrick and Andy's wedding was planned for tomorrow evening and my wife didn't know how to let anyone get married without her deep involvement in every element of the event. Add to those issues Tom wearing his emotional state on his sleeve and Shannon couldn't pick a fire to put out first.

Two, there was nothing I wouldn't do for my wife. If I had to devote the next year to finding Tom a superior alternative to my bonehead brother, I would.

And three, she knew my tricks and tactics. She knew I could find Wes and plank-march his ass to Tom's doorstep.

I smoothed my hand down her ponytail. "Let me make some calls. Okay? I'll see what I can do."

She pressed her palms to my chest, sniffled. "All right. I need to feed Annabelle again."

"I'll make these calls and then I'm taking the baby so you can have some rest." I kissed her forehead. It wasn't going to do any good if Annabelle gained half a pound but Shannon had run herself into the ground in the process.

She stepped back, lifting her hands to her hair to retie her ponytail. "I'll sleep with Annabelle."

"That's funny. You make it seem like you're not going to send nine hundred emails the minute her eyes close."

"I won't," she argued, turning to leave. "I'll take a quick nap."

I snagged her phone out of her back pocket. "Then you don't mind me holding on to this for you. You'll get it back on Monday."

"We'll see about that," she called from the hall.

With the door closed, I tapped Jordan Kaisall's contact on my phone. He answered immediately. "Tell me you're tracking Wes."

"The fact you're asking me this is insulting," Jordan replied.

"Be insulted," I said. "Where is he?"

"The Caribbean," Jordan said. I heard him tapping his keyboard.

"More specifically?"

"One of the small islands. South end. Looks like he's been there nine hours after bouncing down the eastern seaboard and across the islands for about two days. Let me patch Shaw into this call. He'll clean up the signal."

"I'm gonna need a hand with this," I warned.

"Yeah, I'm in the mood to drop everything and collect your brother from the Caribbean. No problem," he said with a groan. "Let me ping my mother and tell her to start rearranging my schedule."

"Say hi to Mama Trish for me," I replied.

"She doesn't want to talk to you."

"Come on. Do it anyway. She loves me," I argued.

"We could send the kidnap and rescue team," he said.

"All right. Shaw's on. We need clean coordinates on the target I'm tracking."

"Hey, Shaw," I said. "Yeah, Kaisall. We *could* send a K&R squad but let me ask you this: when was the last time we sent them to pick up a SEAL-turned-CIA-operative? Those boys bring in some serious coin. I don't want to risk putting any of them on the injured reserve because my brother knocked the snot out of them."

"I'll remind you he has one good arm," Jordan said.

"I'll remind you he left a trail of bodies behind him on his last mission, and that was with one good arm and an open gunshot wound."

"Point taken," Jordan grumbled.

"Montserrat," Shaw announced. "Sending exact coordinates now."

"What's the level of urgency on this?" Jordan asked. "I have a couple of meetings today I won't be able to reschedule for a month or two."

"What's the flight time to—where are we going again?" I asked.

"About two thousand miles," Shaw said. "I'd estimate five or six hours by private jet. Closer to seven or eight, including stops, on commercial."

"I don't know how to fly commercial," Jordan snapped.

"Because your life is so strenuous," I murmured. As much as Shannon wanted this resolved right fucking now, I couldn't catch a flight to the Caribbean tonight. Nights were the toughest for her. Abby had teeth coming in and slept miserably. Even if Annabelle believed in sleeping more than a few hours at a time, Shannon was committed to the double feeding schedule. And there was a goddamn family wedding tomorrow night. "Wheels up at four hundred hours. We'll be there and back before sunset. I'll have some hell to pay if I'm late for this wedding."

"I'll call the hangar," Jordan said.

Shannon: I'm sending you the floor plan of the Lyman Estate.

Will: What the hell are you talking about, peanut?

Shannon: The Lyman Estate is where the wedding is being held.

Shannon: Tonight.

Shannon: The wedding I'm expecting you to attend in a tux, not cargo pants, boots, and a thigh holster.

Will: You love the thigh holster.

Shannon: Not at weddings.

Will: I'll put this intel to good use.

Will: Both pieces.

Shannon: There's a cocktail hour before the ceremony. That would be a wonderful time to sneak in. If you come after that point, please avoid the ballroom. The last thing Andy needs is you hulking around in the background of her ceremony photos.

Will: I'll work on it, peanut.

Will: How are my girls?

Shannon: Napping, thankfully. They'll be full of energy for when Ellie arrives to babysit.

Will: How late do we have Ellie tonight?

Shannon: She's staying over.
Will: And my parents will be there after the wedding.
Shannon: Correct.
Will: How would you like to spend a child-free evening in the city with your husband? If we have my parents and Ellie, plus the twenty gallons of breastmilk you've socked away in the fridge, we're all set. Right?
Shannon: That depends on how this operation turns out.
Will: Peanut. Please. You know I have this under control.
Shannon: I'll believe it when I see it.
Will: Are you saying you doubt me?
Shannon: I trust you completely. It's anyone's ability to bring Wes around right now that I doubt.
Will: You should trust me enough to pack a bag for the night.

JORDAN HELD UP HIS PHONE, pointing to a pin on the map Shaw sent. "This way."

The humidity was killing me. My t-shirt was soaked with sweat and we'd landed on Montserrat less than an hour ago.

I frowned at the tree canopy and thick undergrowth separating the land from the beach. Only the slightest suggestion of a trail was visible. We'd tracked Wes to the west side of Montserrat, on the south side of Bransby Point. As far as the local government was concerned, that area was off-limits. Eruptions from the Soufrière Hills volcano had destroyed the south end of the island along with its urban center, leading the government to strictly enforce an exclusion zone.

Save for wildlife, this part of the island was abandoned. "He's really roughing it, isn't he?"

An impatient noise rattled in Jordan's throat as he started along the trail. "That's the genius of your brother. He knows how to get lost." He ducked under a branch. "It's also really fucking irritating because we're the ones who have to find his ass."

"Let's hope this is the last time," I said, mostly to myself. The beach came into view, and with it, a welcome breath of fresh, salty air.

"There he is." Jordan pointed at the man sprawled on the sand like driftwood. "What's the plan here?"

I spotted two empty bottles of liquor beside Wes and another clutched in his hand. "He has to come willingly."

"That's not going to work but I'm excited to see you try," Jordan replied. "When you've run out of breath, I'll knock him over the head with one of those bottles and we'll toss him in the jeep."

Before we could argue our strategy further, Wes called from the sand, "You fuckers chipped me, didn't you?"

"In my defense, I did it expecting the FSB to snatch you off the street," Jordan shouted. "I was trying to make the job easier in the event we had to find your ass again. That's where it is, by the way. Left cheek."

"And what the fuck are you two doing here?"

"We're thinking about buying the joint," Jordan replied. "Volcanic exclusion zones are perfect for special ops training grounds."

"And we came to talk," I said. "If you don't mind."

"Sir, yes, sir," he snapped.

"That's a great fuckin' sign," Jordan muttered.

We closed the distance between the trail and Wes, dropping down onto the sand beside him.

"You are sunburnt as fuck." Jordan pointed at Wes's bare chest. "I know you've been in Russia a long time but you do realize the sun will fry your ass down here, right? That's gonna hurt somethin' fierce tomorrow."

"You sound like Mama Trish right now," I murmured. "Did you say hi to your mother for me?"

"I did not." Jordan snickered. "Mama Trish would grab this sorry fool by the ear and drag him home for a cold tea bath. I will be doing neither, thank you."

Wes lifted his arm, a long, leathery scar traveling from wrist to elbow. The scar glowed pinkish-white while the rest of his arm was red verging on purple. "I hadn't noticed," he replied. "This is fine. Everything is fine."

"Can I ask why you felt the volcano-ravaged side of an island was the best place to vacation?" Jordan glanced around. "I can appreciate the desire for peace and quiet, especially after being at Halsted's house for more than ten minutes, but this is downright primitive."

"Just wanted to get away from all that shit," he said. "After my last few months on the job, I had a vacation coming to me."

"That's why you're here?" I asked. "Post-mission leave?"

"I still can't believe I was kicked out of the CIA," Wes grumbled, fully avoiding the opening I gave him to talk about Tom. This fool only wanted to do it the most difficult way. "After *years* of that fuckery."

I turned my face to the sun and rolled my eyes.

"I can't believe you're surprised," Jordan said. "We told you this would happen when you left the SEAL Teams for that intelligence community alphabet soup outfit. Any program that far off the books ends badly for the operatives and you should know—"

"You should consider this warning a friendly courtesy," Wes said, edging his sunglasses down to glare at Jordan. "Because if you go on with that bullshit, I'm gonna drag your ass into the ocean and waterboard you."

And because Jordan had no fucking sense whatsoever, he replied, "It's the truth, brother."

I flattened a hand to Wes's chest, keeping him on the sand. "Listen," I started, glaring at my business partner, "it shouldn't have gone down this way. You know it and they know it. You also know these agencies cover asses first and look after operatives later. At the end of the day, even the best of them burn out. And the ones they keep? They get desk jobs where they're buried in fuckin' paperwork and red tape and bureaucratic bullshit. You'd sooner waterboard yourself than choose that life."

He gathered a handful of sand and let it slide through his fingers. "You're probably right about that."

"Of course we're right," Jordan replied. "Why don't you come head up our new espionage team? If we're going to buy the pumice stone side of this island, we need someone to get our spycraft house up and running."

Wes let out a hard laugh. "I don't want to spend the rest of my life teaching mercenaries how to throw knives."

"First of all, brother, they come to us with a full complement of knife-throwing skills," Jordan said. "We don't dedicate a minute to that noise. Second, and no disrespect, but the last thing we'd use you for is hand-to-hand combat training."

"Not when we have April," I added.

"This is true," Jordan replied with a nod.

Wes glared at us for a beat, eventually asking, "Where did you find her?"

"You're gonna love this. She found him," I said, "because she had a contract on him."

My brother peered at Jordan. "That's special. Like, real special. How long did it take you to figure that out?"

"A story for another day," he replied.

"And the reason we need you," I said. "SEALs, Green Berets, Delta Force, these guys don't know spycraft. You know that fact as well as I do. They can play the game enough to carry out a mission but they're not infiltrating shit." When Wes didn't take that opportunity to insult me, Jordan, or the business we ran, I continued. "Whatever they taught you in that off-book, deniable as fuck intelligence program, we need you to teach it to our squads."

"No part of me is interested in that shit." Wes shook his head. "Thank you, next."

Jordan scoffed. "So, you wouldn't want to run spy-game ops? Because that's what we're talking about."

"Sounds amazing. Cool, cool, cool. But I have so many

things I have to fix before I can even think about a job," Wes admitted. "I've said a lot of dumb shit—"

"Yep," Jordan agreed. "The entirety of this conversation comes to mind."

Wes shot him a glower before continuing, "I've done some dumb shit too—"

"Yep," I agreed. "Skipping out in the middle of the night when there is a long line of people who care about you would be a fine example."

"You two together are a real pain in my ass," he snapped. "I'm just saying the job is the least of my worries. Whenever I run out of rum and decide to get off this beach, and whatever I do, I'll land on my feet and I don't need handouts from either of you."

Jordan shot me his usual *I'm bored and this is wasting my time* glare over Wes's head. I glanced at my watch. We were cutting it close and Shannon was going to have my ass if I wasn't back in time for this wedding. She'd also have my ass if my brother wasn't in tow.

"Listen, Wes. We didn't come all this way for you to piss and moan," I said. "We're looking to put together an espionage team and we need someone with your skill set to lead it. If you want to stay here, we're not going to stop you."

"We're not?" Jordan asked.

"No. We're buggin' out." I met Jordan's confused stare with a pointed glance at my brother. "Like I told you on the ride down here, Kaisall, Shannon's brother is getting married in a few hours. I promised her I'd be there on time."

"Right, right," Jordan murmured. "I forgot about that."

"It's because you block out all conversation when marriage and weddings are involved," I said. "You know, given your current inability to get it up in that area."

"I signed up for a snatch-and-grab," Jordan replied. "Not emotional abuse on a lava beach."

Wes lifted the rum to his lips, draining the last of the liquor. He pitched the empty bottle over my head, saying, "If this reunion is supposed to be a snatch-and-grab, you two need a refresher course on the basics of black ops. Aside from burying a microchip in my ass, this showing is shameful."

"Like I said," I continued, "we gotta go. Shannon is alone with both kids and she's dealing with a disaster at the office too."

"What was that about again?" Jordan asked. It was good of him to play along. Finally.

"Her assistant threatened to quit." As far as I knew, that wasn't the case but Wes didn't know that.

From the corner of my eye, I saw Wes's lips part. The muscles in his jaw ticked. His eyes narrowed. Then, he said, "He's not her *assistant*."

Jordan ran his knuckles over his jaw. "What? You know him?"

Wes shot a glare at Jordan. "He's the managing director of operations."

"Yeah, you're right about that. Managing director of operations," I said, nodding. His misplaced rage was beautiful. He was a mess of rum-flavored feelings and it was proof we were getting somewhere. "Anyway, he's going through something right now. He's talking about leaving town."

Wes reached for another bottle of rum but soon realized he was all out. He slapped his palm on the sand.

"She's devastated, of course. He's been working with her since—"

"Years, right?" Jordan asked.

"Yeah, they go back a full decade. She basically adopted him. Gave him a place to stay, put him to work at her firm, sent him to school. He started out as an assistant but worked his way up. She's going to be a wreck if he leaves and it will be a bitch for her to replace him but I can't see it ending any other way. He's been in shambles for a couple of weeks now. Just fuckin' shambles, man."

"That's rough." Jordan pushed to his feet, brushed the sand off his cargo pants. "Let's not add to your wife's issues by showing up late from this wild-goose chase." He held out a hand to Wes. "Take care of yourself, brother. You know how to find us if need be."

"Wait a second," Wes replied, slapping Jordan's hand away. "Enough bullshitting out of you two. What's really going on with Tom? Is he okay?"

I stood, joining my partner in looming over Wes. "You heard what I said."

"Yeah, I did," he snapped, pushing up on an elbow. "And I'm suggesting you stop being a dickhead with a death wish and tell me if he's all right."

I tipped my head in the direction of the jeep. "Come with us and find out for yourself."

Wes flopped back onto the sand. "That's not going to happen."

"What would you say if I told you I know exactly where Tom will be tonight and you could see him for yourself?" I asked.

"I'd say you're minimally good at your job if tracking a guy with a phone and smartwatch in a major metropolitan area is a win for you," he replied.

"You know what? Mom was right. You are an asshole," I said.

"Yeah and we can trace a lot of my issues back to the fact our mother decided I was an asshole toddler," he replied.

"It sounds like you've been reading your psych evals," Jordan said. "Bad move."

With one eye open, Wes peered up at him. "Are you telling me you haven't read yours?"

"Oh, I've read them." Jordan shoved his hands into his pockets. "I stand by what I said. Bad move. If I wanted to feel like dog shit with daddy issues, I'd take on one of the new guys in our training facility's obstacle course. Nothing like going into cardiac arrest after fast-roping to the ground."

"You're not making a strong case for me coming to work with you," Wes said.

"Maybe not but you sure as shit don't want to spend your days running security at the US consulate in Belgium," I said. "Picture it. You'd get a nice walkie-talkie to clip on your belt. Carry a stun gun. Pack your lunch in a little cooler bag. On a good day, you'd get to wrestle a political fanatic to the ground and keep him in a cozy lockup in the basement until the big boys rolled up."

He gathered a handful of sand and flung it at us. "They'd never have me. My Dutch is embarrassing."

"Better than translating memos at the State Department," Jordan added. "If you're lucky, you'll get to park your ass at a desk and read social media posts all day. I hear jihadist slang is a language unto itself."

"I hate you guys so much," Wes said, groaning.

I traded a glance with Jordan. He shook his head, saying, "Time to go."

"Yeah. We're out," I said. "Anything you'd like me to pass along to Tom?"

"Go fuck yourself," Wes rasped.

"Are you sure you want me to say that? I doubt it'll go over well," I replied.

"If you're asking me to kick your ass, I will," he said. "Kaisall too."

Jordan tapped my arm. "This kid isn't budging and I'm too afraid of your wife to send you home late. Let's hit the road."

I followed as he moved up the beach. Over my shoulder, I called to Wes, "One more thing. Did you know Tom's bringing a date to this wedding?"

"You're mean," Jordan murmured.

I shot him an exasperated glance. "I'm out of options. If this doesn't work, we're hog-tying him and leaving him to cool off in the luggage bay."

Jordan shook his head as he shuffled forward, his limp

more pronounced than usual. "I knew I should've packed a tranq gun."

"While that would've been a great way to get him on the plane, it would've left us with the same miserable son of a bitch but with the added bonus of a sedative hangover."

"Yeah and I would've shot him again," he replied. "Dump him on the boyfriend's doorstep and be done. We're in the snatch-and-grab business for a reason, Halsted. We're not qualified for snatch-and-grab-and-solve-everyone's-personal-problems."

"This is a one-off situation," I said. "But we should come back here sometime. This is a nice place. Shannon would love it and I'm sure your wife—oh, wait, you still haven't asked April to marry you. Forget it."

"Your brother was right," he replied. "You're a dickhead with a death wish."

"I might be," I said, inclining my head toward the beach. The sound of feet slapping against sand rose behind us. "But I'm an effective dickhead."

Wes came streaking past, shouting, "I'm going to need a suit."

"We came prepared," I called to his sunburned back.

26

WES

FIVE HOURS on Kaisall's plane was almost enough time to sober up but not nearly enough to get my head on right. I'd squeezed into a suit of Will's and did my best to wash the salt water and rum from my body in the lavatory but I hadn't sorted out what I wanted to say to Tom. All I knew was my nose was going to peel like a motherfucker and I was a week overdue for a haircut, and he'd notice both.

What was I supposed to say? *I'm an idiot. You're a stubborn brat. I'm a fool. You're also kind of impossible sometimes and I'm afraid I'll never be enough for you. I'm wrong about everything and I don't enjoy admitting that. I want to figure this out. I want to figure this out with you.*

None of that seemed right. It was something but it wasn't *right*. Nothing was right.

Maybe *I* wasn't right. That was a strong possibility. I wasn't right for Tom. He needed someone who was already there, who know how to...be. I didn't know how to be—at least, I didn't know how to be me.

Will consulted his watch as I paced the parking lot. "Fifteen minutes until the ceremony is due to start. Guests are congregated in the main parlor on the northwest side of the estate. Follow the central hallway there."

"Did you study the schematics?" I asked. "Are you that crazy?"

"Shannon forwarded me the floor plan on the flight down."

"In that case, she's the crazy one?" I asked.

He shook his head. "Behave yourself."

I shrugged him off. "The night is young. Let's not put restrictions on ourselves this early."

"Let's not ruin anyone's wedding," he argued.

"I'm not going to ruin a wedding." I smoothed a hand down my lapels. "But that's all I can promise you."

"Jesus Christ." Will pinched the bridge of his nose as he blew out a breath. "I have to find Shannon. Behave yourself."

"You're the one who needs to behave," I called after him. "Do your wife a favor and stay off her. The woman doesn't need you knocking her up again."

He shot both middle fingers into the air as he stepped through the doorway.

I marched back and forth, shaking out my hands at my sides. I didn't know what the hell I was doing. No plan, no strategy. I was going in blind and I didn't think I'd be able to bear it if I couldn't execute. I wouldn't recover if Tom turned me away.

Finally gathering a burst of confidence, I strode through the mansion's entrance and headed toward the parlor. With one glance, I spotted Tom on the far side of the room, his back to the guests as he stared out at the grounds. A champagne flute dangled from his fingers. Even from here, the sweet curve of his ass made my fingers itch. He had one ankle crossed over the other, the red sole of his shoe shining like a flag before a bull.

Come and get me.

"Wes! Hi! Where have you been? What's going on with you? I haven't heard from you since that time we met up in Vienna."

It took full seconds to tear my attention away from Tom and focus on the woman blocking my way. There was a brusque response waiting on the tip of my tongue and I nearly let it fly before realizing the woman was my old expat friend, the one who'd once vowed to never stop roaming, never return home for more than moments wedged between the decades. "Erin fucking Walsh." I gathered her up in a tight hug and then held her away from me to get a good look at her. "How the hell are you, girl?"

"I think the better question is how the hell are you?" she replied, matching my once-over glance. "Nick told me about, you know, everything you've been through."

It seemed doctor-patient confidentiality didn't apply where extended family was involved.

"I'm alive and I'm here, and that's about all I can ask for," I admitted, squeezing her forearms. "And I really need to understand how all this"—I stepped back and pointed at her and Nick, the doctor husband with the nice accent coming up behind her—"came to be. I want the long form explanation, okay? Because I've clearly missed a memo or two, as well as an invitation to your bachelorette party. But I have to go throw myself at a very precious man's feet and I can't hear about your abandonment of team nomad until after that's resolved. Sound good?"

Erin pressed her hands to my chest and gave me a gentle shove. "Go," she said. "We'll steal a bottle of sambuca later and catch up."

"Not the sambuca. I had a hangover for six days the last time we drank sambuca."

"Go," she repeated, laughing. "And be sure to bring him back with you."

"Believe me, I'm going to try."

I crossed the room with single-minded focus, weaving through the gathered guests and ignoring greetings. When I reached him, I didn't hold back. I curled my hand around his bicep and turned him to face me. "Don't make me dick-slap that pout off your face," I said. "Come on. I have to do something."

He shook out of my grip with a gasp. "How—what are you doing? Where did you come from and why do you look like a sun-dried tomato?"

I took his hand, laced my fingers with his, and kissed his knuckles. "I'll explain everything later but right now, I'm apologizing. I'm throwing myself at your feet. I'm telling you I don't have all the answers and I'm scared I'll never have the ones you want but I'm also admitting I was wrong and wrong and, oh yeah, even more wrong. And I'm admitting I don't know what I'm doing or where I'm going or who I'm going to be when I grow up but I know I like what I'm doing and where I'm going and who I am when I'm with you. I like that you force me to think about those things and even though it drives me fucking crazy and you're more than a little stubborn, I like that you expect big things from me. And even though there's a choice comment about my cock waiting to be made, I have to do something before this wedding kicks off and you need to be there for it."

Snatching his hand back, he hissed, "Don't you dare propose to me here. That is completely unacceptable."

"There's no way to say this without sounding like a massive dick weasel but I'm not proposing to you." I reached under his tuxedo jacket, flattening my hand on his back. I couldn't handle standing here without touching him. Scowling, he shuffled closer. "We'll talk about the marriage stuff later but I know I want to figure it out. With you."

"I already know what you think. You don't want to get married."

"Yeah, that's what I said before," I admitted. "I've had some time in the bottom of a rum bottle to reconsider. To start, I was thinking we might give it a shot by moving in together. I want to learn. I want to do better. I'm unemployed and my skills don't transfer to many civilian jobs and none of that sounds promising but we could try. We could go anywhere you want. I promise I'd take good care of you, Tom."

He shook his head and blinked away. "I can't," he whispered, tears heavy in his voice. "I *can't* be your secret."

I reached for his hand again. "Do you trust me?"

He sobbed out a laugh. "That's a question with many answers, Wes."

"If you trust me at all, come with me now."

He rested his forehead on my chest for a moment. "All right," he whispered.

Our fingers laced together, I led him across the room. We blew past Shannon and Will, Matt and Lauren, Nick and Erin. We ignored everyone. Then, with my breath coming in jagged pants and bile in my throat and sweat soaking my shirt and my life flashing before my eyes, we stopped.

"Mom. Dad. I want you to meet someone." I met Tom's wide-eyed gaze and the whooshing in my head slowed a bit. I'd nearly died a few months ago but this didn't feel like that. This felt much worse, as if my vital organs were shivering, bracing for impact. "You already know Tom but you haven't met my…my boyfriend."

My mother squeaked in surprise and her face split into an enormous smile. I'd anticipated some version of that. My father, though, he was a different story. He blinked at us and that split-second pause did a number on my heart. But then he reached out, set a hand on each of our shoulders, and said, "I can't wait to get to know you both."

A leaden, decades-held breath wheezed out of me. If I hadn't been rooted in place by Tom's grip on my hand and my father's hold on my shoulder, I would've fallen flat on my ass. That was the only way to cope with the world tilting under my feet.

"Oh, look at you two. You're just darling together." My mother pushed her way into our circle and cupped Tom's cheek. To him, she said, "I've always liked you."

"Have you?" he asked, laughing.

She gave his cheek a loving pat. "Yes. You're bright and you don't take any nonsense. You're a sharp dresser too. I like that."

He glanced at me, an eyebrow arched and the corner of his mouth tipping up in a smile. "You're right about the nonsense."

I felt like a roughly shaken bottle of champagne, everything swirling and bubbling and the pressure building all around. If I blinked or breathed, the cork would pop and I'd dissolve into a fizzy puddle because this wasn't real. This wasn't my life. Things didn't work out like this for me.

As my mother made noise about getting a photo of us for her blog and folded us into a group hug, Tom leaned his temple to my cheek, whispering, "Don't freak out on me now. We've got this." He squeezed my hand again, hard enough to snap my attention away from everything else. "I've got you."

27

TOM

AS I PUSHED through the crowd with Wes close behind me, two things were clear to me.

First, Wes was freaking out.

And second, if I didn't reel in the freak-out within three minutes, he'd hyperventilate his way through the ceremony.

When we reached the bar, I yanked off his suit coat and pushed him into a chair. "Sit, take some deep breaths, and notice the things around you."

Wes snorted out a laugh. "Tom, I love you and I hate to disappoint but if you're asking me to stop and smell the roses, it's time you know I can't *not* smell the roses...and count the thorns and leaves, and track the ants crawling up the stems and keep an eye on the bees overhead. I know everything that's happening in the garden. I don't know how to do anything but notice the things around me. Occupational hazard, baby. Well, I guess that's *former* occupation now."

He didn't mean that. The first part. He meant all the things after those three words. He wasn't talking about real, true, messy love. Forever love. He was being his glib, exaggerated self. I shook my head, scattering those sticky, invasive thoughts of being wanted enough for permanence and commitment and family before they took root. They would, if I allowed it. They'd twist around every last needy piece of me, the ones still raw and bruised from being thrown away, and I'd soothe the hurt with those glib, exaggerated words.

I shook my head again, harder this time. "Think about your toes. How do they feel against your socks? Wiggle each one. Count them. Out loud. Talk to me, okay?" I rubbed a hand between his shoulder blades as I said to the bartender, "Can I get a whiskey? Two, three fingers, on the rocks."

"That's a dangerous idea," Wes said. "I might still be drunk from…other things."

"You haven't counted a single toe," I said, accepting a tumbler from the bartender. I knelt down in front of Wes. Of all the things to level him, it was acceptance. It was overwhelming after expecting the opposite, even if I knew the opposite would never happen. "Talk to me about your toes, sweetheart."

"Ten toes in shamrock green argyle socks and shoes borrowed from my brother which is not my preferred operating procedure," he replied, his arms braced on his thighs and his head low. "Not that you asked but there are five exits from this location, two on your left, one on the far right, and the other two down the hallway. Speaking of the hallway, three people are in there and one of them is very concerned about the amount of red wine on hand. And someone's pacing in the room next door. I'm guessing it's the groom." He blew out a breath, lifted his head, and met my gaze. "If I had to get out of here, I'd take the far-right door. It's farther away than the exits on your left but better proximity to the parking lot."

"Do you need to? Get out of here right now?"

He reached for the tumbler, took a sip. "No. This wedding matters to you."

"You matter to me," I replied. "If you need to leave, we'll leave."

"I've spent—oh, I don't know—twenty-five years expecting my father to tell me he won't tolerate me and people like me." Another sip. "But he didn't."

I brushed my fingers over his forehead. "No, he didn't."

"He looked at me the same as always," Wes continued, tears filling his eyes. "Like it was fine. Like I was fine. And I'm going to need another minute to process that because I've spent the past five hours—and *every day* since I realized this about myself—visualizing that conversation and never once did I see it going that way. I was never fine."

"I know. It's a lot to take in." Still kneeling before him, I wrapped my hands around his forearms, stroking and squeezing over his shirtsleeves.

He dropped his forehead against mine and released a long, shuddering breath. "Tom, baby, I love you"—*he doesn't mean it, he doesn't mean it, he doesn't mean it*—"but that really fucking hurts."

I blinked at him, confused. There was no getting past

those three little words, eight letters to change my world. "I'm sorry? What?"

"I have a wicked bad sunburn," he said with a rueful laugh. "Don't stop touching me but—"

I yanked at his tie and flipped open the buttons at his neck to reveal more inflamed skin under his shirt. "I'd assumed it was only your face," I murmured, pressing my palm to his sternum. "How did this happen?"

"It fits under the umbrella of my wrongs," he replied.

Cupping the back of his neck, I brought his forehead back to mine. He needed a haircut but we'd address that tomorrow. "I shouldn't have criticized you. That day, over lunch. I shouldn't have said any of it. Your reality belongs to you and it doesn't matter whether I perceive it differently. It doesn't matter whether I'd handle it differently. I never should've told you how to experience your emotions, even if your parents reacted exactly as I'd expected—"

"The way you say 'I told you so' is extremely cute," he murmured.

"Even if they reacted as I'd expected, I shouldn't have told you how to feel your feelings. If anyone should know what it's like to have emotions invalidated, it should be me and I should've done better," I said. "I won't do that again. I'm sorry."

"I was wrong to say you wouldn't be happy until your family accepted you," he said. "I put a lot of my issues, a lot of my fears onto you."

I shrugged. "You weren't completely wrong," I conceded. "I, uh, I emailed my sister."

He reared back, blinking rapidly. "What happened?"

"Allow me to restate that. I sent my sister a long, rambling rant. The tone landed somewhere between shrill and oppositional defiance."

"Seems legit." He jerked his chin up. "Well? What happened?"

I fished my phone out of my breast pocket and called up the message I'd received last night. "Take a look."

Wes squinted at the screen, reading aloud, "'Tom, you're right. Ma isn't about to change and she'll never admit she was wrong but she was wrong. I'm sorry. Best, Joy.'" He swiped the screen before glancing up at me. "That's it? 'I'm sorry'? No offer to—I don't know—make it right? And who the hell thinks 'best' is a good way to end emails? Honest to god, I'd rather some blowhardy 'cheers' or 'peace' over 'best.' '*Best*.' What the fuck is that about?" He reached into my jacket, tucked my phone away. "Say the word and I'll have twenty wild turkeys dropped at her door tonight. She'll know what it means to be sorry after that."

"Turkeys?"

"Fuck yeah. Old-school intimidation tactic. It's surprisingly effective," he said. "Coyotes, bobcats, mountain lions, raccoons. Or goats. Goats always work."

"Don't do that," I said, laughing. "She has kids."

"They won't eat the kids," he replied. "Not much."

"No wild animals." I offered him a weak smile as I lifted my hands and let them fall. "This is enough. It's more than enough. I said all the things I'd stored up for years, and by itself, that was an accomplishment. I didn't expect to hear back from her but now I know where she stands. She knows it was fucked-up, she knows my mother won't change, and she's only able to offer an apology. And I'm okay with it. I don't need a family to be happy."

"We'll make our own family," he whispered. "If you'll have me."

We stayed there while the bartender argued with someone about red wine and then grumbled about fetching five more cases from wherever they hid the good stuff around here. We stayed while someone barked orders about centerpieces and someone else asked where they wanted the cake set up.

The rustle of fabric to my right caught my attention and I turned my head to find myself staring at the gorgeous Miss Andy Asani in an enormous tulle ball gown. It wasn't white because why would it be? Instead, it was the deepest, darkest plum at her waist, the color dissolving down the skirt and up the bodice into pale, smoky violet. It was nothing I'd expected from her but completely perfect at the same time.

"Hi," she said, gesturing toward us with a bouquet of paper flowers. "I am delighted this is happening and I don't want to interrupt your moment but if I don't walk down this aisle in the next minute or two, Patrick will rip doors off hinges. As much as possible, I'd rather he not destroy our wedding venue." She glanced over her shoulder and then back at us. "And I know those doors and their casings are old. Restoring them would be a pain in my ass."

"Do you want us to go inside?" I asked, looking up at her from the floor. "Or go calm Patrick down?"

"Inside." She tapped a finger to her cherry red lips, humming. "I'll handle Patrick."

Wes extended a hand in her direction, saying, "I don't think I was invited but thank you for having me, ma'am."

Andy grinned at her bouquet, letting out a sharp laugh as she studied the paper petals. "You settle up with your guy, Tom. I'll settle up with mine."

We watched her go, a fog of smoky tulle and dark, curly hair floating around her as she slipped into the room next door.

"What did she mean by that?" Wes asked.

I pushed to my feet and brushed off the legs of my trousers but the damage was already done. "You were invited *and* I put you down as my plus-one. You're my date."

"So, *that* was what Will meant. Okay. One less grave to dig." Nodding, he said, "I'm not used to being anywhere legitimately. I have a lot of adjusting to do tonight." He stood, looped his arm around my waist. I let him steer me toward the ceremony location. "Thanks for grounding me back there."

"Anytime." I pointed toward a pair of empty seats in the second to last row.

"And thanks for the push. I needed it."

He took my hand as we shuffled single file between the rows, passing his parents as we went. Not even a flinch from him. We sat down in separate seats but there was nothing separate about this. He wrapped his arm around my shoulders, shifted my body into his, and pressed his lips to my forehead.

"I meant it," he whispered. "What I said earlier, I meant it."

Those sticky thoughts returned, liquefied, spilled into

every corner of my existence. I had to force myself to smirk when everything inside me wanted to swoon. "Babe, you've said many things this evening. I'm going to need you to be much more specific."

He ran his tongue over the crease of his lips, his gaze fixed on mine. "I love you," he said, every word ringing with challenge.

"You don't have to say that. It might seem like the right thing because of"—I waved a hand at him and the ceremony space—"this. But there's no obligation to—"

"I'm messy as fuck and I don't know what I'm doing and I don't know who I am when I'm not a spy and not halfway in the closet but I love you," he interrupted. "I want to be the man who gets to love you, Tom. I want that job. I want the right to call you mine and I want to be yours, and I want to do this with you."

"I love—" I nearly choked on the word. Wes tugged me closer, resting my head on his shoulder. "I love you too."

"We don't have to stay in this city if you don't want to," he said. "I'll go wherever you decide."

I shifted, looking up at him. "What? Why wouldn't I want to stay here?"

Wes searched me with wide, confused eyes for a moment before running a hand over his brow. "I'm gonna kill my brother."

"We've talked about this. We can't run around murdering people or making offhand comments about murder. Not everyone understands the Halsted way of life."

"Right, right. I'll work on it," he murmured. He exhaled, holding me tighter. After a beat of silence, he asked, "Is this what it feels like to breathe normally? To not worry about everything, all the time? It's fuckin' weird."

I smiled into his neck. "Get used to it, sweetheart."

Another breath whooshed out. "Give me a couple of months to figure it all out. To figure *me* out, okay?"

"And then what?"

The string quartet ended a drowsy bit of background music and launched full force into a louder, more dramatic piece that prompted the guests to stand. The doors in the back of the room swept open, revealing Andy and Patrick, their hands clasped. With his eyes narrowed and his lips twisted in an expression I couldn't decipher, he stared at her as everyone shifted to face them. She met his stare with an arched eyebrow and a wisp of a smile. Our spot near the back allowed me to see her cock her head toward the altar and his slow nod in response. As they walked down the aisle together, a knot of emotion filled my throat.

"And then what?" I repeated, my words high and watery.

He hooked his finger around my belt, jerking me toward him. He leaned down, his lips hovering over mine. "And then, if I haven't made a bigger mess and you still tolerate me, we'll find an aisle we want to walk down together."

"I'm going to require a better proposal than that," I said.

He brushed his lips against mine in a too-quick kiss. "And you'll get it. You'll get it all."

EPILOGUE

TOM

THE NEXT SUMMER

I COUNTED OUT five pairs of boxer briefs and then another five. One set of posh, one set of hiking-grade. One did not hike mountains in the same underwear worn under tuxedos. It simply was not done. Wes didn't know it yet but I was correcting his underwear selection, not that he adhered to my organizational philosophies on the matter.

"How many ties do I need again?" he called from the other side of our apartment. We still lived in the South End, in the only place that'd ever felt like mine. Now, it was ours.

"I gave you a checklist," I replied.

"Pretend for a second you didn't."

I set the appropriate allotment of undies beside his open suitcase. "Four, not including a bowtie."

"Four? Why four?"

"Where is your checklist?" I asked. "I put all the information on your checklist."

Footsteps sounded on the hardwood floor and soon, Wes's broad shoulders filled the doorway to our bedroom. Because Jesus loved me very much, Wes was wearing a beanie and boxers, and not a stitch more save for the ties draped over his arm. That limb still gave him trouble but it'd improved in the year and a half since the injury. And it wasn't like I minded scrubbing his back for him when he needed it.

He held out his hand, ticking his fingers as he said, "A tie for Kaisall's wedding, a bowtie for Riley's wedding, and then maybe another one for while we're in Switzerland. How do you get four from that?"

"Add in two rehearsal dinners, babe," I said. "You should probably grab one more for backup."

He glanced down at his hand, scowling as if he found this tally personally insulting. "What is there to rehearse?"

"Nothing, really. It's just an opportunity to have another party."

"That I understand," he replied, crossing the room with his arm extended in my direction. "Make this easier on me and choose the ones you like."

"I told you I'd pack for both of us," I murmured as I made my selections. "You've had more than enough going on these past few weeks."

"You're one to talk." Wes collected the ties from me and set them beside his suitcase. He dropped the remainders on his bedside table. "You've had planning board and preservation society meetings every night."

"It's not like you were home alone, honey. You were plenty busy running around with the spy boys in Virginia all week and in Quebec the week before," I countered.

He studied the piles of clothing beside his suitcase. "They are *not* my spy boys. They're Will's. They're Kaisall's. Not mine."

"You can admit you like working with them," I said as lightly as I could manage.

"Small doses, honey. I tolerate them in *small doses*." He eyed the underwear before dropping the stack into his luggage. "I won't miss them while we're traveling."

"Of course not," I agreed. Allowing him to keep up the pretense of hating the work he did for Will and Jordan's company was important for all involved. It fed the strange siblings-and-SEALs dynamic they had going and granted them more opportunities to relentlessly bust each other's balls. It was healthy. Or something like that.

"I'm happy to finally have you all to myself for the next five weeks," he said without meeting my eyes, still occupied with his clothes. "No early mornings, no planning board meetings, no realtors calling to haggle over a deal during our dinner parties."

I tossed a pair of socks at his head. "That happened once and it was an eight-figure deal. Those are allowed to interrupt dinner parties because they *pay* for five weeks of international travel, my love."

He scoffed at that before chucking the socks back in my direction. But…it wasn't socks. It was a little box. I turned it over in my hand. "What is this?"

Wes arched an eyebrow up as he ran his tongue between his lips. "Open it."

Always a challenge with this one. "Okay. Sure. No problem, I'll just—" I stared down at the pair of black bands, understanding exactly what I was seeing but also understanding nothing. Because—because we'd always talked about the next steps in a fanciful sort of way. An autumn wedding, an island honeymoon. Or maybe a summer wedding and a mountain honeymoon. Or an island wedding and a mountain honeymoon. Who knew? Certainly not us. We'd always talked about *someday* and I couldn't believe my someday was coming, it was here. I still couldn't believe this was mine. That it was for keeping. "What is this?" I repeated.

Gesturing toward the box, Wes said, "We're going to Montauk for Jordan's wedding and you're going to meet everyone from the company. I know those fools and I know I don't want to introduce you to them as my boyfriend. I wanted to introduce them to *my fiancé* and—"

It felt like the floor disappeared from beneath my feet because only Wesley Halsted could propose like this. And I loved it. And I loved him. *I loved him.* "Oh my god."

"—but then we're going to Lake Tahoe for Riley's wedding," Wes continued, strolling to my side of the bed like this was a casual conversation about where to go for brunch tomorrow and not one about being his husband. "And I don't know what we're getting into there but I wasn't taking any chances." He looped his arms around my waist. "You're off the market, baby, and I wasn't about to give NorCal any mixed signals on that front."

I blinked down at the box. "So, you bought matching rings for us? To keep the NorCal boys off my ass?"

Wes plucked the smaller band from its casing. "These are temporary," he said, holding it up. "Between the fishing trip we're taking with my dad after Jordan's wedding, the hikes we've planned around Lake Tahoe before Riley's wedding, and the climbs in Switzerland, I knew you'd worry about scratching up a nice ring. These silicone bands seemed like a decent—though temporary—compromise because I didn't want you to worry."

All those *someday* conversations, I'd believed them to live in a someday far from here. Perhaps I'd been fortifying myself against the possibility Wes would need years to come around to the idea. Lowering my expectations to protect myself. And what did he do? He quietly collected those fortifications and protections and replaced them with a proposal that sounded like a military briefing.

Naturally, I burst into messy, sobbing laughter which led Wes to drop the band, bring both hands to my face, and ask, "Do you hate it? You don't have to wear it if you hate it and I'll just—"

"I love it," I managed. "I love all of it."

"Are you sure?"

Nodding, I tangled my arms around his neck, still laughing and sobbing as he sank down to the floor. I shifted in his lap, saying, "And I love how you never once *asked* me to marry you."

He thumbed sloppy tears off my cheek. "Do you need the question?"

Smiling as wide as I'd ever smiled in my life, I said, "I don't."

With that sharp, curt nod I'd come to adore, he replied, "I didn't think so."

I squeezed my fiancé as tight as I could and he gave it right back to me—until a wet nose prodded my arm. "Someone is feeling excluded," I said, sniffling.

"Come on, there's room for you too," Wes said, beckoning to Winnie Pancakes, the nine year old goldendoodle we adopted from a rescue shelter last Christmas. She scampered over, ducking her head to meet his palm. "You should know Dame Winnie helped me pick out your ring."

I ran a hand down her coat. "She has amazing taste."

"I'm going to miss you while we're gone," he said to Winnie. "You are our favorite girl but we'll bring you treats from all the places we visit. Deal?"

"Max and Jory will take great care of her," I said. "And we'll make sure to FaceTime with her so she doesn't forget us."

"Forget us? I figured you'd be more concerned with them cooking her salmon correctly or hiding her vitamins in the good cheese she likes."

I shrugged. "I mean, yes, that too. I've already sent Jory detailed directions. He'll know what to do."

After a moment, Wes asked, "I've never done this before. Did I get it right? Is the answer yes?"

"You're perfect." I pressed my lips to his. "Of course it's yes. Always yes."

***Thank you for reading! I hope you enjoyed Wes and Tom and their journey to finding each other. If you want more from Shannon and Will or Jordan and April, turn the page to find excerpts from* The Cornerstone *and* Coastal Elite.**

Join Kate Canterbary's Office Memos mailing list for occasional news and updates, as well as new release alerts, exclusive extended epilogues and bonus scenes, and more.

If newsletters aren't your thing, follow Kate on BookBub for preorder and new release alerts.

Visit Kate's private reader group, Kate Canterbary's Tales, for exclusive giveaways, sneak previews of upcoming releases, and book talk.

EXCERPT FROM THE CORNERSTONE

WILL

Surveillance wasn't my thing.

I hated all the waiting and watching. Don't get me wrong—keeping track of a bossy redhead who didn't know how to mind her own business was one of the easiest gigs to ever fall into my lap, but it was tedious as fuck. This was why I couldn't do protection ops. I was a scalpel: perfect for quick, quiet attacks, the kinds that were measured and rehearsed for the greatest impact.

I was about ready to bind and gag Shannon Walsh, and then lock her in a closet until the wedding was over. Listening in from the far end of the bar while she quizzed the bartender on his stock of craft beers only reaffirmed it.

She couldn't go five minutes without flitting between the Walsh encampments, and that was on top of her routine cross-examination of the inn staff. She wanted to know when they were pitching the reception tent, where the blue hydrangea centerpieces were being housed for the night, whether they'd prepared extra scallops wrapped in bacon for the cocktail hour.

Apparently those were the groom's favorite, and if her tone was any indication, the catering manager could expect Shannon's fancy high heel to find a home in his small intestine if he underdelivered.

I had to hand it to her—the bitch had balls.

And maybe I was a little punchy. I'd been traveling for the past seventy hours and my body and brain were still in mission mode. There was a gravity associated with coming off deployment. All sailors experienced it, but everyone experienced it differently. For me—after nearly three *years* hunting terrorists—it was the sudden, shocking loss of purpose. Without the constant chatter of comms in my ear, the familiar weight of body armor and weapons, the adrenaline of running exceedingly dangerous ops, the dual responsibilities of guarding my country and getting my men home safely…without all that, I didn't know what to do with myself.

Instead of figuring out how to shake off the culture shock, I fixated on Shannon. She was the expensive, refined kind of beautiful. High maintenance. Diamond earrings bigger than most mortar shells. She couldn't go thirty seconds without checking her phone.

Amazingly enough, that wasn't the most annoying part.

No, it was that this woman didn't even *like* beer. I refused to believe she could. This chick was too high society for beer, even weird hipster beer.

"What about Upper Case?" she asked. There was no hint of impatience or condescension in her voice, and that was the secret weapon. She was calm and relatively pleasant, but it was obvious in the sharp angle of her eyebrow that she was ready to climb over the bar, show this guy how to do his job, and shrivel his dick off with little more than a tight grimace. "Or Congress Street? Triple Sunshine?"

The bartender studied the taps in front of him and then crouched low to inspect the bottles lined up in the refrigerator. He stood, shaking his head. "I've got Smuttynose, and...and Slumbrew."

She drummed her fingers against the bar while she contemplated those options. I was actually concerned the bartender was wilting under her glare. She was a dictator dressed as a socialite, and I doubted she wilted under anything. "What about Sea Hag?"

He snapped his fingers and pointed at the fridge, smiling with relief. Hell, *I* was relieved on his behalf. "*That* I can do for you."

"I knew you'd come through for me, Barry." She sent him a wink as he slid the uncapped bottle toward her. He high tailed it to the other end of the bar, presumably to dislodge his nuts from wherever Shannon shoved them.

I was expecting her to dart back to Lo's side or hunt down other staff members to harass or just go the fuck to bed because it was past midnight and even the wicked required rest, but that all changed when she turned her gaze on me. She collected her bottle and marched my way, offering a bright, plastic smile as she approached.

"I have a thing for IPAs," she said, her voice a conspiratorial whisper. Skinny silver bracelets encased her wrist, and they clanged against each other whenever she moved. From where I was sitting, it looked and sounded like she was accessorizing with a Slinky. "A list of the best local breweries was published last month, and my goal for the summer is to try each one." Unbidden, she tucked herself into the seat beside me. "We met earlier, but I know there are a lot of us and things have been so hectic. I'm Shannon, Matt's sister."

I accepted her outstretched hand, and as our palms met, I realized she was a tiny little thing. She was just a peanut. At first glance, she didn't seem small, not with that feisty attitude and fiery hair, but she was the definition of petite. Slim fingers, smooth skin, trim, compact body, and...freckles. So many freckles.

It was as if Strawberry Shortcake fucked Winston Churchill, and nine months later, Shannon Walsh was born.

"Right," I said. "Will."

"Are you an India Pale Ale fan, Will?" Her eyes dropped to the Corona bottle beside me and she forced that fake smile again. It was obvious she did this with frequency—handling people, subtly manipulating them, getting her way while letting everyone think it was their idea—and it annoyed the fuck out of me. "Oh, that's just silly."

"Is it?"

"Yes," she said, then called down the bar, "Barry! Get my friend a Summer Ale."

Barry didn't react quickly enough for Shannon, and his shift was probably long since over but he didn't know how to break that news to her. With a sigh about wanting things done right meant doing them herself, she stepped behind the bar, grabbed the bottle, popped the top, and placed it in front of me.

"Put it on my tab," she yelled as she settled back into her seat. Barry gave us his best deer-in-the-headlights look and went back to restocking. It was late, and he was the only one manning the patio bar. My money was on him counting the seconds until this rowdy crew cleared out. "So I started my IPA adventure with an Olivette from Paisley Pines and then I discovered Lost Highway Breweries, and now I'm dying to try the Veridien from Banded Horn Brewery."

Bound. Gagged. Closet.

"So tell me, Will," she said, inclining her head toward me. "What's your poison?"

An image of Shannon bent over my knee flashed into my mind, and *fuuuuuck* that had to stop right now. I swallowed it down, drowning that thought in cold beer. "Whatever's on tap," I growled.

In all fairness to my dick, this was nothing more than a natural reaction to being off-base and in the presence of gorgeous women who were free to dress however they pleased. Hell, I hadn't seen a lady in heels like Shannon's, with ribbons lacing all the way up her leg, since…ever.

I sent a silent prayer to my cock, begging it to calm the fuck down.

"There you are," Shannon said as Lo draped her arm over my shoulder.

"Hey, Will, this is my friend Andy. She works with Matt," she said, gesturing to the brunette beside her.

"Will Halsted," I said. She shook my hand without saying a word. "You're not related to this crew?"

"No," Andy said, and her gaze traveled over the patio area to settle on Patrick, the oldest Walsh. He was one stoic motherfucker. I'd only picked up general details about the family Lo was marrying into, and I knew Riley was the fool, Sam was the playboy, Patrick was the hard-ass, Nick wasn't related but came with the package, and Matt was the golden retriever: obedient, loyal, and couldn't keep his tongue in his mouth.

Andy ordered a glass of wine, and thank God Barry was able to meet her request without much discussion. I doubted Shannon cared whether she was empowered to fire him or not; she'd make it happen.

"Finally, an impartial witness. Sit down," I said, pulling up a chair.

If I could get Andy talking, I knew Shannon would go looking for attention elsewhere. That meant I could get some history on these people and distance from Shortcake. Seemed like a win.

But Andy turned away from Patrick a second before he pivoted. A quick inspection of the patio told me that everyone else saw it too. I couldn't understand how she missed his hot stare.

So that's how it is with them.

"Are we not having a conversation?" Shannon asked, and *fuck*. Just...fuck. If I had the time or interest, her mouth would be too busy with my cock to make those comments. And no, I did not want to be interested but post-deployment horny didn't discriminate against viper-women who inspired fear in wolves and inadequate men.

"Apparently she didn't take the hint," I muttered but Andy ignored me. Incidentally, my dick was ignoring me too.

Lo shot me a venomous glare, mouthed "Be nice," and linked her elbow with Andy's. She flipped me off as they walked across the patio to where Wes was seated with Erin, or—as I preferred to call her—the quiet one.

I definitely drew the short straw in this activity.

"I don't spend nearly enough time listening to harpies." I gestured for Shannon to finish her story, and hoped my remarks were enough to send her back to her room for the night. That was my exit strategy, and she was providing more than enough material to work with. "By all means, continue. I'm certain there are some frat boys brewing their own basement lager that you haven't mentioned yet, and I won't be able to sleep tonight without your assessment of their operation."

"The things I do for my brothers," Shannon said under her breath.

I expected another book report on the history of brewing but she stayed silent. She watched as Lo and Andy returned to the inn, and then her attention shifted to Erin. Shannon was putting a lot of effort into making her glances seem casual, and failing miserably.

Her thumb swept back and forth over the bottle's neck, and for a moment, I was transfixed by an image of those fingers on my cock. They were so small and slim, I bet they wouldn't fit all the way around my shaft.

And fuck me, I couldn't stop watching her stroke that bottle. I closed my eyes, and I could feel it, I could feel her skin against mine, and *fucking hell,* it had been too long.

"Give me that," I said, grabbing the beer away. It was barely cold and I couldn't say I enjoyed beer this hoppy but I drank it anyway.

"We could have ordered you one, dearie," she said.

"Unlikely," I said. "You scared the piss out of Barry, and probably everyone else at this place."

Her laugh was a soft, breathy sound, and it was the most honest thing I'd heard from her all night. "You can't say I don't get shit done."

I couldn't stay seated any longer. I needed something to do, a way to expel the misplaced desire hammering in my veins, and I was half ready to dive into the ocean and swim until I washed up on the shore. At least then I'd be too exhausted to think about wrapping all that red hair around my fist and forcing her to her knees.

Stepping behind the bar, I grabbed our empty bottles and tossed them in the bin. Sam was drunkenly corralling his brothers—plus Wes, Erin, and Nick, the doctor who'd asked me an unending series of questions about tribal healthcare conditions in Pakistan and Afghanistan earlier in the evening—and leading them down the beach toward his cottage.

That was the bullet I was taking for this team tonight: Wes was gathering intel on Lo's in-laws while eyeing Erin, and I was left keeping a leash on Shortcake.

But then I noticed her tracking *me,* and I realized this little girl and I were playing the same fucking game. How could I have missed such overt scrutiny? And no, of course she didn't have a thing for IPAs.

Yeah, the bitch had *balls*.

"So you're the tail."

"I'm what?" she snapped, and it seemed plausible that she'd have a trophy case packed with all the assholes she'd torn up.

"The tail," I repeated. "I know my objective here...but what's yours?"

She crossed her arms over her chest, jangling those stupid Slinky bracelets in the process. "Your sister seems to believe you're going to kidnap and torture my brother. She wanted to prevent that."

"It's called enhanced interrogation," I said. "And that's not my wheelhouse."

"That's right," she murmured. "I'm told you're quite the commando."

I bristled. There was a lot of mythology surrounding special operations teams, and most of it was inaccurate or exaggerated. "We aren't fond of that term, ma'am."

"In that case, I'm quite fond of it." She eyed me up and down, visibly taking stock of my dive watch, the Gatorz sunglasses hanging from the neck of my t-shirt, and the frog skeleton tattoo peeking out from my sleeve. "What kind of commando activities have you been up to recently?"

You wouldn't be able to sleep at night if I told you. "Afraid that's classified, ma'am."

She stared at me as if she wasn't accustomed to being refused anything, ever. And look at her. Those pouty lips, the ones that ordered everyone around as if they were on her payroll and they should be fucking thrilled to have that honor. That stubborn chin, angled just enough to communicate her superiority. And those eyes, big and dark, dark mossy green, twinkling as if she was amused by my insubordination.

This woman was lethal.

Tearing my gaze away from Shannon, I surveyed the beer selection and opted for another Summer Ale. "Why is Matt in such a hurry to marry my sister?"

Before seeing Lo or meeting her fiancé, Wes and I endured one of the most stern lectures my father had delivered in years. It seemed the Commodore was drunk on the Matthew Walsh Koolaid. At the very minimum, my mother was force-feeding it to him. He officially warned us off any initiatives aimed at interrogating or otherwise scaring the shit out of our future brother-in-law. That didn't mean I wasn't free to collect intel.

Shannon smiled, and for the first time, it was authentic. "Because they have crazy, filthy love for each other." She wandered behind the bar and inspected every bottle in stock before selecting a Sam Adams. She leaned against the counter, staring at me while she sipped.

Okay, so maybe she wasn't too much of a socialite for beer.

"Really? Do you even like beer?" I shook my head as she drained the bottle and reached for another. "And whatever happened to your blessed IPAs? You should know Barry's off crying in a corner somewhere."

She held the bottle in front of her face and studied the label. "I'll leave him a generous tip. Nothing a few months of psychotherapy won't solve." I couldn't repress the surprised laughter that bubbled up from my chest. "Now explain to me why you have a problem with Matt."

"I don't trust him," I said. "It's really fucking simple."

"Do you trust Lauren?"

"Of course," I said, reaching for my beard and once again finding it missing. "Without a doubt."

"Obviously not," Shannon laughed. She tugged her sweater's sleeves down from where they'd been bunched at her elbows, and now they hung over her fingers. There was absolutely no reason why I'd find that sexy, but...post-deployment horny. That's all it was. "If you trusted her judgment, you'd also trust her choice of husband."

I leaned back against the counter, mirroring her stance. My goal was keeping my eyes on her face and away from her legs and fingers, but then I noticed the way her sweater was always sliding off one shoulder. That shoulder...I couldn't stop staring at it. "I don't trust any guy with my sister."

She tossed the empty bottle into the trash and went for another. "You're a misogynistic meathead," she said.

"If you want to hit me with meathead, I'll own that, but I'm not taking misogynistic. I can respect, admire, and champion the fuck out of women, but that doesn't mean I can't also protect my sister. That doesn't mean I can't make it clear he'll have to deal with me if she's ever harmed in any way."

"That was a lot of words for you all at once. I'm kind of impressed." Shannon ran a hand through her hair, and I noticed we were completely alone. "Let me tell you something about Lauren: she is a badass chick. You want to talk about torture? She put Matt through all kinds of hell."

"Good," I said. "It builds character. And he probably deserved it."

"While your last point is most likely accurate," Shannon said, "you need to lighten up, commando. Not all womenfolk need looking after."

"Someone should be looking after you," I murmured before draining my beer. Too often, the world wasn't very nice to females, and yeah, we needed to deal with that shit straightaway. But no one was going to tell me to stop standing up for the women in my life.

"Erroneous." Her lips curled into a smile that walked the line between playful and demonic, and she shook her head. "If anything, I'm the one who does the looking-after around here."

"In other words, your brothers are lazy sacks of shit," I said, and I knew there was a reason I didn't like those guys.

Her pale brows drew together in a vicious scowl, and I recognized I was wrong about Shannon. She wasn't a socialite, not at all. She was a fighter, and a scrappy one at that.

"In other words," she said, "I run this town and I don't need any help doing it."

She shrugged and now that shoulder was all the way exposed. A wild splash of freckles ran across her skin, and I was too tired, too fed up with this conversation, too tightly wound to do anything but imagine tasting her right there. I pushed off from the counter and stared out at the sea, all while searching for enough discipline to make it back to my room without doing something unbelievably stupid.

But instead of leaving the bar right then, I stopped beside Shannon and studied those freckles. "Like the tail of a comet," I murmured.

I reached out and traced a line from the ball of her shoulder across her collarbone. Then my gaze shifted to her mouth and those defiant, sinful lips, and my other hand was sliding up her neck and into her hair.

I didn't know why I did it. Maybe it had been too long since I touched a woman. Maybe I couldn't handle the post-deployment horny as well as I used to. Or maybe...maybe I wanted to get into a power struggle.

My forehead rested against Shannon's as I moved into her space, crowding her and feeling all five-foot-nothing of her pressed against me.

"What are you doing?" she whispered.

"Waiting for you to stop me," I said against her lips.

She sighed, and I couldn't tell if the sound originated from pleasure or pain. Then she shook her head and it was highly probable her knee would be connecting with my groin any minute. I felt every single second tick by, each one heavier than the one before.

"Will," she finally said, my name no more than a gasp.

I stole those last syllables from Shannon when my mouth met hers. She tasted like beer and sweetness, and just that quickly, my entire world condensed down to her skin, her hair, her scent. We dropped into an easy rhythm of kisses; sweet and simple, and perfectly right for the dark of night at the beach.

But then she bit my tongue and the gauntlet was thrown. Lips and tongues and teeth all fought for control, and oh holy fuck, I was bringing this girl to her knees tonight. I didn't care what it took, she was going to surrender to me. I pulled that plump bottom lip of hers between my teeth, nipping and scraping as my hands moved down her body. Her ass fit right in my palms and I jerked her against me, my fingers squeezing that taut skin until she yelped.

"Not nice," she murmured against my lips. Her hands traveled up my chest and over my shoulders, and the fire in her eyes was enough to get me as hard as a goddamn lamppost.

"The last thing I'm going to be to you is nice," I said.

The Cornerstone ***is available now!***

AN EXCERPT FROM COASTAL ELITE

JORDAN

"I'm taking you out tonight," I said while she poured some cream into her coffee. "Be ready. How does eight sound?"

She offered me a crooked smile and sipped her coffee. "I'm not really an out-to-dinner girl," she said.

"Then what kind of girl are you?" I asked.

Coffee set aside, she pursed her lips as she reached back and started braiding her hair. "I'm the 'walks on the beach, toss all the leftovers into a salad, fall asleep reading' kind of girl."

I spread my hands out in front of me as if our answer was as plain as day. "We'll walk on the beach and eat salads and read until you let me fuck you again, and then we'll fall asleep. Be ready."

She cast her gaze to the floor, her lips folding into a grim line as she continued braiding. I'd said too much. Pushed too hard. Coming on too strong wasn't something I'd ever been accused of, but I'd never met a woman like April before. She was quiet and capable, but also funny and sensual. She didn't want anything from me either. She wasn't grabbing for money or contacts or status. I didn't even know what to do with all that, other than talk to her for hours and claim her body as my home away from home.

"Look, that didn't come out right," I said. "Maybe it came out exactly as it should've, but it made you back away and I don't like that. I want to hang out with you, and my current state of affairs would be greatly improved if you wanted to hang out with me, too. Salads, books, whatever you want."

April pinched her hair with one hand and used the other to wave at my leg. "I want to get some pins in you," she replied. "I think it would help."

I gestured to my torso. "Are you suggesting there were issues with my performance? I'll bend you over that couch right now and show you how much help I need."

She rolled her eyes. "And you'd do it without putting any weight on your right leg," she said. "That's why I spent so much time on your left hip and shoulder last night. You need to address the core problem, and treat the ancillary problems you're creating."

I threw my hands up in surrender. "You got it," I conceded. "Give me the full treatment, and then we'll have a salad and read some books. Later, I'll see to your aches."

April resumed braiding her hair, but she couldn't repress a grin. "I have appointments after I finish up at the bakery, and then I'm teaching a class," she said, twisting a rubber band off her wrist and around her dark strands. "I'll be free around eight again."

I nodded, matching her smile now. Her gaze settled on my bare chest, and her teeth raked over her lower lip.

You can't hide much from me, beautiful.

"What can I bring?" I asked. "If I can't take you out, there's no way in hell I'm showing up empty-handed. My mother would sooner tan my hide than allow such a thing."

She slipped on a pair of athletic shoes and knelt to tie the laces. "She'd whip your six-foot-four, two-hundred-and-fifty-odd-pound hide?"

"She certainly would," I replied, laughing but dead serious.

"Bring some wine," April said after another glance at my chest. She stood and produced my long-abandoned t-shirt from the massage table. She tossed it to me, but I didn't pull it on. "Whatever you like. I'm not picky."

I looked over my shoulder at the stacks of books piled on her trunk. "And what are we reading?"

She drummed her fingertips against her hips. "Don't judge," she warned, wagging a finger at me. "I'm currently on a historical romance kick. You know, dukes, highlanders, viscounts. It's good stuff."

"Right," I said, slightly confused. "Yeah. Sounds great. I'll just head to the bookstore down the street, and pick up a, uh—"

She held up her hand, cutting me off as she crossed the room. "Have this one," she said, chucking a paperback in my direction.

Charming the Duke, it read. I thumbed through the pages, nodding as I went. I could do this. She laughed as she watched my reactions, and it was obvious that she didn't think I'd go along with this.

"I see that smirk," I said. "That smirk says you don't think I'm going to read this book." I tapped the cover, where a guy who looked like an extra from the cast of Hamilton was pawing a chick in a fancy gown. "I'm all over this. I've got a task and purpose, ma'am, and I'm all over it."

April pointed to the watch on her wrist. "Wedding season in the Hamptons waits for no one," she said. "I have a date with ten pounds of fondant."

"And me." The book and my shirt in hand, I stalked toward her until she was backed against the edge of the countertop. "Don't forget about that date with me."

She looked up, her eyes narrowing in challenge. "What do you think you're doing?" she asked.

I nipped at the corner of her mouth. "Getting a taste of you to tide me over until tonight."

"Are you always this"—she arched up, her hands on my shoulders as her lips captured mine for a brief second —“hungry?"

I leaned into her, kissing her with more heat and meaning than I knew I had to give. "Not until now," I said, my lips hovering over hers.

***Coastal Elite* is available now!**

ALSO BY KATE CANTERBARY

The Walsh Series

Underneath It All – Matt and Lauren
The Space Between – Patrick and Andy
Necessary Restorations – Sam and Tiel
The Cornerstone – Shannon and Will
Restored — Sam and Tiel
The Spire — Erin and Nick
Preservation — Riley and Alexandra
Thresholds — The Walsh Family

Walsh Series Spinoff Novels

Coastal Elite
Before Girl
Missing In Action

Talbott's Cove

Fresh Catch
Hard Pressed
Far Cry
Rough Sketch

Adventures in Modern Dating

The Magnolia Chronicles
The Ash Affair—arriving June 2020

Get exclusive sneak previews of upcoming releases through Kate's newsletter and private reader group, The Canterbary Tales, on Facebook.

ACKNOWLEDGMENTS

I don't usually write about *how* I write books but this one was a short eternity in the making and it seems to necessitate this kind of recap. Here goes.

It's never taken me this long to write a book, especially a book I could see from start to finish. All told, *Missing In Action* required more than eighteen months to write. Most of my books come in closer to three or four months of sit-down-and-write time. But this one...I could see it but I couldn't hear it. I knew the moments but not the voices. And I waited a terribly long time to hear Wes's voice.

In the end, it wasn't Wes who talked to me. It was Tom. Unlike characters like Patrick, Shannon, Erin—the ones I knew in my blood and bones—or Andy, Riley, Stremmel—the ones who yelled and screamed and demanded I write them—Tom was quiet. And slowly, so slowly, Wes showed me himself through everyone else. Through Jordan and

April, Shannon and Will, Judy and the Commodore, even the babies.

In other words, every time I responded to questions about whether I was writing Wes by saying he didn't talk to me—that was the damn truth. The boy did not talk to me and I've never struggled to hear a character's voice as much as I did in this book.

This was an extensive journey and I have to thank all the readers who've patiently (and some not-so-patiently) waited. The requests for Wes's story started not long after he appeared in *The Space Between*...which released in 2014. Thank you for sticking with me.

And a giant thank you to the people who've quietly cheered this process on for actual *years*. My editors, my beta readers, my amazing support squad—thank you. And thank you for putting up with me every time I said "I think I have it this time."

ABOUT KATE

USA Today Bestseller Kate Canterbary writes smart, steamy contemporary romances loaded with heat, heart, and happy ever afters. Kate lives on the New England coast with her husband and daughter.

You can find Kate at www.katecanterbary.com

Made in the USA
Columbia, SC
16 April 2020